Complications:
The Deputies Book 1

A novel of the Wild West

Chuck
"Charlie MacNeil"
Buchanan

Sisley Creek Press
Durkee, Oregon

Sisley CreekPress
33369 Sisley Creek Road
Durkee, Oregon 97905

Copyright © 2009, Chuck Buchanan
All rights reserved

This is a work of fiction. Any resemblance between the characters and any person, living or dead, is purely coincidence.

ISBN **978-0-9824580-0-6**

To Cheryl:

Thanks for helping me follow my dream.

One

Harvey Palmer was a simple man who had spent his entire thirty-four years of life avoiding complications; that was all about to change, which was quite probably the last thing he wanted. He wasn't by customary definition an especially good man, but he wasn't a bad man, either--except in the sense that he was a bad man to tangle with--he just wasn't exactly what anyone might call a goody two-shoes, either. Consequently, when Harvey came upon four masked riders holding up the afternoon stage to Ellsworth, he reined his horse out of sight behind a nearby tangle of alders and sat back to watch: it never occurred to him to try to stop the robbery, as he figured that it wasn't any of his business. When the gunmen had relieved the stage company of its strongbox and mail sack, and the driver, guard, and three passengers of their valuables, they cut the six-horse hitch loose from the traces and rode off, yelling and driving the horses in front of them. Complications began to arise when they inadvertently rode straight toward Harvey.

The first robber spotted Harvey and immediately fired a shot at him. It was obvious to Harvey that the masked bandit wasn't very smart; a man sitting on a stopped horse is a whole lot more likely to hit a moving target than a rider on a galloping horse is to hit a sitting target. To make matters worse, two of the other three outlaws began firing their pistols as well--and when bullets come a man's way, his first instinct is to shoot back. Harvey pulled out his Colt, took careful aim, and quickly dispatched the two closest riders. They rolled from their saddles, dropping their guns as well as the strongbox and mail sack, directly in front of the third gunman, whose horse stumbled over their crumpled forms. The robber was thrown from his saddle, landing hard and knocking himself out cold on a rock right at the feet of Harvey's big dun horse. The fourth rider veered sharply and escaped into the trees along a nearby creek bed.

It wasn't long before the stage driver and express rider retrieved their guns and came running to the site of the gun battle. Harvey stepped off of his horse and checked the two men he had shot. Since both of them were dead, he picked up their guns and the unconscious third robber's pistol. He was sitting calmly on the trunk of a fallen alder tree when the coachmen arrived on the scene.

"Mister, I gotta thank you for stoppin' those fellers! They just robbed us!" the driver panted. Of course, that was pretty obvious to somebody who had just witnessed the whole thing. Harvey told them that no thanks were needed, then stood and watched as the stage men picked up the dropped sacks of money and mail.

"Mind if I keep their guns? I could sell 'em for

some ridin' around money," he suggested. "Unless you want 'em for evidence."

"No, no, you go ahead and keep 'em, mister. You earned that much an' more!" the driver exclaimed. Harvey rolled the guns up in his blankets, tied the bundle behind the cantle of his saddle and mounted his horse. He nodded at the two men and as he turned to ride away, the stage driver called after him, "Wait a minute, mister. You might have some reward money comin', an' I don't even know your name."

Harvey turned in the saddle and spoke softly. "Name's Harvey Palmer. I'll be in Ellsworth for a few days, and I'll let the folks at your office know where I'm stayin'."

Two days later, Harvey sat in the corner of the Alhambra Saloon in Ellsworth, enjoying the company of a lady of questionable morals and what was left of a bottle of *Oh Be Joyful*. Two rough-looking men with low-slung guns slammed through the saloon's batwing doors and approached his table; the buck-toothed redhead on the left asked Harvey if he was the one who had killed two stage robbers a few days before. When he cautiously admitted that he was, Harvey suddenly found himself being drawn on by both men. The saloon girl screamed and threw herself off Harvey's lap right into the buck-toothed gunhand, who shoved her violently to the side. As he did, his body twisted half away from Harvey, and he stumbled over the sobbing woman, falling headlong to the floor. His gun skittered across the boards and came to rest under a nearby table. Harvey took advantage of the confusion and rolled off his chair, pulling his own gun as he went, and shot the second gunslinger through the throat. The first gunman, still tangled with the woman on the floor, heard the shot and felt the sprinkle of blood on his face; he frantically hollered, "I ain't got no gun!" and threw up his hands, certain he'd be the next to die.

With the capture of two desperados, and now this third killing in three days, Harvey Palmer had unintentionally managed to shoot his way into western folklore. He became an instant hero when he saved the money and mail from the stage robbery-- the legend grew further when he killed the gunman in the Alhambra Saloon. It also made Harvey an instant target for anyone trying to build a reputation with a gun. Every young buck with a fast gun would be on Harvey's trail, looking to try his luck. If that weren't enough, the reward of $750 he received from the stage company for the holdup men he killed made Harvey a man of means and notoriety; unfortunately, that meant that he was also facing what to him was sure to be a life of unwelcome complications.

Two

Jesse Thompson was twenty years old when he rode into Ellsworth with his worn Mexican spurs jingling on either side of a bony hammer-headed roan. He wore black canvas pants, canvas suspenders, and a sun-faded blue shirt that showed the effects of days of travel on dusty trails in heat-scorched country. His flat-crowned, sweat-stained gray hat was tilted forward to shade his eyes from the bright midday sun, and a tattered neckerchief fluttered in the light breeze that stirred miniature dust devils in the street. He rode with his two ivory-handled Remington New Model Army revolvers tied down to his thighs, and his right hand lay on his leg with his thumb under the hammer thong of the holster there, ready to loose the gun if needed. The scarred stock of a .44 caliber 1860 Henry rifle protruded from the scabbard under his leg. He slouched comfortably in the saddle as he rode, but his eyes were constantly moving under the pulled-down brim of his hat. His hair and mustache, and the week's growth of stubble on his chin and cheeks, were dark against the deep tan of his face and neck.

The young rider figured that a town the size of Ellsworth had to have a livery stable where he could put up his horse and a place where he could get a shave and a bath. His gray eyes soon found a roughly-painted sign advertising *"Horses Boarded, Buggies Rented"* nailed to a tall post in front of a barn up the street, and he heeled the roan into a trot toward the building. He pulled the rangy mustang up in front of the cavernous front door of the weather-bleached barn that stood comfortably slouched in the summer sun. As he stepped down from the saddle, he lifted the thong from the hammer of his right hand gun. He hooked his thumb casually over his belt so that his hand was close to the butt of the pistol; in his line of work, it didn't pay to take chances. There wasn't necessarily any trouble coming his way, but he was going to be ready, just in case; his mother hadn't raised any foolish children, in spite of his father's opinion to the contrary. As he entered the barn, he stepped sideways and put his back against the wall while his eyes adjusted to the darkness inside. When he could see, he called out amiably, "Anyone home?"

"Be right with ye," came a high-pitched voice from the rear of the structure. A short-statured fellow, whose less-than-impressive height was lessened even more by the curve in his spine, came forward with a pitchfork in his hand. "What can I do fer ye, young feller?" he asked.

"I'd like a stall for my horse, if one's to be had, sir," Jesse answered politely, relaxing his demeanor but not his vigilance. "Hay and water, easy on the grain." He pulled a silver dollar out of his vest pocket and flipped it to the man. "How long'll that last?"

The old man snatched the coin out of the air and grinned. "There's a stall to be had, right enough. That's good fer two days, young feller." He caught the look on Jesse's face and the icy glare in his gray eyes, and his grin vanished.

"My name's Jesse, and I'd just as soon be called by it, if you don't mind," Jesse said quietly, keeping his gaze locked on the old man's eyes. Being called "young feller" once he would let slide. Twice was more than he would allow. And three times just wasn't going to happen. The old man nodded carefully and reached gingerly for the roan's reins. "Any place around here a man could get a hot bath?" Jesse asked as he handed his mount to the hostler.

The old man quickly pointed out the door, eager to get out from under the young stranger's gaze. "Down yonder's a bathhouse, just this side of the Alhambra. Ya can git drunk and bathed at the same time, if that's what ye got in mind."

"Thanks." Jesse untied the saddlebags and bedroll from behind the cantle of his saddle then pulled the Henry from its scabbard and started down the street. The liveryman stood for a moment, watching Jesse go and rubbing his chin in thought. That feller looked familiar, or at least his type did. Maybe he just fit the description of somebody. Either way, that boy looked like trouble for somebody; there just wasn't no tellin' who that somebody might be.

The fancy sign on the front of the building the hostler had pointed Jesse toward read *"BATHS"* in big, brightly painted scarlet-and-gold letters. When the tall cowboy stepped through the door into the bathhouse, the first thing to catch his eye was a buxom blond, her hair falling in a long braid down her back, perched in a tall barber chair. He stopped in the doorway, and a grin lifted the corners of his mouth. "My, my, my!" he exclaimed. "Ma'am, are you the barber?"

"I most certainly am!" the lady declared as she stepped down from the chair. "'I'm Maddie Parker, and if you don't mind my saying so, you could sure use a haircut."

"I reckon you're probably right, Miz Parker," Jesse replied. "But I do believe I'd like to get rid of some dirt first. Is there a tub full of hot water hereabouts?"

Maddie turned and pointed to a door at the back of the room. "Back there, stranger." She raised her voice and called, "*JOSÉ! Agua caliente! Andale!*"

"*Sí, señorita,*" came a voice from the back room.

"Head on back there mister," the lady told Jesse. "Jose'll take care of you."

"Obliged, ma'am." Jesse tipped his hat as he followed her directions toward the rear of the shop. He stepped into a short hallway, and a lanky Mexican boy whom Jesse took to be José directed him to a small room where a steaming tub of water stood in the middle of the floor. A side table near the tub held a bar of soap, scrub brush, and washcloth; a large towel hung on a chair nearby.

Jesse pulled up the only other chair in the room and sat down; wearily he tugged off his tall, fancy-stitched bullhide boots and shed his dusty clothes; he was soon submerged up to his neck in hot water. One of his pistols lay atop his clothes on the chair that held the towel. He'd sent José for a pint bottle of brandy that now sat within easy reach on the floor beside the tub.

As he soaked in the hot water, Jesse occasionally

sipped from the bottle while José filled him in on the excitement in the saloon. The young Mexican recounted the story of how Harvey Palmer had taken down the men who had come to kill him, and Jesse had a thoughtful look on his face as he listened to the story. "Harvey Palmer, eh?" he mused. "I've heard of him, but I can't quite place where." Then it dawned on him: the story was spreading all along the trails of how Palmer had faced down the stage robbers and come out on top even though he'd been outnumbered four to one. *Either he's real lucky or he's real good, or both,* Jesse thought. *I may just have to look Mister Palmer up before I leave town.* Making the man's acquaintance just might make his job a bit easier; that was especially true after José told him who it was that Palmer had killed in the saloon that night.

José stepped out of the room; Jesse stood and reached for the towel on the back of the chair. He quickly dried himself and dressed in clean, though wrinkled, clothes from his saddlebags. He strapped his gun belt back around his waist and settled the hand-tooled holsters on his hips; picking up the Henry from its resting place in the corner, Jesse stepped out into the barbershop.

"I declare, I expected you to be half your size after soaking for that long!" the good-looking blond barber exclaimed as she rose from her high-backed, horsehide-covered barber chair. "Are you ready for that haircut now?"

"Yes, ma'am, I am. I'd like to have a shave along with it, if one's available," Jesse replied. He leaned the Henry against the counter nearby and sat down in the chair. After Maddie threw a sheet over him to catch the cut hair, Jesse slipped one of the Remingtons out of its holster and into his lap; he hadn't made it to his twentieth year by taking chances.

Three

When she finished his shave, Maddie Parker doused Jesse's cheeks with toilet water that she said was good for attracting the ladies. "How about you, are you attracted?" he asked her with a wide grin.

"Not to a wandering gunhand, I'm not!" she retorted. "Although, you do clean up pretty good." His hair was cut short enough that he'd have to watch out that his ears didn't get sunburned, his mustache was trimmed up and he smelled sweet. With a wry smile and a tip of his hat, Jesse paid Maddie for the bath, haircut and shave; he tipped generously just because he felt like it. She suggested that he leave his saddlebags and rifle in her shop, and offered to have his dirty, trail-worn clothes cleaned and mended. A man just couldn't beat a deal like that.

Stepping out onto the boardwalk in front of the barbershop, Jesse turned and sauntered toward the nearest beanery, ready for some dinner. After eating his own cooking for at least a week, it was time to put his feet under a table and chew on something that hadn't come out of a frying pan over a juniper or mesquite fire. He pushed open the door to Harry's Hash House and eased into the high-ceilinged room. Several long pine-plank tables covered with red-checked tablecloths and lined with benches stood in ranks on the wide puncheon floor. Men were seated on both sides of the tables; platters of steaks and bowls of potatoes, biscuits, and other fixings were making their way from one diner to the next. The buzz of conversation stopped momentarily when Jesse stepped into the room, but quickly resumed. Ellsworth had seen its share of men with tied-down guns; one more didn't really mean all that much to most of the residents. Jesse was just another face in the crowd here, and that's the way he liked it.

A vacant spot on a bench on the far side of the table nearest the back wall caught his eye. Seated there, his back would be covered and he would be facing the doors and windows. It was the perfect seat. He walked over and looked down at the burly fellow in rough miner's clothing sitting next to the empty spot; "Is this seat taken?" he asked, pointing.

The miner glanced up from his plate long enough to answer, "It is if you sit there," then went back to eating. Jesse slid his legs under the table and sat down. Soon his plate was full and the rattle of his cutlery joined the general hubbub in the room. When Jesse was halfway through a quarter of an apple pie, a well-built man dressed in clean range clothing came through the door, and a call of "Hey Harvey," caught Jesse's attention. It could be that this was the Harvey Palmer he'd heard the stories about. If this cowboy was Palmer, now would be a good time for Jesse to look him over without causing trouble.

Harvey had been in Ellsworth long enough to qualify as a native. He grinned at the room, then nodded and spoke quietly to a couple of acquaintances. He took a seat kitty-corner from the kid in the gray hat. Taking the plate that was placed in front of him, he wiped it with his sleeve then set it on the table and filled it with food from the passing bowls and platters. As he ate, Harvey was aware of the stranger across the table to his left, who was watching every move that he made.

Dammit, Harvey thought to himself, *I hope this ain't another friend of those gunhands from the other day... and I really hope he ain't a relative.* Harvey knew that if this gent was trouble, he couldn't do a whole lot about it until the fellow in question decided to make a move, so he settled in to eat. When he was comfortably stuffed with beef and biscuits, Harvey stood up and carried his plate to the low table next to the kitchen door. On one end of the table sat a bucket into which the diners scraped any leavings from their plates. When he had money, Harvey didn't have any leavings to speak of; there were fewer when he didn't have money. He glanced back at the room; his gaze swept once more over the tall, lean gent across the table. Harvey still had no clue who that fella might be, but since the kid hadn't so much as spoken to him, Harvey dismissed his concerns and walked out into the street, closing the door behind him. His thoughts went to the prospect of a drink over at the Bit O' Luck, and maybe a night with Alice or Mae. He turned in the direction of the saloon just as the taunting words of a challenge rang out behind him.

"Harvey Palmer! You killed my cousin, and you killed a friend of mine!" Harvey turned slowly around, expecting to see the fellow from the table. Instead, he found himself facing a lean whip of a man sporting a pencil-thin mustache and a pair of shiny, nickel-plated Colts. Before Harvey had gotten completely turned around, the man reached for his guns; caught off-guard and off-balance, Harvey could only throw himself to the ground as he grabbed for the Colt on his hip. Two shots blasted, echoing from the false-fronted buildings of the street, but he felt no bullet's impact; he could hardly believe his luck! As the thin gunman fell away from him, Harvey realized that someone else had stepped out into the street and saved his bacon; it was the kid from the beanery. As he calmly reloaded his gun, the stranger commented simply, "It looked like he had you at a disadvantage; I hope you don't mind my stepping in to help."

"Mister, I can't remember a time when I minded less about someone stickin' his nose into my affairs!" Harvey declared as he scrambled to his feet. "Can I buy you a drink? Maybe even two?"

Four

The man the diners called Harvey ate quietly across the table; while Jesse waited for him to finish eating, he nursed a rapidly cooling cup of black coffee and considered how to go about getting a chance to talk to him about the men Harvey had killed. Harvey rose from the table and walked toward the kitchen where he scraped his plate into the wreck pan. Jesse waited a moment longer, then stood and did the same. He dropped two bits on the cloth-covered dining table and sauntered toward the door, wanting to exit after Harvey.

Jesse lingered inside the door as Harvey stepped outside and turned toward the saloon; he stepped out onto the boardwalk just in time to hear the thin man with the shiny Colts call Harvey Palmer's name and draw his pistols. As Harvey threw himself to the ground, clawing for his gun, Jesse stepped to one side. The thin man saw the movement in his peripheral vision and swung his guns toward Jesse; one of the Remingtons appeared in Jesse's hand and a big .44 slug slammed into the shooter's chest and tore through his heart. The gunman's own bullet went into the dust of the street as he fell.

As Jesse punched out the empty shell and filled the chamber with a loaded cartridge from his belt, Harvey stood and holstered his gun then tried to beat the dust out of his clothes. "I think I can handle a drink or two," Jesse replied. "But we might want to head that way kinda fast. There'll be a crowd here shortly." He nodded toward the faces pressed against the café window. "And I really don't think you fancy buying drinks for the whole bunch." He grinned and holstered the reloaded Remington, then held out his hand in a gesture of "after you". Harvey nodded wordlessly and led the way down the street. Since the law would more than likely be looking them up fairly shortly, they might as well have a drink while they waited.

Introductions were made, and the two men stood elbow to elbow at the worn bar in the Bit O' Luck and toasted long life and good health. "I sure hope I got a long life ahead," muttered Harvey morosely. "I'm startin' to wonder. Ever since I had to shoot those fellas the other day, I've been dodgin' one dang thing after another." He sipped his whiskey, then set the glass solidly back on the bar.

"Want to tell me about it?" Jesse asked quietly. The bar was lined with drinkers, and two white-shirted bartenders were kept busy filling glasses. Several scantily-clad ladies of the evening wended their way through the crowded room, carrying trays of drinks and artfully dodging the reaching hands of the patrons at the tables that dotted the spur-scarred pine floor. A faro table beyond the bar was surrounded by men eager to "buck the tiger", while other customers bet their hard-earned pay on the roulette wheel. The rattle of coins and the slap of cards underlay the hubbub of voices that rose in a variety of accents in the smoky air of the room.

"There's not much to tell," Harvey replied. "I was just ridin' along, mindin' my own business, when I come on these fellas robbin' the stage out south of here. They weren't hurtin' me none, and I didn't know nobody on that coach, so I just kinda sat back there in the brush and waited for 'em to get finished. If they'd've gone the other way, they never would've seen me settin' there. But they did see me, and they started in to shootin' their guns at me. I started shootin' back, just so they'd leave me alone, and I dusted a couple of 'em. I really wasn't lookin' for trouble, but I'm startin' to think I shoulda let 'em shoot me; it would've been a whole lot simpler." He signaled a bartender for a refill of both glasses before he went on.

"Two more men jumped me in here the other night, and I ended up killin' one of 'em. I'd be the first to admit that it was more luck than skill. Now I find out I'm considered a real bad man--some kind of gunfightin' hero or some such. I'm glad I got some money out of this whole fiasco, but I also got a lot of complications." He took a long swallow from his drink. "An', mister, there ain't nothin' in this world I want less than complications."

Jesse sipped his second drink. Unfortunately for Harvey, his life was going to get even more complicated, whether he liked it or not. "Uh, you do realize, I guess, that the character you shot in here the other night has six brothers, right?" he asked Harvey.

Harvey stared unbelievingly at Jesse. "Oh no!"

Harvey groaned as he stood up away from the bar and pushed his hat back on his head. "You've gotta be joshin'! Or I hope you are!"

Nope," Jesse answered. "According to José down at the bathhouse, that fella you shot in here the other night was Verl Baxter. Surely you've heard of Howdy Baxter, haven't you?" Without waiting for an answer Jesse went on. "Howdy is Verl's older brother. And Howdy's kind of partial to havin' his whole family alive, if you follow my drift."

As the color began to drain from Harvey's face, the two men heard heavy footsteps on the boardwalk in front of the saloon. The batwing doors slammed open, and a deep voice boomed, "I'll have them guns, young feller!" Jesse's jaw clenched and his gaze turned to ice in the mirror back of the bar as a slovenly, unshaven fellow with a tarnished star pinned to the lapel of his gravy-stained vest stomped across the room. The heavyset star-packer reached out for Jesse's shoulder, intending to spin him around. Jesse turned of his own accord; as he did, one of his Remingtons turned with him and the muzzle found a home under the fellow's chin.

"I'll thank you to keep your hands to yourself, mister," Jesse rasped through clenched teeth. "You got a name?"

The man swallowed loudly then answered with some difficulty due to the gun muzzle's position, "Uh, it's Barnes. Chandler Barnes."

"Well, Mister, uh, Barnyard, did you say?" Jesse said loudly. "I really don't believe that the good people of Ellsworth would make you the sheriff, so where'd you get the star and the attitude?"

Barnes swallowed nervously again, his Adam's

apple bobbing. "I'm, uh, I'm actin' sheriff while Sheriff Johnson's outta town. An' yer under arrest fer murder."

"Murder of whom, may I ask?" Jesse inquired formally while a smile tugged at his lips. "Surely you don't mean that fancy-pants with the nickel-plated Colts who fell down dead on the boardwalk down by the café?" The man tried to nod, but again he was having some difficulty due to the muzzle of the Remington. "Wrong answer, Mister Barnyard," Jesse told him. "Fancy Pants drew first. He was planning on shooting Mister Palmer here in the back. I merely acted in self-defense when that fella turned his pistols on me. Just ask any of those folks I saw with their faces glued to the glass down yonder. Surely you don't expect me to just stand there and let him shoot me, do you?" Barnes shook his head no. "I thought not. Now then, why don't you go on about your business and leave us to our drinks?" Barnes nodded carefully, not trusting his voice. "Have a nice day, Mister Barnyard. And leave the star here. It's only going to get you hurt." Jesse reached down with his free hand, unpinned the star from Barnes' vest, and tossed it on the bar. "Now, git!"

Barnes turned to leave, scuttling toward the scarred batwings as the crowd applauded. Apparently Barnes wasn't very popular with the residents of Ellsworth. In a moment he had disappeared out the door with his tail tucked figuratively between his legs. Like most bullies, once somebody stood up to him his true colors shone through. As Barnes vanished out the door Jesse holstered his pistol, then turned back to see Harvey looking at him in disbelief. Harvey stood mute for nearly a minute before reaching over and setting his empty glass on the bar. He hitched up his britches, set his hat more firmly on his head, and started for the exit himself.

"*Adios,*" he muttered to Jesse.

Jesse called after his new friend, "Where you goin', Harv?"

Without turning around, Harvey answered, "I've always had a hankerin' to visit Seattle, maybe drift up to Alaska, too. I reckon now's as good a time as any to do just that. See ya."

As he rode out of town a short time later, Harvey was considering the day's events. *That Jesse seemed like a nice enough fella,* he thought to himself. *Might do to ride with, that is if I wasn't going to Seattle.* He grinned. *On second thought, maybe I should go up and look at Sitka. Always wanted to see some really BIG country.*" His horse was a good, long-legged lineback dun he'd had for a couple of years. They understood each other and made it a point to look after each other; that is, if horses make a point of anything. Harvey pondered that question for a few miles, too. The sun went down and they ambled along through the night, taking their time.

In due time the sun rose out of the prairie to the east, and after a water stop at a spring they stumbled upon, man and horse continued putting miles behind them. Around noon, Harvey reined in under a wide-spreading tree at the edge of a small grove and got down to make a bite to eat. The dun cropped the lush grass nearby, and stayed close to the tiny fire that Palmer built. Following fried meat and some pretty bad coffee, Harvey laid back against the bole of a tree. He contemplated the fact that he really did make terrible coffee until he dozed off, which, after the long night of riding, didn't take long. As he slipped off into comfortable slumber, he thought that the Mexicans had sure come up with a good idea when they invented the siesta. With the dun around, he didn't worry about anyone sneaking up on him. That horse could hear a fly buzzing a mile away, and had eyes like a hawk. Harvey dreamed of a girl back in town; never mind which girl. There were several back yonder worth dreaming about.

Five

Jesse watched Harvey disappear out the door. *What's his problem?* he wondered silently. That so-called 'actin' sheriff was nothing to worry about. Jesse shrugged and reached for his glass. It was empty, and he started to raise it to get the bartender's attention then changed his mind and dropped his hand. He hated drinking alone, so he figured that he might as well go to bed, providing of course that he could find a hotel room. Come morning he'd see if Harvey really had ridden out.

In the morning, Jesse went to the livery to check on his horse, and to find out if Harvey had a horse stabled there. The liveryman met him at the door. "I want you to get that demon out of here!" he exclaimed, red-faced, as he stood up to his full, still less-than-impressive height to shake a finger in Jesse's face. "So far that no-good crow bait's tried to bite me twice, and he's kicked the walls out of two stalls for me! I want him out of my barn, and I want him out now!"

"Easy there, old timer," Jesse said placatingly. "I'll pay for the damages, all right?"

"Yer dern tootin' you will!" the stable owner

exclaimed angrily. "And then you and that devil-horse are gettin' out of my stable!"

Jesse quickly paid the man for the damages the roan mustang had done to the barn then saddled then ill-tempered horse. "By the way, mister, do you know what kind of horse Harvey Palmer's ridin'? And could you point me to the stall it was in?"

"Yeah, I know his horse, an' it's a lot better tempered than that one of your'n." The irate stableman pointed across the aisle. "It was over yonder, an' it was a line-back dun."

"Thank you, sir." Jesse ground-tied his roan and walked over to the stall where Palmer's horse had been. He dropped down on one knee and looked the tracks over carefully. After a minute or so, he stood up, with the dun's tracks fixed firmly in his mind. There were a couple of things he needed to talk to Harvey about, so he decided that he'd best get moving. Jesse led the roan outside then stepped into the saddle and started around the barn, intently watching the ground. He figured that Harvey would probably take the most unobtrusive route out of town, and sure enough, the dun's tracks led out from the back door of the livery. In the soft dirt near the water trough an obvious line of tracks pointed to the north. The dun was a big, easy moving mount and would cover a lot of ground. Jesse heeled the roan into a trot and started north, following Harvey Palmer's trail.

Harvey woke up as he always did, whether he was being chased or not: cautiously. He didn't move anything except his eyes until he had figured out what had ruined his nap. He could see that the dun was facing down their back trail; the big horse's ears were up, but he didn't seem unduly alarmed. It must have been the dun's snort that awakened him. Since he was not exactly a trusting sort, Harvey carefully moved his head to look in the direction the dun's ears were pointing. A half a mile or so down the trail, a horse stepped into view, and Harvey peered intently at the rider in an effort to see who it might be. The man on the buckskin was no one that he could recollect, but had a familiar look about him nonetheless . Whoever the rider was, he was holding his rifle across the pommel of his saddle, and appeared to be hunting something or someone.

Keeping to the shade, Harvey eased over to his saddlebags and picked up his Winchester carbine from where it rested against them. Out of habit, he checked the loads in the gun, then got to his feet and moved behind a nearby tree. He spotted a second rider some hundred yards or so behind the first, and a short time later two more riders came into view. All of the men carried rifles in their hands; it looked for all the world as if there was a hunting party on his back trail.

Harvey thought back to what Jesse had told him about Verl Baxter having a lot of friends and relatives; he quickly stuffed his gear into his saddlebags and tied them behind the cantle of his saddle. He kicked dirt over the fire and poured the last of his coffee over the dirt; at least his coffee was good for that, even if it was barely drinkable. He didn't figure he had time to do much more to hide his presence. He threw the saddle on the dun, then led the big horse deeper into the trees and stepped aboard. If those men were looking for him, they'd have to work a lot harder than they were at the moment to find him. Harvey figured he might not be good for much, but he was a dang good injun on the trail. He hadn't particularly been trying to hide his trail up to this point, but he was about to start doing exactly that. As he set out, he reflected again that the last thing he wanted from life was complications, but they just seemed to be stacking up more and more all the time.

Six

Jesse gave the roan his head and the horse stepped out in a ground-eating walk. That gelding might be ugly as sin, and have a nasty disposition to boot, but he was out of wild stock and could go all day and then some on a hatful of water and a handful of mesquite beans. As Jesse kept his eyes on the ground, he could tell from the dun's widely spaced tracks that Harvey was more interested in covering ground than in covering his trail, and so he was easy to follow.

It was a couple of hours past noon and the dun's tracks were getting fresher when Jesse reined the roan in abruptly. "Whoa, boy. We better think about this," he said as the horse's ears swiveled. There in front of them, the tracks of several more horses had crossed over the top of Harvey's tracks and the new tracks swerved to follow the trail the dun had left.

Smoothly, Jesse shucked his Henry out of the scabbard and laid it across his lap. His fingers were tucked into the lever, ready to jack a round into the chamber quickly if need be. Tipping his hat back from his forehead, Jesse sat and contemplated; from the tracks, four riders appeared to be on Harvey's trail. The complications did seem to be stacking up, whether Harvey wanted them to or not.

Jesse tickled the roan with his spurs and the horse stepped out again, walking easily. Jesse figured there was no sense making a lot of noise for the characters on Harvey's trail to hear. In the far distance, a small copse of trees and brush indicated the presence of water, and it looked like a good resting place if a fellow was in mind to have a siesta. All of the tracks were pointed in that direction, so Jesse headed that way, too. Ahead of him, Jesse could make out several riders through the haze of the midday heat. As near as he could tell the men all had their rifles ready, and they were spread out in a skirmish line, like they were hunting; as far as Jesse knew, the only thing out here to hunt Harvey Palmer.

Over to the west, a small draw seemed to point to a rocky ridge which appeared to peter out near the grove of alders; Jesse reined the roan over toward the crease in the ground. He figured that if he hurried, he could skirt around the trail through the draw and get to that little grove of trees yonder at about the same time as, or a little after, the riders. If he could manage that, he could ride down from the north and make it look as though he was just passing through. It was also possible that he might find Harvey's trail in the process, if Harvey had kept going north. It was a pretty sure bet that a man as canny as Harvey wasn't going to be in those trees by the time the hunters got there, if he'd even been there at all.

The roan slid on its haunches down into the draw, and Jesse booted the horse into a shambling trot.

The bottom of the draw was soft sand which would muffle the sounds of the roan's hooves. After only a few minutes travel, the small wash came to an end in a cluster of bushes. Jesse drew rein in the shadows of a large clump of head-high greasewood and looked around for the men he was trying to flank. He spotted them near the thicket. Through the trees of the little grove, they looked to be milling around the remains of a small campfire. One of the men was kneeling by the ashes feeling for heat, while another circled slowly around the area trying to locate tracks. The remaining two riders sat their horses, rifles at the ready across their laps.

The line of brush Jesse was behind continued for roughly another hundred yards before it ended just to the north of the clearing where the men searched. As Jesse walked his horse toward the trees he levered a round into the Henry's chamber then let the hammer down to half-cock; he had no idea who the searchers were, and if he needed the rifle he would need it in a hurry. As he came down through the trees and pulled the roan to a stop, he called out, "Hello, the camp! Mind if I come in?" At the sound of his voice the two men on the ground grabbed for their holstered pistols; the two who were mounted dropped to the ground on the far side of their horses. A rifle barrel appeared over one of the saddles.

Jesse raised his left hand and tipped his hat back a little. His other hand stayed wrapped around the Henry with his thumb on the hammer. "Now hold on a minute there, pards, no need to get hasty," he said calmly. "I'm just passin' through, lookin' to water my horse. I ain't lookin' for trouble."

He could see now that the big, dark-haired

man kneeling by the fire was Marty Bannon. A saddle partner of Howdy Baxter, Bannon took care of things Howdy didn't think he had time to mess with himself. "You see anybody heading north from here, mister?" the big gunman asked roughly. He stood and faced Jesse belligerently.

"Can't say as I did, friend," Jesse answered truthfully. He really hadn't seen anybody. "Who're you looking for?"

"We're lookin' for a man by the name of Harvey Palmer," Bannon told him. "He killed a friend of our'n, an' we're lookin' ta talk to 'im about it."

"Harvey Palmer, eh? I hear he's a real bad feller to tangle with. You gents might want to rethink what you're doing." Jesse gave Bannon a smile that stopped short of his cold gray eyes.

"Ain't no rethinkin' needed, boy!" Bannon retorted, heat in his voice. "We're plannin' on killin' him! So why don't you just ride on?"

At the word "boy" Jesse's horse suddenly shifted its feet, turning sideways to where Bannon stood. When the horse halted, the Henry in Jesse's hand just happened to be pointing at Marty Bannon's belt buckle; the hammer was eared back. "This here Henry ain't no boy, Mister Bannon," Jesse said softly, with frost icing his voice. Bannon gave him a startled look. "Yes, I know who you are, and you've got a reputation as a hard man, but you'd best be careful who you try to push. And you can tell that man over yonder with the rifle that if he even so much as thinks about shootin' me, I'm gonna put a .44 slug in your belly. I just came up here to water my horse. There's no call for hostilities."

It was obvious that Bannon wasn't afraid of the rifle pointed at him. It was equally as obvious that right at that moment he didn't feel that getting shot was in his best interest. "Montez, back off," he said. "Let this gent water his horse and be on his way." Instantly the rifle disappeared.

"*Sí*, Marty," the rifleman answered in a thick Spanish accent.

"That's right considerate of you, Mister Bannon," Jesse remarked. He stepped down and led his horse toward a small pool of water which sustained a bit of green around its edge. The Henry never wavered as the horse drank and Jesse filled his canteen. Jesse stepped back into the saddle then backed the roan away from the men. "You gents take care now, hear?" He whirled the roan and spurred him around the far side of the small grove of trees. At any second he expected to hear gunshots and the whine of lead bees around his ears, but the only thing he heard was the thudding of the roan's hooves.

Seven

Out of sight and rifle range on the other side of the trees, Jesse slowed the roan and looked around. Off to his left, a wash meandered toward a low line of hills that loomed blue in the distance; Jesse turned the horse toward the wash, looking for a place to hole up and see what transpired with the men hunting Harvey. His first impulse had been to try to find Harvey's tracks, but that would only lead the hunters to the trail. He decided it might be better to hang back and let the hunters lead him.

A cow trail cut in the steep side of the wash led Jesse and the roan down onto the hard packed sand in the bottom of the sculpted defile. Jesse loosened his saddle's cinch then ground tied the roan in the shade of the bank and took a spyglass out of his saddlebag. He scrambled back up the side of the draw and came to rest with his eyes just clearing the edge and his head between two small clumps of sage. He tipped his hat off and let it hang by the rawhide chinstrap. Bringing the spyglass to his eye, Jesse braced his elbows on the bank in front of him.

The hunting party, with Bannon in the lead, swam into focus through the heat waves. The big man was riding slowly, looking intently at the ground, trying to find some sign of where Harvey had gone. Apparently, the hunters believed that Harvey had ridden north, in spite of Jesse telling them that he hadn't seen anyone. There was no way for them to know that Jesse hadn't actually come in from that direction, but apparently they hadn't believed what he'd said. It was possible that one of them had seen the tracks of Jesse's horse, but he didn't think so, because Bannon and his men were angling away from Jesse's trail, and they seemed to have forgotten him altogether.

The four men were spread out and were casting their eyes from side to side; all of them were searching for signs now. Apparently, Harvey had done a good job of hiding his tracks. As Jesse watched through the glass, the men stopped near a clump of greasewood and Bannon leaned down from the saddle to pluck something from the end of a branch. Jesse couldn't tell for sure, but through the glass, it looked like a tuft of hair from a horse's tail. It wasn't long before the men moved out of sight, and Jesse slid down the bank to his horse. He stowed the spyglass, then pulled the cinch tight. "Come on, horse," he told the roan. "Let's us move on up the country and see if we can follow those boys without being spotted."

Near the top of a rocky knoll, miles to the north of where Jesse was following the hunters, Harvey rested the big dun. With only the top of his head showing among the rocks, he could see a good distance down his back trail. Far to the south, a thin trace of dust rose into the air, letting him know he was still being followed, albeit slowly. Those boys were having more than a little bit of trouble following the trail. Harvey sighed wearily, touched the dun with his spurs and moved the horse out onto the trail leading north.

Jesse was behind the hunters now, and he chuckled to himself as he watched them. Either they were having a devil of a time finding Harvey's trail, or Bannon wasn't as good an injun as he thought he was. Whatever the case, at the rate they were traveling it was going to be a long time before those yahoos caught up with Harvey. Jesse decided that it was about time to start having a little fun with them; he figured he could maybe slow them down even more. He reined the roan behind a small rise, then stepped down and shucked the Henry from the boot. One of the roan's virtues was that he would stand fast, come hell or high water, gunfire or no gunfire. Jesse levered a cartridge into the chamber of the rifle, tipped up the ladder sight, and contemplated the distance to the nearest rider. It was a fair piece, but Jesse wasn't really worried about precision shooting; he was just out to stir the pot, so to speak.

The first man Jesse got his sights on was Marty Bannon. The outlaw was standing behind a tall clump of greasewood; from his posture, it was obvious that he was answering the call of nature, his bridle reins gripped in his right hand. About the time he figured that things should have been going good, Jesse lifted the Henry to his shoulder and fired. Throwing the lever and triggering as fast as he could, Jesse dusted the area around Bannon. The outlaw disappeared for a moment then reappeared, scrambling to hang onto his horse. One of Jesse's shots must have burned the horse somewhere because the bay started bucking then ran off with his head up and tilted to one side to keep from stepping on the bridle reins. The bay's startled owner ran after it, cussing and yelling. Obviously, Bannon's horse wasn't as well trained as the roan. It took Bannon's companions a moment or two to come out from under cover and get themselves organized enough to ride in pursuit of the runaway.

Jesse laughed out loud as he reloaded the Henry. He moved over to where the roan patiently waited for the fusillade to end and slid the Henry back into the scabbard. Jesse gathered the reins, mounted and headed north. Now he wanted to get ahead of these fellas, and see what other kind of mischief he could dream up.

An hour later Jesse reined up in the shade of a bushy mahogany that grew out of a crack in a large boulder. He took out his spyglass and brought it to his eye. Focusing through the heat waves, he could see the hunters coming slowly, once again spread out in a skirmish line with their rifles ready. One of the hunters was intently scanning the ground, looking for tracks, while the others kept an eye out for an ambush, which was just exactly what Jesse had in mind. Once again the Henry came out; at the first shot, the tracker's horse shied away from the spurt of dust. Levering quickly, Jesse again sprayed the area with bullets, holding higher this time. He wasn't out to kill anybody; he just wanted to make them think a little. One of the men suddenly grabbed the side of his head and swayed in the saddle.

"Damn, Marty, that SOB shot my ear off!" Hank Jenkins yelled, clapping a hand to the side of his head. The men dropped from their horses, sheltering themselves with their mounts between them and the distant puffs of powder smoke. "We gotta do somethin'!"

Bannon stood on the lee side of his horse, cussing steadily under his breath. "I swear, I'll hang that no good Palmer's hide from a tree! I'm gettin' tired of this crap!" Suddenly, Bannon's horse gave a lunge and tried to bolt. Only a swift wrench on the bridle reins kept him in control of the startled animal. He jerked the bay back in front of him. He noticed something dripping from the far side of the horse, and he cussed again. "That rotten bastard shot my horse!" he raged. "I'll skin him alive and stake him to an anthill!"

The last echoes of the shooting died away, and the men cautiously peered over their saddles in the direction of the shooting. "I theenk he goes," the Mexican, Montez, ventured. "He ain' shooteen' no more."

After a few more minutes passed with no more rifle fire, Bannon ventured out. "I think you're right, Cholo. You boys keep watch. I gotta check on my horse." Bannon pulled the horse around to assess its wounds and swore again. Water was dripping from a bullet hole in the canteen he had slung from his saddle horn; his horse was unhurt, but his canteen was dripping its last.

Eight

The lonesome howl of a solitary coyote drifted across the darkened landscape. The whoosh of wings, and a sudden squeak, announced the demise of a deer mouse as an owl found one last bit of food before heading to its roost for the day. "Dammit!" Harvey's low curse alerted the denizens of the night to the presence of man. He cursed again as he stumbled over another rock in the predawn darkness. The eastern sky showed a rim of light, but the hilly terrain he stumbled through was still cloaked in velvety black, faintly lit by the brightness of stars overhead. He stopped for a moment and looked back over his shoulder at his horse's silhouette; the big dun, always game, limped up to Harvey and nudged his shoulder with its nose, urging him up the rocky trail. "Alright, alright, I'm goin'," Harvey mumbled as he went on. "Don't be so impatient."

Harvey's original intention had been to skirt around the nearby town of Watsonville and continue on to the north. At least that *had* been his plan until the dun's left front shoe had busted while they were picking their way through a patch of rocks some miles back. The shoe hadn't broken clean, and before Harvey realized something was wrong the big horse began favoring its left foreleg. Harvey had stepped down and used his belt knife to pry off the broken shoe; he'd been as gentle as he could, but the damage was already done. They would have to go into town and get a new shoe and rest the hoof. Harvey had quietly cursed again, to himself, resigned to going where he didn't really want to go. He had grub and water, and he really preferred to stay as far as possible ahead of the men hunting him. That was no longer an option, and meant more complications…

Hitching his holstered Colt into a more comfortable position, Harvey contemplated what he knew about Watsonville as he walked. The last time he'd been through this part of the world, the town had consisted of a saloon, a beanery, and a blacksmith shop. The blacksmith, Lars Johansen, was a good friend of his; the big Norwegian was also part-time postmaster, taking care of the few letters that arrived for the outlying ranches. A freighter brought in what supplies the local folks ordered, but nobody in the town kept much of a stock of goods on hand, other than a few staples such as coffee and flour. Consequently, when he topped out on a rise west of the town Harvey was surprised to see what looked to him like a bustling metropolis spread out in front of him. Since he'd last been here, a store, what appeared to be a hotel, and even a church had been built. It was truly amazing what the passage of a little time could bring to a town. *Somebody must have struck it rich,* he thought to himself

By now Harvey was limping and half-lame himself. His riding boots weren't exactly made for hiking, and he'd been walking, or rather stumbling, in the dark through some pretty rough terrain for most of the night. He was glad the blacksmith shop was on this end of town; the sore-footed dun and his owner didn't have much further to walk. In the shop a match flared, and the upwelling of light as a lamp was lit announced the arrival of the smith at his place of business. By the time Harvey limped up to the door of the rambling building, a thin thread of smoke was drifting from the forge's chimney as Lars kindled a fire and got ready for the day's work.

The forge was built to one side of an open alley that ran completely through the shop to end in a small wagon yard out back. Lars Johansen, his thickly-muscled arms and chest straining the seams of his blue gingham shirt, had his back to the door. He was blowing on the small flame that licked at the slivers of pitchwood lying nestled in the charcoal of the forge bed. The glow of the fire grew stronger as the flames greedily consumed the tinder; soon the charcoal itself began to glow. Carefully Lars worked the bellows, blowing more air into the fire bed and stoking up the heat. Presently, he grunted in satisfaction and turned to look out the door of the smithy.

"Mornin'," Harvey greeted him. "How ya doin', Lars?"

"Harvey Palmer, I svear," the big Swede replied. "I t'ought you vas det."

"Not yet, I ain't," Harvey said with a grin. He stepped forward to shake the big, fair-haired smith's hand. "Although a few folks have been tryin' lately to put me in the ground."

"Oh?" Lars said, one eyebrow raised quizzically. He took note of Harvey's trail-worn appearance, then continued. "So vhat brings ye to our fair city, eh? Problems, I'll vager."

"Complications, more like," Harvey said. "There's some men on my backtrail, and I was plannin' on avoiding civilization for a while, but the dun came up lame. He broke a shoe last night and I think it may have bruised the frog before I noticed it."

Lars rushed solicitously to Harvey's mount; he'd raised the dun from a colt, and he'd sold Harvey that horse. The big horse stood quietly, holding its weight off the sore hoof, making it easy to tell where to look. Lars picked up the hoof and felt it gingerly. "I can poot on a new shoe, and maybe bar it oop a bit," he told Harvey. "He's gonna be sore for a few days. If ye vant, ye can lay 'im oop in my back corral out of sight. Not much goes back dere, and dere's a goot spring and some grass." He let the hoof down and reached for the cinch. "Poot yer gear in de back storage room. Dere ain't no rats back dere."

"Much obliged, Lars," Harvey said tiredly. He stripped the gear off of the dun then carried it to the room Lars had indicated. He stood the saddle on its tail in the corner and spread the blankets, horse side up, on top of the saddle to dry. He hung his bridle on a hook and went back to where the dun stood patiently waiting. So well trained was the dun that the thin horsehair *mecate*, or lead rope, on the ground held him hard and fast. Harvey had his rifle and saddlebags in his left hand. "Is the hotel any good, Lars? I feel like I been walkin' for a week."

The big smith chuckled. "Yah, it ain' too bat. Pretty vidow voman runnin' it, too." He gave Harvey a grin and pointed out the door. "Go get some rest. De dun'll be finished een a yiffy and I'll poot 'im out back."

Nine

At the young age of thirty, Lila Foster was indeed a widow, and she was pretty. She had married later than most women of her day; she'd spent most of her twenties waiting for the man she truly loved to decide that she was the only woman for him, but that hope had gone south. Instead, the man she wanted to marry had run from commitment as hard and as fast as he could. Approaching what was considered old-maid-hood and desperately wanting a family, she had married Bertram Foster. Bertram had talked a good line, but he'd had too much trouble cutting his momma's apron strings to be a good husband.

After two childless years of marriage, Bertram and Lila had decided to go west from their native Ohio; they'd taken up with a wagon train leaving for the gold camps in California. Having grown up on a farm near the hamlet of Palmer's Creek, Lila had handled wagon teams most of her life; it fell to her to do most of the wagon driving while Bertram complained. He complained about the dust, the bugs, and the weather; he complained about most anything else he could think of to complain about. Lila did her best to make his passage as painless as possible, all the while rapidly coming to the conclusion that marrying for the reasons she had, and especially marrying the man she had married, had been a serious mistake.

On the advice of a somewhat unsavory scout, the wagon train had taken a less-traveled trail, arriving in Watsonville in the late fall. The year was far gone; if they continued on toward California, they risked being caught in the mountains by the winter blizzards. The weary travelers had decided that discretion was better than derring-do, so they had stopped for the winter and built temporary shelters. In that regard as well, Bertram had performed less than adequately, as he had never been much of a hand with tools. Just as winter was wearing itself out, Bertram had contracted pneumonia; he died shortly thereafter.

In a land where women were scarce, and especially women of quality, Lila had found herself the object of numerous proposals of marriage and other less proper arrangements. Rather than taking any of the offers, Lila had instead used her remaining cash, along with what she could get from the sale of her team and wagon, to finance the building of a small four-room hotel she called the Desert Inn. It was into this hotel that Harvey walked, looking for a place to rest while his horse was re-shod.

Harvey stepped into the lobby of the Desert Inn and looked around. He saw a small room with two armchairs to one side, nestled around a small trestle table. An ashtray, several well-thumbed magazines, and a small potted juniper tree decorated the tabletop. The tree's disheveled appearance belied the hardy little evergreen's lust for life; it simply refused to turn up its roots and expire. Across the room a counter hardly large enough to merit the name held a guest register and a small bell sitting in front of a hand-printed sign: *"Ring bell for service"*. Seeing no one in sight, Harvey reached out and tapped the bell. The tinny chiming brought a scurry of movement from behind a door in the wall back of the desk. A moment later, the door opened and Lila Foster hurried into the room; her right hand worked at tucking an errant strand of her fine brown hair back into place before greeting her customer. Little did she know who that customer would be.

The moment her dark brown eyes found the face of the figure across the counter, Lila's hand froze and she stopped stock-still; with his saddlebags and rifle slung carelessly over his shoulder, Harvey Palmer brought her quiet, ordered life to a sudden standstill. Her eyes went wide as Harvey's "Hello, Lila," greeted her in the smooth baritone voice that had thrilled her for all the years that she had known him.

As Lila's world stood still for a moment, her unbelieving gaze took in the unexpected apparition in front of her. *Harvey was here?* Her overwhelmed mind could barely comprehend what her eyes were telling her. *Harvey was here!* She'd never, in her wildest imaginings, dreamed that the only man she had ever truly loved would re-enter her life after six years, but here he was. His clothes were trail-worn and dusty, and several days worth of beard stubble covered his face, but none of that mattered to Lila; only the fact that he was there made any difference at all. Lila tried to speak but her throat was dry and not a sound escaped her soft, pink lips. She swallowed quickly, trying desperately to hide the emotions surging through her. As calmly as she could, she replied, "Hello, Harvey. What brings you to my hotel?"

She's as beautiful as ever, Harvey thought. Just the sight of her shortened his breath. All the years of running, and all the miles he'd put behind him, disappeared in a heartbeat as he suddenly realized how he truly felt about the lovely woman standing before him. He knew now what, subconsciously, he had always known: that everything that truly mattered in his life was to be found in the woman he now faced across a hotel counter. He took a deep breath and said softly, "I'm just passin' through, Lila. I didn't even know you were here. The last I heard you were still back in Ohio, and you were recently married. How the devil did you end up in Watsonville?"

"It's a long story, Harvey," she replied coolly. "I'll tell it to you some time."

"What will your husband think?" Harvey asked her, afraid to hear the answer...

"My husband is dead," Lila said, with little emotion coloring her tone. "Pneumonia took him two winters ago."

Relief washed over Harvey like an ocean wave and left him feeling weak, but he kept his voice neutral as he said softly, "I'm sorry, Lila. I didn't know."

Lila shrugged off the momentary melancholy that always came over her at the mention of Bertram. She smiled warmly and said, "You look well, Harvey-- aside from needing a bath and a shave."

"You look pretty good yourself, Lila," Harvey replied. "That hairstyle becomes you." At his words Lila unconsciously lifted a hand to her hair then stopped in mid-gesture and brought her hands back together in front of her. An uncomfortable silence filled the room, broken only by the distant thump of a hammer driving nails and the busy clucking of a hen scratching for bugs in the dust outside the room's open window. Their eyes met; Harvey lowered his saddlebags and rifle to the floor and stepped forward. Lila stood entranced, and then she was in his arms. Their lips touched in a kiss that lasted only a moment but seemed to go on for all eternity. For a fleeting moment, one word coursed through Harvey's brain: *Complications...*

The sound of boots on the boardwalk out front pushed the couple apart. Lila's face reddened; she turned away and hurried behind the counter as the blacksmith came through the hotel door. "Ah, dere you are, my friend," Lars said to Harvey. "Your horse is shod, and vaiting vhere I told ye."

"You came all the way down here to tell me that?" Harvey asked, an undertone of irritation rising in his voice.

Lars grinned as he took in the sight of Lila's pink cheeks and Harvey's sheepish expression. "No, I vas yust on my vay to de post office, and t'ought I'd stop by to tell ye. Did I interrupt someting?"

"Just go on and get your mail," Harvey growled. "I need to get some sleep."

"Pleasant dreams," Lars said, laughter ringing in his voice as he left.

Harvey turned back to the counter where Lila was holding out a key. "Never mind him," he said. "He's always thought he was pretty funny." He took the key from her hand, thanked her, then picked up his rifle and saddlebags and started down the hall. The key had a number on the leather tag, and he compared room numbers to the tag as he went. Lila watched him go, still dumbfounded at his appearance in Watsonville; her lips still tingled from his kiss. When he came to the last room, Harvey stood for a minute, checking for exits; no rat trusts himself to a hole with only one escape route. A door at the end of the hall appeared to lead outside. Satisfied that he could bail out if necessary, Harvey stepped inside the room and closed the door.

Ten

Harvey sat on the bed in his room in the Desert Inn with his left boot in his hand. He was dead tired, but still he sat there with one boot on and one boot off as his jumbled thoughts whirled through his brain. Lila was here, in Watsonville. That one brief kiss had proved beyond a doubt that it was really her, and Harvey was at a loss for his next move. On the one hand, he had the urge to run like he always had; to head for Johansen's, saddle the dun, and be gone. But another side of him wanted to stay. He'd been footloose and fancy-free since he'd left home all those years ago, going wherever life took him, but he'd never quite been able to get Lila out of his head. No matter how hard he tried, she was always there. And now she was here, just down the hall.

A small niggling voice in his brain kept saying, "Don't be a fool. That's a good woman, and she'd marry you in a heartbeat. You've got some money, buy a place and settle down." And right now that didn't sound half bad, except for the fact that Howdy Baxter was probably out to get him, and had more than likely sent those men who were following Harvey's trail. *Complications*, he thought once again as he took off his other boot, lay back on the bed, and closed his eyes...

Jesse was sleeping in this morning. He'd rolled out his bed deep in the brush near a spring where the sun couldn't reach him for a while. He'd had a busy night, as the hunters were probably just now finding out.

Shortly before midnight, Jesse left the roan tethered to a bush a half-mile from the hunters' camp and walked in from there, his moccasin-clad feet making no sound on the dry ground. He carried only his tied-down Remingtons and the antler handled skinning knife on his belt. He figured that if anything did happen, it would be up close and personal; the long-barreled Henry would just be in the way.

When he got to Bannon's camp, the first thing he did was look for the men's horses. Conveniently for Jesse, the outlaws had strung a picket line between two trees, and the horses were all tied side by side a short distance from where the last few embers of a supper fire still glowed. A battered coffeepot stood on a rock to one side of the fire with a few faint wisps of steam still drifting from the spout. Here and there in the fire circle a coal winked faintly, but it was likely that the men would have to build a new fire in the morning; this one was going to be out. That fit perfectly into Jesse's plans.

A lone sentry sat on a boulder at the edge of the camp; his back was to the camp and the remuda *as if he felt that anyone coming at them would come from out yonder. The steeple-crowned silhouette of the sentry's hat meant that it was the Mexican,*

Montez; the tilt of the silhouette meant that he was asleep. Jesse drifted into the camp like a shadow, and his open hand went to his cartridge belt. He squatted at the edge of the fire ring and brought his now closed hand down from his belt toward the last remaining embers. The momentary gleam of brass in the faint starlight disappeared while he felt around with his other hand for a moment; he picked up a blackened stick that had been used to stir the fire, and used it to carefully bury a handful of cartridges in the coolest part of the fire bed. The ring of rocks around the ashes was small; when the outlaws built any size fire at all, it would heat up those .44's, and those boys would be in for a surprise.

A sharp intake of breath froze Jesse in place. He slowly looked around for the source of the sound as one of the Remingtons appeared in his hand. He heard a belch and a grumble from one of the lumpy bedrolls scattered around the camp, but a snore soon followed. The outlaws must have been tired. Silence settled again over the camp and Jesse relaxed, quietly holstering the Remington. He picked up the coffeepot and drank a few swallows of the strong black liquid from the spout before he stood and stole silently to the stretched picket line.

Jesse moved quietly along the picket line, untying the horses from the stretched rope. On his way into the camp, he had seen a long ribbon of sand leading away from the camp toward the south. He slowly and carefully eased the horses over to the sand, where the sound of their hooves would be muffled. Grabbing a handful of mane, he vaulted to the back of Bannon's horse and led the rest of the remuda away from the camp. A mile or so later, he slipped the halters off all of the horses and, driving them in front of him, pushed them on. One by one, the animals slipped away and disappeared into the darkness; Jesse let them go wherever they wanted.

Several miles to the west, he stopped Bannon's horse, slid to the ground, and slipped off its halter as well. He slapped the bay on the rump to get it moving, then made his way back to where he had left his own horse. Bannon and his men wouldn't have too much trouble getting their horses back, but it would take them a while. Jesse decided that as soon as he got some sleep, it would be time to head for that town he'd seen on the map, a little place called Watsonville. If it was on the map, it was pretty likely to have a restaurant of some sort. Some hot food would be nice; jerky was okay in a pinch, but a good steak was hard to beat.

A breaking twig snapped Jesse's eyes open under the down-tilted brim of his hat. Jesse's breathing didn't change, but as he listened for the source of the noise, his right hand was on the Remington beside him under the blanket. After a minute or two of listening he relaxed, deciding that the roan had been the source of the noise. He sat up and tipped his hat back off of his forehead then threw off the blanket. He had removed only the moccasins he'd worn to the outlaw camp when he'd gone to bed in the wee hours of the morning; his boots stood alongside the saddle he'd used for a pillow. He reached over to the boots and turned them upside down one at a time, shaking them to remove any tenants who may have moved in during the night. He dumped a large spider out of the right boot then tugged it on. The spider scurried off as Jesse chuckled and told the retreating arachnid, "On your way, pardner. That ain't a safe place for either one of us." The left boot turned out to be unoccupied, so he pulled it on, then rose to his feet, picked up his gun belt and strapped it on.

Jesse quickly rolled his bed and tied it to his saddle, then pulled the picket pin and coiled the picket rope. He led the roan over to where his gear was stacked and was soon ready to hit the trail to Watsonville; he figured he had about ten miles to ride before he could get breakfast.

The morning hadn't been quite so peaceful in Marty Bannon's camp. The first dim light of day was stealing over the camp when the pain in his bullet-torn ear roused Hank Jenkins from a fitful sleep. He reached blearily for the bottle of "pain-killer" next to the saddle he was using for a pillow, and his eyes suddenly opened wide as they took in the sight of the vacant picket line. Sitting up and rubbing his eyes didn't do a thing to make the horses reappear. He mumbled a quick "Ah, crap!", then reached over to the heap of blankets nearby. He shook the shoulder of the recumbent figure there and said urgently, "Marty! Marty! Wake up! The horses is gone!" Grumbling, Bannon rose up on one elbow with his Colt in his hand and pointed in Jenkins' general direction.

"What are you chirpin' about, Hank?" the big outlaw demanded. Hank pointed a shaking finger at the empty picket line. Bannon turned his head to follow the vibrating digit, and witnessed the sight that had greeted Hank. He scrambled ungracefully out of his blankets and onto his feet and proceeded to cuss Harvey Palmer, Hank Jenkins, the horses, and anyone and anything else that came to mind. As he was describing the ancestry and potential future of his subjects in vivid detail, Bannon was stomping around in his long underwear and socks, with the Colt dangling, momentarily forgotten, in his hand. Montez slunk into sight with his eyes downcast. "Where were you when the horses was bein' stolen?" Bannon roared. The Colt in his hand jerked up suddenly, and the gaping muzzle centered on Montez' face. "You were supposed to be watchin'!"

"I mus' have fall asleep, Marty," Montez mumbled; he was pretty sure that he was about to die. The hammer clicked back on the Colt, and Bannon's finger was white on the trigger, as he struggled with the urge to scatter what few brains Montez appeared to have all over the camp. After a few tense moments that had Montez nearly paralyzed with fear, Marty let down the hammer on the Colt and lowered his hand to his side. "Shootin' you wouldn't bring the horses back, even if it would make me feel better," he growled. "Somebody get a fire goin' and put some coffee on. We'll start trackin' when it gets lighter." He moved to his bedroll, picked up his pants and started to dress while Rule Carson squatted down and started building a fire.

Carson pulled up a handful of dry grass and put it in the fire ring, then laid a few dry twigs on top. He scratched a match alight on a rock and lit the grass. A burst of flame began to lick greedily at the twigs, and Carson added some larger sticks to the growing fire. Flames began to crackle merrily. Carson reached for his canteen and the bag of Arbuckle's that lay nearby. He dumped the dregs from the coffeepot, filled it with fresh water, and tossed in a couple of handfuls of the coarsely-crushed coffee beans from the bag. The pot went into the ring near the now healthy fire, and Carson sat back on his haunches to wait for things to come to a boil, which they soon did.

By the time the fire was ready for the coffee pot, the small amount of dirt and ashes that Jesse had used to cover up the .44's he'd buried was heating rapidly; it wasn't long before the cartridges started to explode. Without a gun barrel around them, the bullets traveled with less than their usual speed, but the one that ricocheted off one of the surrounding rocks and hit Carson in the middle of the forehead had enough speed to knock him over, split the skin of his forehead, and start a flood of blood down his face.

Jenkins, Montez, and Bannon all dove to the ground with their guns in their hands, looking around wildly for whoever was doing the shooting, but no one was in sight. After a few seconds that seemed a great deal longer, the "gunfire" stopped and everybody looked around, checking for casualties. They immediately saw Carson lying on his back near the fire, out cold, with blood streaming down his face; steam was rising from the punctured coffeepot as its contents rapidly drained out into the fire ring. Cautiously, they moved toward Carson, trying to look everywhere at once. Bannon got to Carson just as that unfortunate individual moaned, tried to wipe his eyes clean, and struggled to sit up. "What the hell was that?" he groaned. "My head hurts."

"That was a present from somebody who thinks he's mighty funny!" Bannon snarled. "And I intend to pay back the joke real soon! Somebody patch up this joker's head, and let's go find the horses!" He stomped off as Hank dug into a saddlebag for some bandages, and wrapped a pad around Carson's forehead.

Montez was first to find one of the runaway

mounts. Bannon's bay was nibbling on a clump of rabbit brush near a small seep. The Mexican outlaw's feet hurt; he was thirsty and a long way from camp, so he was happy to see anything with four legs. He talked softly to the horse as he stepped closer with his hand outstretched. The bay tensed, ready to bolt, but the familiar scent of the man relaxed him. Montez had saddled the horse several times and had always taken the time to fuss over it, pulling burrs out of its tail and brushing it all over, and the bay was a horse that liked to be fussed over.

Flipping the loop of the lariat in his hand over the bay's head, Montez quickly fashioned a makeshift hackamore. He grabbed a handful of mane to vault aboard the broad back, then caught sight of the small pool of water and decided that he'd better maybe get a drink of that *agua* while he was here; it had been a long walk and his throat was dry. Montez knelt down and scooped up a mouthful of water in his cupped left hand. Out of the corner of his eye, the bandit suddenly caught a glimpse of something he hadn't noticed while standing beside the horse. He tipped his head to one side and made out what had gotten his attention. Off to his left, under the edge of the brush, a small patch of grass was mashed down and there were numerous horse tracks as if someone's horse had been picketed there for quite a while.

Montez sipped the water from his cupped hand, then rose to his feet with his Colt in his hand and went to investigate. It didn't take long for him to realize that he had found someone's recently-vacated camp. Like many of those who rode the owlhoot trail, Montez had started life as an honest cowhand, but had rapidly discovered that honest work just wasn't his style. He had learned to read and remember tracks, however, and those horse tracks looked familiar. He thought for a moment and then it came to him; that kid they'd talked to a couple of days back! The one who said he was headed south, riding a hammer-headed roan that looked like evil incarnate. Those were the roan's tracks! Montez jumped onto the bay and headed for their camp at a trot; Marty would want to know about this.

Eleven

Kitty Moynahan was the apple of her father's eye and the sweetheart of Watsonville. Her waist-length hair, which she generally wore in a thick braid down her back, was the shiny blue-black of a sun-splashed raven's wing, and was a legacy from her Mexican mother. Her laughing blue eyes and porcelain skin she inherited from her father.

Dennis Moynahan had come north out of the Big Thicket country of Texas. The big Irishman had ridden north with a cantankerous herd of longhorn cattle, a crew of hard-bitten riders, a pretty Mexican wife, and a *remuda* he'd mostly appropriated from Mexican horse thieves below the border. A few of the horses already wore his brand when he "reclaimed" them. His chuckwagon had been driven by a one-legged man who had lost his leg below the knee in a horse wreck years before; nowadays that same cook presided over the cookhouse at Moynahan's Bar M ranch.

Dennis had settled here when the only people

for miles around were Indians. He had made friends with those he could make friends with, and had fought those he couldn't, and the graveyard on the knoll back of the house held the bodies of six warriors as proof that his crew could fight. The graveyard also contained the remains of two rustlers they'd hung and one young ranch hand who got caught out in an early blizzard and froze to death. The small cemetery was also the final resting place of Dennis' beloved wife Juana, who had died of smallpox when Kitty was small.

Kitty grew up riding the range. After her mother died, she could have become a spoiled brat; she had her doting father, and a whole crew of cowhands, wrapped around her little finger. She had inherited her mother's fiery Latino temper, but it was leavened with her father's levelheaded common sense. As she grew, she gained both patience and knowledge, and by the time she was fourteen, she knew as much about the day-to-day operation of the Bar M as Dennis did. She was a mature nineteen when she rode into Jesse Thompson's life. It would soon become obvious that Harvey Palmer wasn't the only one whose life was about to get complicated.

Jesse turned the roan into a corral at Johansen's smithy, then slung his saddle and bridle up onto the top rail of the fence. The blue sky held no hint of rain, so his gear would be safe enough for the moment. He forked some hay into the manger in the corner. The roan immediately trotted to a patch of dust in the middle of the corral and dropped to his knees, then rolled to his back. With all four feet in the air he wriggled with pleasure, rubbing his sweaty back against the dirt. He rolled back to his feet and shook the majority of the dust from his coat in a cloud that made him sneeze.

Jesse grinned at the horse's antics as he untied his saddlebags from behind the cantle of his slick-fork saddle, then lifted the Henry from the scabbard. He'd given the rifle a rudimentary cleaning the day before, but he really needed to strip it down and give it a thorough scrubbing before rust started to set in; that would be the first order of business, after he ate.

Jesse stepped inside the barn and asked the smith, "Mind if I leave my rifle and saddlebags here while I go find some place to get myself something to eat?"

"Yah, be my guest," Lars said. "De last gent who helped himself to someone else's gear ended up hangin' from dat cottonwood yonder. Yer t'ings should be safe enough."

"Much obliged," Jesse said. He stood the Henry in the corner under the ladder to the loft and leaned the saddlebags against it. Touching the brim of his hat with a finger, he sauntered out the door. Jesse's gray eyes missed nothing as he strolled down the street, looking for a place to get some grub. A sign reading *"EATS"* caught his eye, so he headed in that direction. He had just stepped up onto the short stretch of boardwalk fronting the Bluebonnet Café, and was reaching for the doorknob, when he heard the sound of a fast-stepping horse coming toward him. He stopped and turned casually, slipping back into the shadows against the café wall more out of habit than anything else.

The sight that greeted Jesse was one that would be etched into his brain forever. Trotting down the street astride a tall, easy-moving Appaloosa gelding was the most beautiful girl he had ever seen. The horse's mottled blue coloring faded to a brilliant splash of white that covered its hindquarters, where the shining white of its rump was spotted with deep blue-gray patches of color the size of double eagles. A white stocking covered the gelding's off hind leg to the knee. The silver on the fancy-carved bridle adorning the horse's finely-shaped head flashed brilliantly in the noonday sunlight. But it wasn't the horse that riveted Jesse's attention; it was the beautiful girl in the hand-carved slick-fork saddle. Kitty Moynahan had elected to wear her hair loose this day, and it flowed around her shoulders and down her back like a velvet robe of purest ebony. Her creamy-white, open-crowned hat was held in place by a buckskin chinstrap sporting a polished turquoise slide that complemented her flashing eyes. The pale blue neckerchief tied at her throat fluttered gaily in the breeze of her passing.

The open-necked gingham blouse Kitty wore hugged her trim figure, and her divided buckskin riding skirt and highly polished boots completed a picture straight out of Jesse's dreams. He was so entranced with the vision before him that he didn't immediately notice the Colt in the crossdraw holster snugged around the young woman's waist. All he knew was that this was the only girl for him, and somehow he had to meet her. He ignored the small voice in his head that was gleefully repeating one word over and over: *"Complications..."*

Twelve

Kitty glanced over at the slim figure leaning against the café wall as her horse, Socorro, trotted past the Bluebonnet. His hat brim was pulled down so that all of his face was in shadow except for the mustache and a quirky smile. She unconsciously checked the Appaloosa for a moment, then went on; the stranger touched the brim of his hat with a finger and turned to enter the café.

Reining up in front of the Watsonville Emporium, Kitty dismounted and tied Socorro to the rail. She stepped onto the porch and entered the store, where bolts of fabric, tools, ready-made clothing, and all the usual fixings of a general store were stacked neatly on shelves around the room. Barrels of flour, sacks of coffee beans and even a pickle barrel stood in neat rows, awaiting the next customer. Perched on one end of the counter were several jars of hard candy; a big wheel of cheese with a knife stuck in it sat under glass at the other end, inviting shoppers to help themselves to a sample. Behind the counter, waiting on an elderly customer who couldn't decide between the pink and the blue bolts of calico cloth spread in front of her, was a slightly-built blond girl of Kitty's age. Melody Hoskins had grown up in Watsonville; her father had started the Emporium as a freight line, running essentials into the area many years before. She and Kitty had been friends since they were little girls.

"Have you seen any strangers in town lately, Melody?" Kitty asked cautiously when Melody looked up at her and smiled warmly over the head of her customer.

Melody excused herself, saying, "I think the blue might be better for what you have in mind, Missus Swain. Please let me know what you decide, and how much of it you'd like," and moved down the counter. She looked across the candy display at Kitty. "Why, no I haven't, Kitty. Why do you ask?"

"Oh, no reason," Kitty replied, with a coy expression spreading across her face.

"I know you better than that, Kitty Moynahan!" Melody declared. "Now you tell me what's going on!"

"Oh, there's really nothing going on," Kitty answered casually. "There was just a stranger entering the café when I rode by, and I was wondering if you'd seen him. One can't be too careful about wandering gunhands and such, you know."

"All right, spill it!" Melody said with a smile. "What did he look like, and why are you so concerned with him?"

"I'm not concerned at all," Kitty countered defensively; her expression declared otherwise. "I just wondered if you'd seen him."

Melody gave her a knowing smile as she turned back to Missus Swain, who had made up her mind about the calico. "I believe I'll take three yards of the blue, Miss Hoskins," the elderly lady called. Melody quickly measured and cut the material, then wrapped it in brown paper and tied the package with string. She made change and handed it to the woman, along with the package. Missus Swain thanked Melody and walked out the door, pleased with her purchase.

Moving back along the counter to where Kitty stood absently fingering the bolt of cloth that lay there, Melody watched her friend for a moment with a bemused expression on her face. "That young man must have left quite an impression," she commented dryly with a hint of laughter in her voice. "Maybe I'll go down to the café and see what's so intriguing about him."

Kitty looked up quickly. "Oh no, you mustn't!" she exclaimed. "If he finds out you're my friend, he'll think I sent you!"

"How in the world will he find out we're friends?" Melody challenged, chuckling. "He doesn't even know who you are yet. Or does he?"

"Oh, no!" Kitty blurted in dismay. "We haven't even spoken to each other. How could he?"

At that particular moment, Jesse was more interested in the beefsteak on the plate in front of him than he was in whom the beautiful young girl's friends might be. The vision was still there, front and center in his mind's eye, but he had decided to wait to announce their engagement until he at least knew her name. For the moment, filling his belly occupied his time. After a steak, potatoes, several biscuits, and a number of cups of coffee, there would be time enough to discover the identity of the raven-haired beauty he'd seen in the street.

Thirteen

Marty Bannon heard the sound of the bay's hooves and stood up with his hand on his holstered Colt. He had been staring into the fire with a sour look on his face, grimly contemplating the events of the last few days, and he was ready to kill something. When he and the others had left Howdy Baxter's road ranch in the mountains, they'd only planned on being gone a couple of days; it surely couldn't take more than that to run Harvey Palmer to ground and kill him. But they'd already been on the trail for four days; first the sniper, and now the disappearance of their horses, had slowed them down, and they were no closer to catching Palmer than they had been when they left Baxter's ranch. "Marty, I foun' your horse!" Montez exclaimed as he slid the bay to a stop just outside the camp. "An' I foun' sometheeng else! I foun' a camp, an' it look like eet was that keed we talk to sout' of here--the one on the roan *caballo*." He dropped the rope, ground tying the bay, and strode hurriedly up to Bannon.

"I can see you got my horse, but what's the rest of this stuff you're cacklin' about? You sound like an old hen layin' an egg! Slow down and make sense." Bannon glared at Montez until the man regained his composure. The Mexican was so relieved to find something that might take some of the heat off himself that he'd been talking a mile a minute.

Montez stopped his babbling, counted to ten silently, and started again. "I foun' your *caballo* at a leetle spring a couple miles or so from here. He let me put the *jaquima* on heem, an' I was starting to get on hees back, when I decide to get a drink of the *agua*. So, when I kneel down for a dreenk, I see horse tracks, an' a camp back een the bushes. The tracks belong to that roan *caballo diablo* that keed we talk to was riding. You know, the one who say he was going sout', an' seen nobody? You theenk maybe he's the *hombre* who been shooting at us? An' the one who run off *los caballos*?"

Bannon contemplated Montez' story for several moments. "Sounds like a good possibility. That kid never really said which way he was headin'- he just said he hadn't seen nobody. We just took it that he was headin' south." He paused, then asked, "Where'd he go from there?"

"I no look too far," Montez said. "I was want to let you know, an' I feegure we can go back there when we find all the *caballos*."

"Good point," Bannon grudgingly admitted. "You can find your way back there, right?"

"Oh *sí*, Marty!" Montez declared. "No *problema!* I take you right to eet."

"Alright, we'll wait until Jenkins and Carson get here; then we'll go find out which way the kid headed." Bannon sat down to wait for the other two outlaws to come back.

Carson and Jenkins returned to the camp, each riding his own horse. Hank was leading Montez' grulla. They slid stiffly to the ground; neither of the two had ridden a horse bareback in a long while. "Damn, I forgot just how much work it is to ride one of these nags without a saddle," Hank grumbled. "I'm 'bout near crippled."

"Quit your complainin', and get saddled up," Bannon commanded. "We got some trailin' to do. Montez here found the tracks of the fella he's pretty sure ran off our horses. And he says it's that kid we talked to over north of Ellsworth."

"How come that kid run off the horses?" Hank wanted to know. Carson started saddling his buckskin, ignoring his cohort's simple-minded question.

"How the hell should I know?" Bannon snarled. "Get that rack of bones saddled, and we'll go find him an' ask him, real polite-like!"

In short order the four horses were saddled, bedrolls were tied behind saddles and the smoldering fire was doused. After a short ride, the four men pulled up at the spring where Montez had found Jesse's tracks. Carson, the best tracker of the bunch, knelt on the ground and ran his fingertips over the tracks. "It was him, alright," he told Bannon. "That roan of his has one hind foot that toes out, and the shoe's worn down more on the inside than the outside. Looks like he was here for a while, and pulled out after daylight." He reached up and touched the bandage on his still aching head. "He probably laughed all the way up the trail about this. Well, I plan on makin' sure he don't have the last laugh." Carson moved to his horse and mounted, leading the way out of the little pocket of brush. "Looks like he's headed for Watsonville."

Fourteen

Harvey woke and glanced toward the window. The slant of the sun around the edge of the roller shade told him it was mid-afternoon. As near as he could tell, he'd awakened in the same position in which he'd fallen asleep. "Damn, I musta been tired," he said quietly to himself. Yawning mightily, he tried to stretch the stiffness of four days in the saddle from his aching muscles. As he swung his feet over the side of the bed and reached for his boots, a growl from behind his belt buckle made him grimace. It had been quite a while since he'd eaten, and his stomach was acting as if his throat had been cut. *Best remedy that pretty quick,* he thought. Harvey stood and stamped his feet into his boots, then swung his gun belt around his hips. He settled it into place and pulled the Colt from the leather, checking to make sure it was still loaded. As far as he knew, he'd been the only one in the room and checking the gun was probably unnecessary, but old habits were hard to break. This particular one had saved his life more than once, so he saw no reason to change now.

He glanced in the cracked mirror on the dresser behind the basin and pitcher, and decided that Lila was right; he needed a close shave and a hot bath--a man with four killers on his back trail had little time for personal grooming. He rinsed his mouth with water from the pitcher, then slicked back his hair with a piece of comb he took from his vest pocket. Harvey set his hat on his head, then removed the chair from its position under the doorknob. The door opened silently on well-oiled hinges; he stepped carefully out into the hallway and pulled the door shut behind him. As he passed through the lobby he glanced around for Lila, but she was nowhere in sight and he was disinclined to interrupt whatever she might be doing. First, he'd go find a restaurant--he'd always had trouble concentrating when his stomach was empty--and if possible a bathhouse, then come back and talk to her later.

The sight that greeted Harvey's bloodshot eyes when he stepped outside stopped him in mid-stride. A long, lean figure was propped up against the wall of the hotel in a ladderback chair. Harvey stared in disbelief. "Why Harvey Palmer, as I live and breathe!" Jesse Thompson exclaimed cheerfully. "Just how the heck are you?"

"What in hell are you doin' in Watsonville?" Harvey demanded gruffly. His sleep-fogged brain was having trouble believing what his eyes were telling it.

"Right at the moment, I'm settin' here enjoying the afternoon," Jesse replied brightly. "How 'bout yourself?"

Harvey just shook his head in disgust then stepped around Jesse, heading toward the "*EATS*" sign down the street. The chair thumped to the boardwalk, and the sound of boot heels on pine and the jingle of spurs followed his footsteps. "Aren't ya even gonna invite me for coffee, ol' buddy?" Jesse asked lightly as he stepped up alongside Harvey and matched him stride for stride. "I did save your life, you know."

"Huh," Harvey grunted. "I did buy you a drink back in Ellsworth, you know," he said sarcastically. "Just before you stuck your gun barrel up that wannabe sheriff's nose."

"Yeah, I know, that probably wasn't the best thing to do," Jesse grinned. He didn't seem to be the least bit repentant. "So now why don't you buy me some coffee, an' I'll tell ya why I'm here. Surely your life's worth that much. That gent had it comin', anyway. He was just a little too full of himself."

"I think I know somebody else like that," Harvey growled, "but it's a free country. I reckon you can go to the café same's I can. Ain't nothin' I can do to stop you." Jesse just grinned again and walked down the street with Harvey. At the door to the café, Jesse quickly stepped forward and pushed the door open before Harvey could get there. He bowed and gestured for Harvey to enter the restaurant ahead of him. It occurred to Jesse that it was time to level with Harvey. Fun was fun; but sometimes a fella had to get serious. From the set of Harvey's shoulders and the expression on his unshaven face, it looked like the time to be serious had come.

A small round table in the rear corner of the café was vacant except for a soiled plate and a cup half full of cold coffee shoved to the center. Two chairs flanked the table, and the two men crossed the room to seat themselves. Each waited for the other to take a chair, until Jesse finally said with a grin, "We're gonna look awful silly standing here drinking coffee. Now, do you wanna sit down, or do you wanna dance?"

Harvey grinned sheepishly and reached for a chair. "All right, you win." He sat down with his back to the wall. Since the table was in a corner, they could both sit against a wall and still look at each other. The waitress, a tired-looking brunette in her forties, brought a pot of coffee and two cups. She set them on the table with a thump, wordlessly scooped up the dirty dishes and turned back toward the kitchen.

"Howdy to you too, ma'am," Jesse drawled toward the waitress's retreating back. She stiffened and turned on her heel, primed to bite this impudent young buck's head off. Before she could light into him, the sight of his cheerful grin cooled her temper, and she simply shook her head, returned his smile and resumed her trip to the wreck pan at the end of the counter.

Jesse poured coffee for both Harvey and himself then took a sip of the hot brew. He'd discovered earlier that the cooks here made pretty good coffee. He swallowed and set his cup down on the table as Harvey watched him over the rim of his heavy porcelain mug. He took a sip and commented, with the cup still to his lips, "So how 'bout explainin' to me why you followed me here, and why I shouldn't just get up and walk out of here and leave you here all by your lonesome."

Jesse reached into a pocket on the inside of his vest and pulled out a metallic object that glinted in the afternoon sunlight. Keeping it cupped in his fingers, he tilted his hand enough for Harvey to recognize the star then quickly slipped it back into his pocket. "Is that what I think it is?" Harvey asked in amazement.

"It is," Jesse nodded. "Have you ever heard

of Judge Randolph Martin, presiding judge for the territorial court over in Laramie?" The startled look on Harvey's face was answer enough. "Well, I'm one of six special deputies for Judge Martin."

"But you killed that character in Ellsworth!" Harvey exclaimed, confused.

"It was either that or let him shoot us both," Jesse retorted. "I wouldn't do the judge a whole lot of good in Boot Hill, would I?"

"And what about the way you treated that so-called sheriff in the saloon?"

"Well, I guess him grabbing me like that upset me more than it should have. I really shouldn't have done that. I was tired, and I just didn't think," Jesse said apologetically. "Judge Martin's told me more than once that I need to keep a tighter rein on my temper. It doesn't slip very often, but once in a while it gets away from me."

"Okay, so now I know who you are, but that still doesn't tell me why you followed me to Watsonville," Harvey said.

"That's kind of a long story," Jesse replied. "The short version is this: I was hopin' that Howdy Baxter would be the one comin' after you, but he sent Marty Bannon instead. I've got a warrant for Baxter, but it's kinda hard to serve a warrant when you're in the middle of thirty or forty gunhands, you know?"

"You used me for bait?!" Harvey asked incredulously, outraged at Jesse's audacity. He shoved himself to his feet, knocking his chair over with a crash.

With a hint of steel in his voice, Jesse snapped, "You're making a scene! Sit down and let me finish!" His tone of voice and the sudden change in his demeanor stopped Harvey cold. It was the first time he'd heard anything but humor in the young deputy's voice, and it made him wonder if maybe he'd misjudged Jesse Thompson.

Righting his chair and dropping into it, Harvey gazed at Jesse and was shocked by what he saw. Until now, all he'd seen was a smiling, devil-may-care kid--albeit one who went armed to the teeth--but the tight-lipped man who sat across the table from him now was someone else entirely. Here was someone he really didn't know at all. Gone was the easy vernacular of the frontier, its place taken by precise language and a stern expression.

"Are you ready to listen to me now?" Jesse demanded in a low voice. Harvey nodded silently. "I told you I've got a warrant for Howdy Baxter--it's in my pocket. But I had to have some way to get him out of his fort in the mountains. When I learned that you killed Baxter's brother, I decided you were just what I needed. Unfortunately for me, Baxter sent Bannon instead."

Jesse took a swallow of coffee, and continued his explanation. "Bannon and three other men are following you, and they could show up here in Watsonville any time. I slowed them up some on my way here, but they're still coming. I have to figure out a way to send him back to Baxter in sorry enough shape to draw Baxter out, preferably without thirty gunhands to back him up." Jesse looked straight at Harvey. "So now you know what I'm about, and I'm asking for your help."

Harvey sat back in his chair, then picked up his cup and took a thoughtful sip. While they talked, the afternoon sun was declining and their corner was now in shadow. The pair heard the clatter of hooves on the hard-packed dirt of the street, and both men turned to look out the windows in time to see Marty Bannon leading his little cavalcade past the windows of the Bluebonnet Café.

Harvey watched the four men pass by. Bannon, his massive shape draped in a dirty, wrinkled shirt, looked as big as a house. Harvey looked from Bannon's bulk to Jesse's lean, muscular form, cleared his throat quietly, and stated dryly, "I know you can shoot. How are you with your fists?" Jesse looked startled, then thoughtful. Now that was an interesting question.

"I take it you're thinking of Bannon?"

"Yeah, I am," Harvey answered. "Maybe if you whip up on him bad enough, his boys'll haul him back to Baxter, and Baxter will come down here himself to take care of you. When he does, you can arrest him. Whadda ya think?"

"Why don't *you* whip up on Bannon, as you so eloquently put it, and let Baxter come after *you*?" Jesse wanted to know.

"Because you're the one who's been pestering Bannon, not me!" Harvey answered emphatically. "He'd be more apt to try to shoot me, but he might enjoy the idea of poundin' you into the ground headfirst with his hands. He's got a reputation as a brawler, y'know. So, back to my original question: can you fight with your hands, or just those Remingtons?"

Fifteen

Jesse Thompson's childhood was an easy one; his family was well off, and Jesse attended a private school for young gentlemen for a number of years. On the occasion of his sixteenth birthday, he suddenly got the urge to roam. He told his parents as much and so, while his father ignored him and his mother wrung her hands and cried in protest, he saddled his horse and took his leave. He really didn't want to be the lawyer his parents wanted him to be, so he decided to head west. At the last minute, his father relented enough to hand him two hundred dollars, shake his hand and wish him Godspeed.

Jesse was naturally gifted with strength and coordination, and he'd boxed and ridden all through school. After he left home, he worked for a year on riverboats, starting out as a deckhand and eventually working his way up to apprentice pilot. During that time he was in his share of fights, augmenting the boxing training he'd had in school. He learned the hard way the "root hog or die", no-holds-barred style of fighting that the men he worked around practiced by getting his ears trimmed several times. He wore his share of battle scars; the most prominent was low down on his right side, just above his belt. A drunken trapper stabbed him with a skinning knife, just before sailing involuntarily over the rail of the promenade deck of the Delta Princess and into the muddy waters of the Mississippi, twenty miles upstream from Natchez. When the knife wound was healed, Jesse decided that a change of occupation, to something less dangerous, was in order; he moved on west, ending up in Laramie.

When he arrived in the thriving Wyoming city, Jesse ran across a handbill advertising for deputies for the territorial court. By this time he was a tall, muscular seventeen. He was a natural shot whose coordination made him fast and accurate with both pistol and rifle; his schooling in philosophy and logic had taught him to look at all sides of a situation. Judge Randolph Martin saw something promising in him, and hired him on the spot.

Two weeks after taking an oath to uphold the law, Jesse brought in his first wanted man. The man was a horse thief Jesse tracked down over yonder in the Nation. The horse thief didn't believe that a kid could possibly be a deputy and consequently paid a stiff price for his unbelief; he came into Laramie tied, belly-down, across his saddle. Jesse had been a deputy going on three years now, and had discovered that he could often solve problems without anyone ending up dead. It didn't always work out that way, but so far, most of the time, it had.

"I reckon I can hold my own," Jesse drawled with a humorous glint in his mischievous eyes. "You think you can hold those other three off me long enough for me to get it done?"

"You just worry about Bannon," Harvey assured him. "I'll take care of the others."

The four outlaws drew rein in front of the blacksmith shop and stepped down to lead their horses to the trough at the front of the building for a much needed drink. Bannon handed his reins to Montez then made his way toward the dark opening into the smithy itself. He could hear the ringing of a hammer on steel so the big man entered the shop.

The shadow crossing the threshold informed Lars that he had visitors. He was putting the finishing touches on a wagon wheel for Old Man Perkins and hadn't heard the horses approach the smithy. He straightened up from his work and turned, his hammer still clenched firmly in his hand. When he saw Bannon, he tensed inside. Lars knew who the man was, and he knew that Bannon left the mountains only on hunting parties. The only hunted man Lars knew about in Watsonville was his old friend Harvey Palmer. Whether Harvey liked it or not, the complications were once again stacking up.

"Vhat can I do for ye, friend?" the smith asked, masking his unease with an amiable smile.

"Need to put up four horses, if you got room," Bannon answered.

"Two bits a night, hay and vater included, corral out yonder." Lars pointed with the hammer.

Bannon reached into his vest pocket, pulled out

two silver dollars and handed them to the smith. "Ain't seen a fella on a dun horse come in here some time in the last day or so, have ya?" he asked gruffly.

Lars lazily scratched his chin with the head of the hammer and replied, "Don't remember a dun horse. Vhy, he stolen or someting?"

"Never you mind why," Bannon said roughly. "Suffice it to say I'm lookin' for the man ridin' him." Bannon turned abruptly and returned to his horse. He took the reins from Montez with a grunted "Out back" and started around the building leading the bay; the others followed suit. Behind the smithy was a large corral with a stack of wild hay at one corner near a manger; a pitchfork stood sentry in the side of the stack. Bannon led his horse up to the fence alongside the gate and looped the reins around a corral pole. He moved to the horse's side and loosened the cinch. A well-made, Texas-rigged saddle was slung on the top pole of the fence, but he paid no attention to it.

Carson, Jenkins, and Montez led their horses up alongside Bannon's and began to unsaddle. As Carson swung his saddle up to the top pole, he stopped dead with his hands on the horn and cantle. He let go of the saddle and stepped to one side, the better to see into the corral. On the far side, in the shade of a small tree, Jesse's roan stood hipshot, dozing while flies buzzed around his head. Carson turned to the others and exclaimed, "That kid's here somewheres! There's his horse!"

Bannon had started to lead the bay through the corral gate, but he stopped and jerked his head toward Carson, who pointed at the roan, then toward the horse. "Are you sure?"

"We followed the tracks most of the way here,

didn't we?" Carson snapped in disgust. "An' he was ridin' a roan horse. 'Course I'm sure. That kid's somewhere in Watsonville!"

"All right," Bannon said. "Turn your horses loose an' fork 'em some hay, then we'll go get a drink an' start lookin' for him. This town ain't so big that we won't be able to find him. Right at the moment, I'm more interested in him than I am in Harvey Palmer. That kid's had a little too much fun at our expense the last few days and it's time for him to pay the piper."

Jesse pushed back his chair and dropped some money on the table as he rose. He picked his hat off the back of the chair where it had hung by the chinstrap, set it on his head, and started walking toward the door. Hearing the thumping of boots on the boardwalk, he stopped and moved back against the wall with his right hand on the butt of his Remington. From the sounds outside, there was more than one man passing by. His hunch was confirmed as Bannon and his men moved past the window on their way to the saloon down the street. They were intent on getting a drink and didn't give the eatery a second glance. "Well, it looks like they're not just passin' through," Jesse commented dryly. "How exactly are you plannin' on keeping those other three cornered while I deal with Bannon?"

"Give me about ten minutes, then make your play," Harvey said. "I need to get something. My guess is they're headed for the Nugget. That's the only saloon on this end of town. It's the only saloon in town, period. If they were after grub, they'd've come in here. See you in a few." Harvey slipped out the back door of the restaurant and hustled toward the Emporium.

Jesse sat back down and poured another cup

of coffee, then slid his old silver watch out of his vest pocket and checked the time. Ten minutes could be short or long, depending on the circumstances. He thought maybe this ten would be of the long variety.

Harvey stepped into the Emporium. His sudden entrance surprised two young ladies who were deep in conversation at one end of the counter. The two turned toward him, and the pretty blond greeted him. "Can I help you?" she asked cordially.

"Yes, ma'am, I believe you can," he replied. "I need a shotgun." He pointed at the rack behind the counter. "That Greener should do nicely. And I'll need some shells, of course--preferably buckshot, if you've got it."

Melody had been raised around firearms, so she didn't hesitate to reach up and take down the gun Harvey had indicated. She lifted the short-barreled Greener coach gun from the rack and swung the latch so that the barrels dropped down. She laid the shotgun on the counter and reached underneath for a box of brass shells. "That will be $15," she said with a polite smile. Harvey would normally have dickered some on the price, but right now he was in a hurry. He reached into his pocket without a second thought and laid three five-dollar gold pieces on the counter. He thanked Melody and picked up the gun, dropped two shells in the chambers, and closed the action. Another handful of shells went into his vest pocket, then he headed for the back door. "What about the rest of your shells?" Melody called after him.

"I'll be back..." The door closed behind Harvey's retreating form.

Hurrying along the backs of the buildings,

Harvey headed for the Nugget. He reached the back door of the saloon in short order, and eased silently up onto the step to listen at the door. Hearing no sound except muted voices from the barroom proper, he eased the door open and stepped into a storeroom. Crates of whiskey, a stack of broken furniture and other detritus were piled haphazardly around the room; cobwebs hung freely from the corners near the ceiling. He slipped silently over to an open doorway and peered around the corner into the main room of the saloon; the outlaws were lined up at the bar, with Bannon at the far end of the line. Besides the bartender, the only other occupants of the room were two teamsters sharing a bottle at a table by the wall, and a down on his luck gambler dressed in a ragged frock coat and dented derby hat who sat by himself at another table dealing solitaire with a deck of grubby cards. *Perfect.* Now all he needed was Jesse.

As if on cue, Jesse strode confidently through the batwings. The creak of the doors caused the outlaws to glance sharply at the mirror behind the bar. When they recognized Jesse, they turned in unison to stare at the cocky young upstart coming toward them. Jesse's step never slowed as he walked straight toward Bannon. He reached up as if to tip his hat back, but instead grasped the front of the brim; sweeping it off his head in one smooth motion, he slapped the burly gunman squarely across the face with the crown of the hat.

The arrogant outlaw had been leaning back with his elbows on the bar, nonchalantly watching Jesse cross the room, as if he hadn't a care in the world. But when Jesse slapped him with his hat Bannon's temper, which was never under the tightest of control at the best of times, erupted like Chinese fireworks. He launched himself from the bar with a growled curse and reached for Jesse, intent on stomping a mud hole in the middle of the cocky young man facing him.

At the same moment, Harvey stepped into the room with the shotgun leveled. Carson, Jenkins, and Montez were stepping away from the bar, intent on helping Bannon pound the young cowboy. Harvey cocked the hammers on the Greener and said quietly, "Ah, ah, ah, none of that. You boys just steady down, and put your hands on the bar where I can see 'em. This here Greener has got hair triggers, and the way you're all lined up there I could get you all with one easy little pull."

The three whirled as one to look at Harvey, then carefully turned and placed their hands flat on the bar. Harvey walked behind them and pulled their pistols from the holsters. He tucked the commandeered guns behind his own belt then retreated to the end of the bar. He crooked a finger at the men and the three outlaws sidled toward him, keeping their hands in sight. The muzzles of the Greener looked like black tunnels big enough to ride into with a hat on. The three men soon stood in a cluster at the end of the bar. "This looks like a good place to watch a fight from," Harvey said with a smile.

Sixteen

Bannon rushed at Jesse with his arms outstretched. He was pawing for a hold on the young man's shirt, intent on pulling him close and mauling him. The young deputy sidestepped and buried his right fist in the outlaw's belly just above the belt. It was a hard blow, but the enraged gunman barely felt it in the depths of his fury. He spun and caught Jesse with a clubbing blow to the shoulder and Jesse staggered. Bannon followed the swinging fist in, still trying to get close. Jesse shoved him back and laid a hard left to his cheek that cut skin and flesh to the bone and started a stream of blood flowing down Bannon's face; he took it coming in.

A crashing shot from Bannon's big left hand drove Jesse back against the bar. The bottle the four outlaws had been sharing tipped over and rolled off the back of the bar to shatter on the floor. The bartender hadn't tried to catch it, because the bartender wasn't there. He had long since disappeared out the back door, leaving the fight to the fighters.

Bannon crowded in, pounding Jesse's ribs and belly. Jesse's body was tough and sinewy from the miles of riding he did on the job and from the sparring he did when he was in Laramie, but the blows hurt nonetheless. Jesse knew that if he didn't get away from the bar quickly, he was going to go down under the rain of punches. Jesse reached up and pounded his cupped palms on his opponent's ears. When the rhythm the outlaw was playing on Jesse's belly slowed for a moment, Jesse grabbed Bannon's ears and yanked his head down in what he'd once heard called a "Liverpool kiss". Jesse's forehead crashed into Bannon's nose and the crunch of breaking bone and cartilage echoed through the room. The bleeding gunman staggered back, his nose a smashed ruin, and Jesse followed. Blood cascaded down over Bannon's mouth and chin and his eyes were rapidly swelling shut from the massive trauma as Jesse continued to pound his face. Jesse moved with him and swung again for the cut on Bannon's cheek. A large knot began to form around the cut, and Jesse's work-hardened fist crashed into the middle of it, splitting the cut wider.

The big, punch-drunk outlaw brought his hands up defensively and moved painfully toward Jesse, circling warily. He'd just been shown in no uncertain terms that the kid in front of him could hit. His eyes were swelled to slits, making it hard for him to see. Jesse was up on his toes, trying to pretend that his ribs weren't making it hard to breathe; several of them were obviously cracked. Jesse's shirt was in shreds and his hands hurt, but surprisingly he felt good. It had been a while since he'd been in a good knuckle-and-skull, knock-down-drag-out fight, and he found himself enjoying this one, even though he knew that tomorrow he would pay dearly for his fun.

The gambler and the two teamsters had made a run for the door when Jesse slapped Bannon with his hat; now the three of them were back, and along with several of the townspeople they were hanging over the batwing doors and the windowsills, eager to watch what mayhem might ensue. There hadn't been any excitement in town in a month of Sundays, and a fight like this one was considered quality entertainment.

The two fighters circled each other, looking for an opening to exploit. The outlaw reached out with a left that Jesse easily blocked. He tried the left again, and again Jesse blocked it. Suddenly, Bannon dropped his hands and charged with his arms widespread. Jesse backpedaled, stabbing a right to the man's lips, mashing them against his teeth; but Bannon charged forward like a maddened bull and wrapped his arms around Jesse, driving him backward. The men crashed onto a table, smashing it to splinters as they fell. Jesse brought his knees up into Bannon's belly; his boot toe caught the big outlaw in the groin and drove a gasp of pain from him. Using his legs, Jesse threw Bannon off and rolled to his feet. The weakened gunman was on hands and knees, pushing himself up, when the heel of Jesse's boot caught him on the side of the jaw. The rowel of Jesse's Mexican spur slashed through the skin as it slid down Bannon's jaw; the outlaw's head snapped to the side and his arms began to fold.

Forcing himself back onto all fours, Bannon struggled to get up and continue the fight. His pain-wracked brain couldn't comprehend what was happening to him. *Gotta... get... this... kid...* stuttered through his head. Jesse watched Bannon fight to get on his feet then took a step and launched a kick to Bannon's midsection that lifted him off the floor and flung him onto his back. The big man groaned, clutching his belly; he struggled to push himself up then fell back to the scarred pine. He lay on his back for a moment, breathing heavily, until a bolt of agony shot through his belly and twisted him onto his side with his knees drawn up in pain.

Jesse leaned down, stifling a gasp as a lance of pain from his cracked ribs shot through him. He picked up his hat and set it gingerly on his head. Sometime during the fight, he'd picked up a considerable knot on the back of his skull. He turned toward the bar, teetering for a moment, then shuffled behind the counter to pick up a bottle of rye. He swallowed a shot, then rinsed his mouth with more of the liquor; the cuts inside his mouth stung from the alcohol.

He moved up the bar to where the other three outlaws stood spellbound under the unwavering stare of Harvey's shotgun. Jesse leaned on the bar and said, "Thanks, Harvey." He gave Harvey's companions a hard look then turned and pointed at the groaning Bannon. "Pick him up, put him on his horse, and take him back to Howdy Baxter. You tell Baxter that next time, he'd better come himself instead of sending a boy to do a man's job. You got that?" The men nodded mutely. Hastily, they moved to where Bannon lay, grabbed him under the arms and hoisted him unsteadily to his feet. It was all the three of them could do to get Bannon's nearly limp form to the door and headed for the smithy.

As soon as the four outlaws were out of sight the onlookers rushed in, all chattering at once about the fight, and bellied up to the bar. The bartender materialized out of thin air and began serving drinks.

Jesse sagged as he rounded the end of the bar and took a step toward Harvey. Harvey had uncocked the Greener when the four outlaws left, and now he dropped it hastily onto the bar. He rushed to catch the young deputy, and moved the battered young man hurriedly to a chair and set him in it. "You all right?" he asked, concern evident in his voice.

"Bannon doesn't know how close he came to winnin' that fight," Jesse gasped, holding his ribs. "If he'd've held out any longer, I might not've gotten him whipped."

"Yeah, but you did. That's the important thing," Harvey said emphatically.

"I just hope it draws Baxter out of his hideout!" Jesse declared. "'Cause otherwise, I'm gonna be hurtin' for nothing."

The grimace on Jesse's face brought a chuckle from Harvey. "Well, we won't know one way or the other for a few days. Let's get you to the Doc's and get your ribs wrapped." Apparently Jesse hadn't heard that a man should be careful what he wishes for, because he just might get it.

Seventeen

Three days after his fight with Jesse, Marty Bannon led his troops into the yard of Howdy Baxter's road ranch in the mountains. Bannon rode hunched over his saddle horn, keeping one arm wrapped around his belly as though he was trying to hold himself together--he grunted in pain with every step his horse took. The cuts on his face were scabbed over, but his black eyes and swollen nose revealed quite a tale for any interested party to read.

Baxter, a lean whip of a man dressed in neat range clothing, sauntered out onto the porch with a glass of whiskey in his hand. He leaned on one of the posts holding up the porch roof and looked Bannon up and down. In a deceptively mild voice he asked, "What the hell happened to you? Fall off your horse and get stepped on?"

Bannon glared at Baxter, then looked away. "Not hardly," he mumbled through split and still-swollen lips. "I got in a fight."

"If you won, I'd hate to see the other guy," Baxter grinned. "You did win, didn't ya?"

Bannon looked through him at an unseen enemy. "No."

Baxter straightened up and stepped away from the post to advance on Bannon. His glass was forgotten in his hand. "What do you mean, no?" he demanded. "I don't pay you to lose fights! And who was this fight with? It wasn't that scum Palmer, was it?"

"No," Bannon repeated sullenly.

By now Baxter's temper was rising, which could be a bad thing for those hapless individuals in front of him. Through tight lips, he hissed, "I hope for your sake Harvey Palmer's dead and you just got in a fight for the hell of it."

This time Bannon's answer was barely audible as he whispered, "No."

Baxter's blue eyes were like chips off a glacier when he looked up at Bannon and seethed, "You get your sorry butt down off that *cayuse*, and you and these other three clowns come in the house. Maybe one of you can explain to me how four so-called gunhands couldn't kill one no-good cowboy, and how my foreman got his butt kicked so bad that he had to run home with his tail tucked between his legs." He looked around for someone to take the men's horses, but the layabouts who had been standing around when Bannon and company rode in had vanished like snowflakes on a hot griddle. "Ah, crap! Leave 'em!" he snarled. "Maybe one of your pals will take care of 'em." Baxter turned and stomped into the house.

Howdy stood with his hands on his hips and a frown twisting his lean features, waiting for his four *pistoleros* to come inside. The four luckless man-hunters pulled chairs out from the table and sat without being told. All but Rule Carson stared down at the knife-scarred trestle table in front of them. Carson looked directly back at Baxter with defiance in his eyes, waiting for what came next. Carson was relatively new to the outfit; he hadn't yet learned how dangerous it could be to defy Howdy when his temper was aroused.

"So," Baxter's voice was deceptively silky, "which one of you cretins is going to tell me what happened?" Carson wasn't really too sure what a cretin was, but he recounted the story anyway. He made it short and not especially sweet. He left nothing out, regardless of the picture his words painted of himself and his fellow gun-hands. Hank had quit wearing the bandage on his ear; the scabbed-over appendage was mute testimony to the truth of Rule's story, as was the healing cut in the center of Carson's own forehead. When he came to the part where Jesse walked up to Bannon and slapped him with his hat, the corners of Baxter's mouth turned up slightly as if hiding a grin, but Baxter said not a word while Carson described the fight that ensued.

"You're trying to tell me that this *kid*, as you call him, walked right up to Marty here and slapped him in the chops with a hat, then proceeded to whip the stuffin's out of him, and none of you did anything?" Baxter asked at last, staring incredulously at his sorry crew.

"We didn't have a choice, Howdy," Hank broke in with a whine. "We was covered by a shotgun!"

"And who, pray tell, was holding that shotgun? The bartender?" Howdy demanded. "I know damn good and well there's no sheriff in Watsonville! And just when *were* you going to tell me about the shotgun?"

"No, it weren't the bartender, it was Harvey

Palmer. Or at least we're purty sure it was." Hank swallowed nervously and went on. "The feller with the shotgun took our guns an' made us stand there an' watch while that kid was fightin' with Marty. Then he made us pick Marty up an' leave town. He kept our guns, too. What was we sposed to do, jump him an' let him cut us in two?"

Baxter stared at Hank, his mouth literally hanging open, as stunned as if his underling had suddenly sprouted another head. He snarled, "You expect me to believe that the man I sent you idiots to kill held you three at gunpoint and made you stand there and watch while this *kid*, whose name you don't even know, kicked Marty's butt? *Are you serious?* How do you know it was Palmer? And why in hell did you come back home and leave those two alive? *What in the world do you think I pay you for?*" he thundered.

Hank stammered, "That k-k-kid called him Harvey. An' the feller had a G-G-Greener, Howdy. He'd 'a k-kilt us all. W-we didn't have no guns, 'cause he t-took 'em."

"I've got half a notion to kill you myself!" Baxter snarled menacingly. "Now, did either of them do or say anything *else* that you may or may not think I should know?"

Bannon had been silent until now. Jesse's parting words, which his three companions had relayed to him when he had regained some semblance of consciousness, had been burning in his brain since they had ridden out of Watsonville. Marty looked up at Baxter and mumbled, "That kid said to tell you not to send a boy to do a man's job next time. I think he's callin' you out, Howdy." Marty dropped his chin back to his chest and waited for the storm that he was sure would break out.

To Bannon's amazement, Howdy began to laugh. At first it was just a chuckle, but it grew louder until Baxter was roaring with hysterical mirth. He was holding his sides as tears rolled down his cheeks. Suddenly his laughter ceased as if a door had slammed on it. "Does this kid have a name?" he asked menacingly, his voice grating in the ensuing silence. Howdy Baxter didn't have a reputation for being especially stable. He had been known to change moods so fast, and so often, that it was downright scary sometimes.

"We never heard his name, Howdy. We wasn't in town that long." Hank whined, cringing and waiting for a blow, or a bullet. When neither came his way, he lifted his head again to look at Howdy.

Baxter paced the floor for a moment, then stopped and leaned on the end of the table with his palms pressed flat to the scarred pine. "Can you at least tell me what he looked like?" he asked mildly. "Or is that too much for you lame-brains?"

Carson was decidedly more humble after Baxter's outburst than he'd been when he first sat down at the table. He described Jesse as best he could remember, including his hammer-headed roan, and finished with, "I'll know him when I see him, and I'll kill him."

Baxter snorted, "Yeah, right! You four couldn't kill a sick jackrabbit!" He walked over to a gun rack on the wall and took down a rifle and a bandoleer of ammunition. "I guess that kid's right. I shouldn't have sent a bunch of boys to do a man's job. This sounds like something I'll have to take care of myself. You four get us some fresh horses and load up some grub. We're going to Watsonville." The four men just stared at him mutely. He turned and glared at them with the muzzle of his rifle pointed in their general direction. "I said MOVE!" he roared.

The four hit the door at approximately the same time, tripping over each other. They finally crashed out onto the stoop then galloped clumsily toward the horse corral. On the way, they snagged their own tired mounts, which still stood ground tied in the yard. As he ran, half hunched over, Marty Bannon felt an itch rising between his shoulder blades. Knowing Baxter the way he did, he half expected to be shot down in his tracks at any moment, but the shot didn't come. They got five fresh horses saddled and a packhorse loaded, then Howdy Baxter and his four man-hunters set out on the trail to Watsonville.

Eighteen

Jesse hung around town waiting for his ribs to heal enough so he could ride and trying to find out what he could about the raven-haired beauty on the big Appaloosa horse. So far, all he'd been able to find out was her name. He wasn't necessarily in a hurry to go anywhere, but he was bored to death and wanted to do something, even if it was wrong. When he took the time to think about it, that often seemed to be the case. On the fourth day after the fight with Marty Bannon, he couldn't handle sitting around any longer and headed down to Johansen's corral to saddle the roan.

Jesse walked up to the corral fence; the roan stood placidly, watching him approach. He untied his lariat from his saddle, shook out a loop, and slipped between the corral poles. The roan eyed him warily with his ears back and his head up. This was an old game, and one the horse enjoyed. Jesse walked closer, with the loop swinging gently in his hand. When he was ten feet from the roan the horse suddenly jumped sideways and began to trot around the corral, watching Jesse from the corner of its eye. Jesse acted like he didn't care one way or the other, then he suddenly hoolihanned the loop out and over the roan's head. He drew in the slack and walked up the rope hand-over-hand, then twisted it into a halter around the roan's nose and led him to the corral gate. With a resigned snort, the horse followed quietly.

A few minutes later, the horse was saddled and bridled and Jesse was ready to go. As he stepped into the saddle, he noticed that there was more slack in the cinch than there really should be if he planned on staying aboard. The wily mustang had sucked in a bellyful of air when Jesse first pulled the cinch tight, and now that the horse had let out its breath, the saddle was loose. Jesse reached for the tail of the latigo to pull the cinch up some more and saw the roan's chest start to swell. "Oh, no you don't, you bandit," Jesse grinned. He quickly stepped in and kneed the horse in the ribs, causing him to exhale. Before the roan could grab another breath Jesse had the cinch tight and his foot in the stirrup. Normally, after a few days of lying around a corral or stall the roan would buck and give Jesse a good workout to start their day. But today it seemed to sense that Jesse really wasn't in the mood. The roan stepped into a jog without so much as a crow hop.

Soon the pair was out of town and headed at a jog across a sagebrush flat toward a nearby string of hills. The blue vault of the sky was cloudless overhead. Small birds prospecting for seeds and insects in the high sage scattered in front of the rangy mustang, quickly resuming their activities after man and horse had passed by. Jesse took a deep breath, glad that his cracked ribs were finally allowing him that luxury, and considered how great it was to be alive. A light breeze blew through the sagebrush and bunchgrass, stirring up small dust clouds. Near the edge of the trail a long-eared jackrabbit sat motionless in the shade of a greasewood clump pretending he wasn't there, on the off chance that Jesse wouldn't notice him. As he rode, Jesse worked his hands, trying to ease the last of the residual stiffness from the joints and muscles. His knuckles still showed some bruises and cuts, but were gradually returning to normal. If Baxter showed up, he'd need his hands at full strength.

Jesse came around a flat-topped butte and saw a faint dust trail a ways off, against the far hills. From where he stood, it was hard to tell what was stirring up the dust. Jesse reached back for his spyglass and brought it to his eye while the roan stood quietly in the shade of a tall juniper. He focused on the distant cloud of dust. For a moment it was hard to determine the source, then several riders came into view--none of them were white.

As Jesse watched, a party of what appeared to be Cheyenne came out of the brush and halted with their horses milling about and stirring up dust. Jesse knew he was pretty much invisible where he sat in the dark shade against the tree, but any movement would give him away. Try as he might, he couldn't tell for sure if the Cheyenne were painted for war or not; they were just too far away. He decided that he'd really rather not find out firsthand. The riders were well armed and led extra horses behind them. Jesse gently drew the roan backward around the tree and faded into a stand of junipers, hoping he hadn't been seen. He turned the roan back toward Watsonville, which was a good hour's ride away. He glanced over his shoulder frequently, checking to see if the war party--if war party it was--had followed him. For the moment it looked like he'd gotten away clean.

Suddenly one of the Cheyenne threw an arm up and pointed in Jesse's direction. With a yip, the Indians booted their horses into a run. Either they were indeed a war party, or a lone white man was just too tempting a target to pass up. Either way, Jesse wasn't planning on staying around to find out. That yip was Jesse's cue to light a shuck, as the saying went, and he put his spurs to the roan. That horse was ugly and slab-sided, but it could run. The touch of Jesse's spurs shot the lanky gelding out of there like a frightened jackrabbit; soon it was stretched out and running for all it was worth.

The trail to Watsonville crossed the big, sage-covered flatland at an angle. Jesse started his run in the northwest corner of the mostly rectangular flat; he would have to travel to the southeast on his return to the relative safety of the town. Unfortunately, the Cheyenne started in the southwest corner of the same rectangle, and pretty much had the angle on him. The terrain was too rough to attempt cutting across; he was better off on the trail. Now everything depended on the roan, and on the quality of the Indians' horses. As he leaned over the roan's neck, it occurred to Jesse once again that complications could come in a lot of different shapes and sizes.

The roan was hammering its heart out, racing up the first of a set of rolling rises between the flatland and the town, when Jesse felt a thump just behind his right leg. He reached down and grabbed the Henry out of the boot and took a secure hold on it as the roan pounded on. Without warning, just below the top of the rise, the roan's front legs folded up; its nose hit the dirt, and Jesse somersaulted through the air. He lit on his shoulder and tumbled head over heels. When he stopped rolling, he scrambled back to lay prone behind the roan's carcass. What had been one hell of a good horse was now relegated to serving as a less than adequate fort for fighting Indians.

When the roan went down, the Cheyenne yipped and howled even louder. They charged in, expecting to find Jesse lying unconscious beyond the dead horse. To their surprise, what they rode into was a hail of lead from Jesse's Henry. He emptied the fifteen-shot magazine in a rolling blast of flame and smoke, relieving two charging ponies of their riders and wounding two other warriors. The remaining warriors yanked their horses to a stop, spun and galloped back out of range. They had no reason to directly challenge shooting like that.

As the Indians fell back, Jesse quickly sat up and reloaded the Henry from his cartridge belt, then counted his remaining rounds by feel. He had ten in the Remingtons, a full magazine in the Henry, and a dozen or so left in his belt. Unfortunately, the rest of his ammunition was in the saddlebag that lay pinned under the roan. Unless he could discourage those Cheyenne in a hurry, he was in deep trouble. Pretty soon they'd send flankers out and he would be hard pressed to hold off the rest when they came charging in, as he was sure they would.

Nineteen

When the Henry was reloaded, Jesse peered over the carcass of the roan to see what the Indians were up to. So far, they were just milling around while they decided what to do. He thought about his situation for a minute, then leaned the Henry against the dead horse and reached back for the broad-bladed knife in the sheath at the back of his belt. He plunged it into the soil near the roan's belly and began to dig, casting frequent glances at the warriors downhill from where he worked. Gradually Jesse's dugout deepened. He knew his time was short and he worked feverishly, hoping to have a depression a couple of feet deep to hunker down in before the attack came.

With a loud, yodeling call, a large warrior on a beautiful paint gelding kicked his horse into motion and charged directly at Jesse. Jesse lifted the Henry and waited. The Indian's rifle was blasting flame and smoke as the paint charged up the slope. Bullets thumped into the roan's carcass and ricocheted off the dirt of the trail.

When the rifle was empty the warrior threw it aside and lifted a lance from the side of the blanket-covered McClellan saddle he rode. The insanely courageous, but soon-to-die Cheyenne charged on, yipping and yelling.

When the brave was a mere fifty feet away Jesse rose up on one knee and brought the Henry to his shoulder. The front blade settled into the notch of the rear sight and Jesse blasted a round into the Indian's chest. The man rolled backwards off the rump of his horse and ran for several steps before Jesse shot him again. He went down on his face. The dead warrior's horse leapt over Jesse and the roan's carcass and disappeared through the tall sagebrush in the wide swale beyond the rise behind Jesse. Jesse watched the Indian closely for several moments but he didn't stir; Jesse laid the Henry down and returned to his digging.

By now the hole was nearly two feet deep and four feet wide; the sandy soil made for easy digging. After killing the charging Cheyenne, Jesse kept an even closer eye on the others who sat in silence at the foot of the rise, but even their horses were still. He stopped his digging and sat cross-legged in the bottom of his excavation. His eyes were level with the top of the carcass in front of him and he sat with his hat off, watching. He saw two of the Cheyenne drop from their horses and slip into the brush, one on each side of the trail. Jesse unholstered the Remingtons and laid them on the brim of his hat, which was perched on the earthen dike in front of him. He kept watch for any disturbance in the surrounding vegetation. At the same time, he kept an eye on the larger group in front of him but they remained motionless.

On Jesse's right, the sage stood back from the trail at least twenty yards. The open area held scattered bunch grass; there was relatively little cover there. On his left, clumps of sage and greasewood grew up to within a few feet of the dead roan's outstretched nose. Jesse kept watch on the open side, figuring the brave on that side would be the boldest.

The minutes passed slowly. Jesse reached up, pulled the canteen from the saddle horn and uncorked it. He took a long drink then drove the stopper back in with the heel of his hand. The sun wasn't especially hot, but there was little breeze, and soon a tiny rivulet of sweat trickled through the hair on Jesse's temple. He reached up to wipe it away just as a magpie flew down toward the dead horse. Jesse's movement spooked the black and white bird and it swooped toward a clump of greasewood at the far edge of the bunch grass to Jesse's right. When the magpie flared away, scolding, Jesse nonchalantly picked up his right-hand pistol, trying not to let on that he'd seen the bird's sudden change in direction.

Concentrating on the area which the magpie had helpfully pointed out, Jesse waited. *There!* The grass had moved just the least bit, even though there was no wind. A moment later, a tiny sound of dried grass stems scraping against leather whispered on the breeze. As quietly as possible, Jesse drew back the hammer of the Remington. The warrior rose out of the grass to Jesse's right. Jesse's shot knocked him to the ground and Jesse quickly pivoted to his left as the second brave came from the sage on the other side of the trail with the knife in his hand drawn back to strike. Jesse slipped the hammer of the Remington, triggering two shots into the chest of the Cheyenne in front of him, then swung back to the first man he had shot. The warrior was just rising to throw his own knife;

his hand was on his belly where Jesse's first bullet had hit. Jesse's shot struck the Indian just below the nose, exiting out the back of his skull, snapping his neck and driving him backward to the ground.

Jesse hastily dropped the pistol back on its perch and picked up the Henry just as the mounted Cheyenne in front of him booted their horses into another charge. He leveled the rifle across the roan and fired in a roll of thunder. One warrior fell from his horse, and another horse went down, throwing its rider over its head. Before the man could run Jesse shot him. The others veered away and retreated again, to go back and reassess the situation one more time.

After a brief parley the Cheyenne reined their horses around and rode away, yelling insults in their native tongue. Jesse heard the sound of hoof beats behind him and he whirled quickly around, bringing the Henry to his shoulder as he turned. Harvey's big dun appeared over the rise, leading the flashy paint horse which had vaulted over Jesse when he shot its rider. Harvey pulled the big horse to a halt and looked down at Jesse where he knelt in a hole in the dirt behind the dead roan. "What exactly are you doin', Jesse?" Harvey asked mildly. "Diggin' to China? Or did you decide to take up gold minin'?"

"I decided this dead horse is a dang lousy fort and that I needed some earthworks!" Jesse retorted. "I didn't see the cavalry comin' so I started diggin'. What took you so long to get here?"

"Well, it sounded like you were havin' so much fun I really hated to interrupt. An' besides which, I was catchin' you a horse." Harvey raised his hand, revealing the horsehair rein that led to the charging brave's spirited paint. "I thought you might rather not walk home."

Jesse stood and dusted off his britches, then holstered his pistols and bent down to uncinch his saddle. "Well, I appreciate that, but are you gonna help me get the saddle off my horse, or were you gonna make me ride that fella's McClellan into town?" Harvey took a turn of the paint's lead rein around the horn of his saddle then stepped down and ground tied the dun. They worked Jesse's gear from under the dead roan, stripped the old McClellan from the paint and put Jesse's saddle in its place. Then the two men headed for town. When they were out of sight beyond the rise, the remaining Cheyenne appeared like wraiths, picked up their dead and galloped back across the wide flat.

Harvey and Jesse rode into Watsonville side by side. The paint gelding was a fast walker and easy to ride. The two men had been silent on the trail; the tracks and cartridge cases around Jesse's dead horse had told enough of the story for Harvey to pretty much figure out what had happened. As the town came into sight Jesse remarked, "I don't think this horse started life in a Cheyenne horse herd. He acts like he's carried a bit in his mouth before."

"I've heard that Indians set a lot of store by a good horse thief," Harvey said thoughtfully. "That horse ain't branded, but I'd be willing to bet that some cowboy somewhere is missin' him." They lapsed into silence again and soon arrived at the livery. They unsaddled their horses and turned them into the corral. This time the dun went in with Jesse's mount; since Harvey's presence in town was common knowledge after the fight in the Nugget, there was no sense trying to hide any longer. "Well, if Howdy Baxter's comin', he'd ought ta be here in the next day or two," Harvey commented as the two headed for the hotel.

"Yep, an' now I've gotta figure out a way to arrest him without gettin' myself shot," Jesse said. "I don't think he's gonna be by himself, and I don't think slappin' him with a hat is gonna work. Those boys are gonna be loaded for bear when they come."

Twenty

Howdy Baxter reined up near a spring at the edge of a live oak thicket and held up his hand. "We'll camp here for the night," he told the others. "We can get an early start in the morning and come into Watsonville just before dark. I'm not giving your *kid* a chance to get set if I don't have to. This time I want him and Palmer dead. There'd better be no slipups, and no fights unless we start them."

Rule Carson unsaddled his horse, led it to water, then picketed the buckskin on a patch of grass. He moved around the edges of the thicket, gathering twigs and sticks for a fire. A ring of fire-blackened rocks near the center of the clearing indicated that others had camped there before Baxter's group. As he worked, Carson kept his thoughts about Jesse to himself; he was determined to be the one to kill Jesse, even if he had to shoot the young man in the back. It wouldn't be the first time he'd done that to somebody he wanted dead. Soon a small fire crackled in the fire ring and thin smoke from the long-dry wood drifted up through the branches overhead, dissipating as it rose. While they went about setting the camp, the outlaws stayed vigilant. Even with the size of their group, it wouldn't do to relax too much--all of their faces graced "Wanted" posters across the territory.

Hank leaned back on his saddle, sipping on a pint bottle of whiskey. His ear still hurt, but it no longer bled when he bumped it. Carson knelt by the fire and sliced bacon into a pan while Montez mixed flour and water into dough nearby. Patting the dough out flat on a rock next to the heat, Montez made a batch of thick tortillas, stacking them off to one side as they were finished.

"Come an' get it 'fore I throw it to the hogs!" Carson called. He moved the pan of bacon off the fire and reached for one of Montez' tortillas. The Mexican might not be able to stay awake on watch too good, but he made good tortillas. Carson wrapped several slices of bacon in the flat bread then stepped away from the fire so the rest could get their share of the grub. He reached down to the steaming pot of coffee standing at the edge of the fire and filled the tin cup from his saddlebag with the hot brew, then stepped over to his saddle and sat down. He leaned back and looked up at the stars. The bright band of the Milky Way laid a brilliant finger of light across the dark expanse of the sky. The North Star twinkled overhead and Carson's thoughts drifted bleakly back to other days and other camps.

Life was good on the small ranch. Rule and Maggie Carson were happily married, and there was a smiling, healthy baby boy for Rule to bounce on his knee at the end of the workday while Maggie cooked dinner. The couple had a good milk cow, a pair of fine cow horses, and a small but expanding cattle herd. Then the cholera struck. The disease took his lovely young wife and his son, and left Rule weak and near death; how he survived was anybody's guess. The loss of his family burned something from him inside. He buried them, burned the cabin and barn and rode away, leaving his blackened, scarred heart behind him in the ashes of his lost life. He left the cattle to fend for themselves and never looked back. A week later, Carson robbed an itinerant peddler of twenty dollars and his horse, turning his life irrevocably down the owlhoot trail. He could never say why he embarked on a life of crime; it just seemed like the thing to do at the time.

Marty Bannon sat sulking by the fire, scarcely touching his food. He knew that Carson wouldn't hesitate to shoot Jesse in the back, but he had no intention of letting that happen. Bannon's size and strength were his weapons; he fully intended to kill the skinny, two-bit kid with his bare hands. Only when Jesse lay, crushed and broken, at his feet, would Bannon have the vengeance he sought.

Howdy Baxter sat away from the rest. His relaxed demeanor hid the rattlesnake coiled inside, ready to strike. His brother was dead and Howdy meant to avenge him. Blood meant everything in his family, and as the oldest son, it was up to him to even the score. The Baxters were members of a feuding family who came from, or were run out of, back in the Tennessee hills, whichever way a person chose to look at it. Howdy didn't think about the past; Harvey Palmer owed a debt that must be paid in the here and now, one that only blood could assuage. That meddling kid must die as well. It didn't matter to Howdy who killed them; the two men owed him, and he would collect. After all, Howdy Baxter had a reputation to uphold.

Twenty-one

Jesse sat alone in the Bluebonnet Café absentmindedly fingering the porcelain of a cup of cold coffee and staring into the unseen distance beyond the walls of the room. He could almost feel Howdy Baxter somewhere out yonder in the dark. He had to bring Baxter to justice, either over his saddle or on it, but he hadn't a clue how to go about it. He'd brought in some hard cases in the short time he'd been one of Judge Martin's deputies, but those men were almost always alone, never surrounded by their friends. He usually managed to get the drop on them and bring them in alive, except for a couple who'd gone for their guns in spite of being covered. But Baxter was the worst he'd ever tried to capture. The list of Baxter's crimes would fill a scroll of Biblical proportions. He was wanted for everything from rustling, to murder and robbery, and for all Jesse knew, maybe even spitting on the sidewalk. Many lawmen had gone after Baxter in the past; they'd all returned draped face-down over the back of a burro. Baxter generally kept the horse the deputy rode in on, adding insult to injury.

Just before Jesse left Laramie, Judge Martin had taken him aside and told him point-blank, "You are one of my best men, Deputy Thompson. I know this is a difficult task, but I have every confidence that you can accomplish it. Good men have failed to bring Baxter in, but I have faith in your abilities. I only have one admonition for you: failure is not an option. Howdy Baxter is one of the worst of the worst, and I plan to either hang him or bury him in Boot Hill, neither of which my predecessor was able to do. Which of these events takes place is up to you." With that, the Judge had shaken Jesse's hand and turned back into his chambers, leaving Jesse staring after him, shaking his head. That was six weeks ago.

Lamps on wrought-iron brackets around the walls of the café shed a golden light, pushing back the dusk that stole through the curtained windows. Soon the room would empty as the patrons headed for home. Western men rose early, as survival out here required a full day's hard labor; consequently, they were also early to retire. The creak of unoiled door hinges interrupted Jesse's reverie, and he and the other customers looked up from their coffee or food to see who the newcomer might be. Kitty Moynahan's smile greeted the tired eyes of the patrons as she stepped into the room, accompanied by her father Dennis. The Moynahans were in town to purchase their monthly supplies; due to the lateness of the hour, they had decided to stay over in the room Dennis kept at the Desert Inn and return home in the morning.

As Dennis seated his daughter at a table across the room, Jesse came to a decision. He pushed back his chair and rose to his feet. Out of habit, he reached for his hat where it hung on the chair next to him, then thought better of it. He ran a hand through his unruly hair, brushed his mustache with a finger and started across the room toward the Moynahans. When Jesse's shadow crossed their table, Dennis looked up at the young deputy. Kitty saw her father look around, and her breath caught in her throat when she realized who had come to their table. "Mister Moynahan, my name is Jesse Thompson..." Jesse began.

Dennis cut him off with a smile. "I know who y'are, young man," he said in an Irish brogue with a hint of the twang of Texas in it. "Ye're famous in these parts after the beatin' ye gave that scoundrel Marty Bannon in the Nugget last week. Not that he hasn't had it comin' for lo these many years. What is it I can do for ye?"

Jesse's face reddened at Dennis' words. "Sir," he started again, "I've seen your lovely daughter riding through the town, and, being much taken by her beauty, I hoped to have your permission to call upon her." He and Kitty both waited expectantly for Dennis' reply.

Dennis looked the young man in front of him up and down. He liked what he saw. Dennis had seen Jesse's fight with Bannon, and he heartily approved of the beating Jesse had given the outlaw. Dennis' green eyes twinkled merrily as he drawled, "Well, now, me young friend, I suppose that would be up to the lass herself. I've no problem with ye comin' to visit, but perhaps you should be gettin' her opinion as well."

Jesse turned hastily toward Kitty, whose eyes were glowing. "Miss Moynahan, may I have your permission to call on you?" Jesse asked. Mentally he was kicking himself for being so formal, but he was so nervous that he found it impossible to speak any other way.

Kitty straightened in her chair and she answered him in the same manner. "I would be honored, Mister Thompson," she said solemnly. "Perhaps you would care to join my father and myself in our repast?" The hint of a smile turned up the corners of her mouth as she indicated a third chair tucked under the edge of their table.

Jesse shook his head and answered politely, "I believe I will turn in, Miss Moynahan. But thank you for your kind offer."

Dennis had observed this stiffly-spoken exchange with a great deal of amusement. "Oh, sit down, Jesse Thompson," he said with a chuckle. "It's too early to be turnin' in, as ye say, and it's obvious to me that my daughter wants to get to know ye better. If that indeed be the case, ye'd best just surrender. It makes it easier on yer constitution in the long run." With a sheepish smile, Jesse sat down in the offered chaired, and Dennis asked the waitress for another cup. Pouring himself a cup of coffee, Jesse looked expectantly at Kitty, as if waiting for her to start the conversation.

Slowly, Kitty drew the story of Jesse's childhood and young adulthood out of him. Her wide eyes and rapt attention soon loosened his tongue, and he found himself talking more than he had talked in a long time. As the time passed, he also heard the story of Dennis' move to the area from Texas and the establishment of the Bar M. Before the trio realized it, three hours had passed. The café was empty of patrons, and the waitress was hovering in the background, waiting for them to leave so she could draw the shades, lock the door and go home herself. Dennis looked at the two young people, who had moved closer together as the evening progressed, and cleared his throat. "We'd best be gettin' out o' here so yon lady can close the place up. An old man like me needs his rest, y'know. Come, daughter. There'll be time t' learn more of this young man when he comes t' call."

Jesse stood and offered his hand first to Dennis, then to Kitty. She held it for just a second longer than might have been entirely proper, but Dennis chose to ignore that fact. He liked the cut of this young man's jib--as his seagoing ancestors might have said--and thought that he would make a fine husband for his Kitty, if such should come to pass. "I'll take my leave, Miss Moynahan..." Jesse began.

"Jesse Thompson, I told you to call me Kitty!" she protested. "And I'll be expecting you for supper tomorrow night at the Bar M." Somewhere in the conversation, Jesse belatedly realized, he'd been invited for the evening meal at the Moynahan's ranch, and had accepted.

"I'll be there, Miss, er, Kitty. Good night, Mister Moynahan." Jesse picked up his hat, which he had retrieved from its original resting place. He settled it on his head and started for the door with his spurs jingling lightly. As he pulled the door open, he turned to glance back at the girl he already felt himself falling in love with. He'd always run from such entanglements in the past, but this time he didn't feel any desire to escape. He stepped lightly out onto the boardwalk and turned toward his bedroll in the loft of the smithy as pleasant thoughts of a bright future with Kitty drifted through his head. Like any young man, he had dreams of a girl and an idyllic life, and the future seemed bright before him...

Twenty-two

Jesse came to with a groan. His right arm was tingling where his cheek was pillowed on it, and a rock was digging into the flesh near his armpit. Shards of rock gouged his ribs. Somewhere in the distance dripping water counted cadence. Jesse tried to force open his left eye, and managed to force the lids apart a tiny bit; the lashes were gummed together with some substance that caked his face and the side of his head. Cold rock and sand under him had chilled him to the bone; as his body tried to maintain some warmth, the resulting shivering had brought him back to a semi-conscious state. Using his left hand, he pushed himself to a sitting position. Another groan parted his lips as a bolt of agony shot through his neck and head. There was a throbbing pain at the back of his neck, and he brought his right hand up to touch the large lump that had formed there. His seeking fingers found a split in the skin over the lump, caked with dried blood, and further exploration revealed other scrapes and scabs on his head and neck.

Jesse dug the caked blood from his left eye then opened it wide to find that he couldn't see his hand in front of his face, except as the faintest of shadows. The darkness around him was nearly complete, and was only mildly tempered by a disc of weak gray light high overhead. His right eye was swollen shut and hot to the touch.

A finger of moist breeze touched Jesse's right cheek. He turned his head stiffly and reached out toward the draft, and his outstretched hand brushed damp rock, then nothing; a passageway appeared to lead toward the dripping water. Jesse came up on his hands and knees, then brought his left foot up under his chest and tried to stand. His spinning brain dropped Jesse back to his knees as his right leg buckled. He knelt on the sand for a moment with his head hanging then forced himself up. His left hand came to rest on the nearby wall of rock, and Jesse held himself there until the world quit revolving around him. He followed the damp flow of air from the passageway, his left hand leading the way. With his right hand brushing the wall of the tunnel he limped through the dark, favoring his right leg. After only a few steps he splashed into water up to his knees, nearly falling again; he held himself upright by sheer force of will.

Jesse dipped a cupped hand into the cold water and lifted it to his lips. He first smelled, then tasted the liquid he held in his palm. The water was sweet, so he began scooping up great handfuls of the precious fluid and pouring them down his parched throat. The cold water cleared some of the cobwebs from his brain, and he stepped up onto the sand surrounding the pool, water running from his pants-legs and boots. Reaching for the holsters tied down on his thighs, he found them empty; the Remingtons were gone. The short-barreled

Remington derringer he normally carried in his boot, and the antler-handled sheath knife he carried at the back of his belt, were gone as well. Someone had checked him thoroughly for weapons before they dumped him into whatever pit he was in.

Gingerly lowering himself to a seat on a rock at the sandy edge of the pool, Jesse wracked his brain in an attempt to figure out where he might be. From his research of the area before he left Laramie, he knew there were numerous abandoned mine shafts in the hills surrounding Watsonville, but determining which one he was in was more than he could handle at the moment; he would be better off to think about how he was going to get out. His attacker--or attackers--had left him little to work with. Many a western man had disappeared without a trace--not always due to foul play--and it was obvious that he was meant to be just one more.

Scattered pictures tumbled through Jesse's aching brain. He remembered leaving the café and turning toward the smithy, distracted by the pleasant hours just past. He dimly recalled being struck from behind, and a gruff voice growling, "Dump him someplace where he ain't gonna be found any time soon." Then he was belly down over the saddle of a horse and his world faded to black. He wracked his brain, trying to place the voice, but soon gave up; there would be time enough for that when he was back on the surface.

Jesse suddenly jerked awake. He'd dozed off in the middle of his cogitations, and he was sure that wasn't a safe thing to do. If he was hurt worse than he suspected, falling asleep could mean dying in this miserable pit. He needed to get on his feet and find a way out of his prison. He pushed himself up, stiff right leg complaining mightily, and it suddenly came to him who the voice belonged to--an owlhoot named Grant Morgan. Their first meeting had been in an Arizona desert...

Jesse had been on the trail of Grant Morgan and Cutter Davis for a week and a half. From the freshness of the tracks in front of him, he was pretty sure he had to be less than an hour behind the pair. He pulled up just below the crest of a hill, slipped off his hat, and gigged the roan forward far enough to see over the top. A mile out in the yucca-covered flat below, two men stood by a horse that lay sprawled on its side on the ground. Its head came up as it struggled to rise. Jesse watched through his spyglass as one of the men drew a pistol; the boom of the shot rang through the still air, and the horse jerked once and lay still. The two men removed the saddlebags from the dead horse, mounted their remaining horse double, and moved off.

Those saddlebags probably held, in addition to dirty shirts and a bottle of whiskey, at least part of the loot from a bank holdup the two had pulled off in Warrenton. They'd taken $4300 from the bank safe, and Davis had killed a teller when the fellow hadn't called the bank manager soon enough to suit the two robbers. Jesse watched them disappear into the heat haze, then cautiously rode down to the dead horse. A badger hole and a broken foreleg told the poor beast's story.

Jesse kept moving, paralleling the men's tracks and staying out of sight. It would be dark before long, and with only one horse between them the robbers would have to camp soon, if only to rest the horse; that's when Jess would make his move.

The moon had been down for several hours when Jesse, his Henry rifle in his hands, moved into the flickering light of a small fire that glowed near a seep of water. Cutter Davis was hunched over, staring into the fire, which is always a mistake if a man plans on keeping his night vision intact. Grant Morgan lay snoring under a rumpled blanket nearby.

"Cutter Davis! This is Deputy Jesse Thompson!" Jesse barked from behind Davis. "Unbuckle your belt and move back, and don't do anything stupid." Davis reached for his belt buckle but Jesse could tell by the way his shoulders hunched that Davis was going to go for his gun. "Don't be a damned fool!" Jesse snapped. "This Henry is pointed at your spine and the hammer's cocked!" As fast as a striking snake, Davis' hand dropped to his holstered Colt; he drew and turned, shooting blindly toward the sound of Jesse's voice. But the deputy had moved as soon as he spoke, and the bullet flew harmlessly into the night. Jesse's foot bumped a frying pan and Davis fired again. His bullet clipped twigs from a tree over Jesse's shoulder, but he wouldn't get another chance.

The Henry blasted, lighting the night. The bullet blew through the robber's heart and his pistol fired into the dirt at his feet as it dropped from his dying hand. Grant Morgan came awake with the first shot, but he was sleeping so deeply that for the moment he was disoriented. By the time he gathered his wits, the warm muzzle of the Henry was touching his upper lip. In the yellow firelight, he could see that the rifle's hammer was eared back. "If you don't want to end up like your partner, you just lay still!" Jesse growled. He bent to pick up the pistol Morgan had been reaching for, stuffing it behind his own belt. "Now you roll over, and cross your wrists behind your back."

"I'll be damned if I will," Morgan grated.

"You'll be even further damned if you don't," Jesse retorted. "You'll end up like your pard over yonder." Morgan grudgingly rolled onto his belly, and Jesse reached into the pocket of his vest for the rawhide pigging string he kept there as a matter of course. He laid the Henry out of reach then quickly bound Morgan's wrists together, tying them to the outlaw's belt.

"All right, you can turn over," Jesse said, picking up the Henry. "As soon as I get your partner loaded on your horse, we're headed for Laramie."

"Are you plumb loco?" Morgan challenged. "It's the middle of the night!"

"It'll be cooler traveling now than it will be tomorrow mornin'," Jesse told him calmly. "Now you just sit still." Jesse quickly saddled the men's lone horse and tied Davis across the seat. He took down his lariat and looped it around Morgan's chest, made sure the fire was doused and led the way out of the camp. Morgan had a long walk ahead of him if they didn't find somebody with a horse for sale pretty soon.

Four days and a horse trade later, Jesse led his little cavalcade into Laramie. The outlaws, both living and dead, were riding. Morgan was delivered to the lockup, cursing and grumbling and vowing to get even with Jesse. Davis was starting to smell by then, but it couldn't be helped. Jesse stopped off at the undertaking parlor where Judge Martin kept an open account and arranged for Davis to be buried.

That had been over a year ago, and Jesse had heard that Morgan had been sent to the territorial prison, but apparently he'd either never made it or had figured out how to escape. Somehow, Morgan had ended up in Watsonville in time to waylay Jesse and have him dumped in here, wherever "here" was.

Twenty-three

The disk of light overhead had brightened considerably; the day was passing fast. Jesse limped to the wall and started looking for a way out. He tested various handholds, then slowly began to climb. With only one leg to help him it was going to be hell, but it had to be done.

By the time Jesse had climbed halfway to the top of the wall, it looked like he'd run out of options. The rock face was smooth for the last twenty feet, with no protrusions visible. Jesse's toes were hooked on a lip of rock only a few inches wide and he looked around, trying to find something, anything, to grab hold of. *There!* Just out of reach above his head was a vertical fissure in the rock barely wide enough for his closed fist. He would have but one chance to reach that crack, and if he missed it he'd be back down in the hole he'd come from--this time probably with something broken. He knew his one try had to count.

He carefully lowered himself as far as possible, then tensed to spring. Pushing with his left leg and pulling with his left hand, Jesse forced himself up and slammed his right fist into the crack. When his full weight came down on his hand and wrist, the bolt of agony shooting through his tortured flesh nearly sent him crashing to the rocks below, but he somehow held on and muscled himself up until he could get a grip on the rock of the crack with his left hand. By sheer grit he forced himself upward until he could get his foot in the crack and give his battered hands and arms a break. When the trembling in his muscles subsided he climbed on, working his way inch by inch toward the beckoning light above. After a grueling hour of desperate labor, he rolled exhaustedly over the lip of the shaft and into bright sunlight to lay gasping, his body covered with sweat. He was out; as soon as he caught his breath, it would be time to figure out where he was.

Jesse's eyelids fluttered open. He lay on cold sand, and the first stars were beginning to twinkle in the twilight sky overhead. He must have passed out again. He was starting to get scared. These fainting spells, or whatever they were, were getting to be a problem. He pushed himself to a sitting position, holding himself there with trembling arms. His head hung down, his chin sagging on his chest, while his breath whistled through his nostrils and his head spun. At last the world came to rest and he decided it was time to see if he could walk.

Jesse crawled to a nearby juniper, grasped a branch and pulled himself to his feet. He stood wobbling for a moment until his legs steadied under him. He looked around for something to use as a staff or walking stick, and finally found a large branch that was approximately the right shape for a crutch.

He managed to reach down and pick up the stick without falling, then started downhill, trending mostly southward. Some instinct told him that Watsonville had to be down there somewhere.

The next several hours were a blur. Jesse fell several times, and each time he went down it was harder to get back on his feet. His right knee was swollen and the pant leg was tight. It was becoming increasingly difficult to bend his leg, so he gave up trying. The dark silhouette of a low ridge bulked in front of him. In the starlight, he couldn't tell how far the ridge went; even though he was weak, he decided it would be easier to go over it than to try to find a way around. He pulled himself up the slope, using brush and small trees as handholds; at last he made the summit and stood trembling in a small opening in the brush. A light breeze tickled the back of Jesse's sweating neck, and chills marched up his spine. Somewhere in the darkness beyond the crest of the ridge a dog barked, and Jesse's head jerked toward the sound. He saw a dim light and prayed that the light came from a house. *The Lord knows I won't make it much further without help*, Jesse told himself.

Mumbling a short prayer, Jesse stumbled down the hill. A few feet from the bottom of the slope he tripped and fell, rolling the remaining distance and crashing into a pole corral fence. Inside the corral horses milled about, startled by his sudden appearance. A cloud of dust drifted away in the light of the quarter moon. Across the corral, a water trough glimmered in the moonlight, and Jesse felt his way around the pole fence to the water. He tipped his hat off his head then plunged his head under the mirrored surface. He came up dripping and snorting. The cold water helped to clear his head, and he took several long swallows. He came back to an upright position then looked around for the source of the light he'd seen. The dog barked again, and across an expanse of light-colored dust Jesse made out the outline of a house. A guttering lantern flame lit the front stoop. He hitched his makeshift crutch into place then started across the ranch yard toward the light.

Twenty-four

The sun was well up when Harvey stepped onto the short stretch of boardwalk fronting the hotel door and went inside. He had recently decided to become fiscally responsible, so rented a house to live in temporarily; he was also making some of his own meals. He was a terrible cook, but he needed to hang onto as much of his ready cash as he could. The Desert Inn was a nice place, but that kind of high living could be hard on the pocketbook. In spite of his newfound thrift, Harvey was in the habit of taking Lila Foster to breakfast at the Bluebonnet Café most mornings, unless she was too busy. As the sole employee of the Inn, Lila's day began early, but she managed to fit breakfast with Harvey into her to-do list more often than not. As it did every day, Lila's lilting "Good morning", followed by her peck on his cheek, lifted his spirits. Harvey realized for the umpteenth time just what this woman truly meant to him. He was no longer sorry that the dun had thrown a shoe and caused him to come to Watsonville instead of going on by. Lila was here, so here he would stay. But time was passing rapidly, and he wanted a place of his own to settle into before winter came. He grinned wryly to himself as a picture came unbidden to his mind of the ice houses, called igloos, that he had read about in a dog-eared copy of Harper's magazine one snowbound winter in Montana. He'd read that the Eskimeaux up north built their igloos out of packed snow, and lived quite comfortably in them, but he couldn't quite see himself dressed in furs, sleeping on a block of ice.

Lila took Harvey's arm and the couple closed the hotel door behind them. They strolled down the street, enjoying the early morning sunshine. At the Bluebonnet, Harvey gallantly opened the door for Lila and motioned her to precede him. They moved to his favorite table in the corner and sat--Harvey with his back to the wall as usual--looking around the room for Jesse. Most mornings, the young deputy was already at the café drinking coffee and eating breakfast when Harvey and Lila arrived, but this morning he was absent. Harvey shrugged off a small, nagging worry, and ordered breakfast. There'd be time enough to look for Jesse after they'd eaten.

By the time the couple finished eating, Harvey was decidedly uneasy. It wasn't like Jesse to be that late for breakfast; that boy liked to eat. *Maybe I'd better go check on him,* Harvey thought to himself as he escorted Lila back to her hotel. After they said their goodbyes, Harvey hurried down the street toward the livery. Jesse was bunking in the loft there, and if he was gone somewhere, the paint he'd taken from the Cheyenne warrior would be gone, too. Harvey rounded the corner of the livery barn and saw the paint standing placidly switching flies in the corral with his own relaxed dun. Harvey walked swiftly into the blacksmith shop, where he could hear a hammer ringing on steel. "Lars, have you seen Jesse this morning?" he called out over the din.

The smith shook his head, no, intent on the red-hot piece of metal he was shaping. After a few more blows of the hammer, Lars nodded his satisfaction with the piece, put down his hammer and quenched the hot metal in a bucket of water near his anvil. "I haven't seen him dis morning, Harvey. Ye're velcome to check de loft if ye vant, but I tink if he vas dere, dis hammer vould vake him up."

Harvey climbed the ladder to the loft. As soon as his eyes rose above the level of the floor it was obvious that Jesse was nowhere around. His blankets were rolled neatly and lay alongside his saddlebags. His coat was hung on a peg. Harvey dropped back to the floor. *Wonder where he's gotten to*, Harvey mused to himself. Then to Lars he said, "If you see him, would you tell him I'm lookin' for him? He was gonna go with me today to look at the Hanneman place. I'm thinkin' about buyin' out Old Man Hanneman."

"Yah, I tell 'im, Harvey," Lars answered, and went back to his work. The more Harvey thought about Jesse, the more worried he became. Watsonville wasn't so big that a person could lose himself in it very easily. He was beginning to suspect that something bad had happened. For whatever reason, Jesse seemed to have a way of getting himself into things that made life a good deal more complicated than Harvey really liked it to be.

Ten o'clock came, and Harvey was out of time.

He'd looked all through the town, in all the outbuildings, and found no sign of Jesse, and he had an appointment to keep with Old Man Hanneman. After waiting as long as he could, he went on to the smithy and saddled the dun. "I'm ridin' out to Hanneman's, Lars," he told the smith. "If Jesse comes in, tell him to stay put, wouldya?"

"Sure t'ing, Harvey. Still no sign of him, eh?" the big blacksmith called.

"Nope." Harvey swung into the saddle, tapped the dun with his spurs and trotted out of town. Orville Hanneman's place was northeast of Watsonville. As he rode, Harvey kept an eye on the country around. Out of habit he stopped occasionally to check his back trail.

He'd asked around about the Hanneman place, and he'd talked to the grizzled owner a few days before when the rancher was in town; taking a chance, Harvey had made an offer for the ranch, sight unseen. At the same time he'd made the appointment for today to look at the place. Old man Hanneman was in his sixties, and had lived on the small ranch for at least twenty years. From all accounts the place wasn't all that big, but it was well-kept. The rancher's wife had passed away recently, and selling the place would enable the old man to move closer to where his daughter, son-in-law and grandchildren lived. As a result, Hanneman was amenable to Harvey's first offer, providing that Harvey liked the look of the ranch.

The sun was directly overhead when Harvey crossed a rise and rode into Hanneman's yard. The ranch buildings lay nestled in a small grass-floored hollow, surrounded by cottonwoods, at the base of a low hill. A row of poplars, planted as a windbreak, grew along one open side of the hollow; a set of pole corrals lay along the other. A trickle of smoke rose from the chimney of a low stone house sitting at the base of the hill. Across the packed-dirt yard stood a combination storage shed and blacksmith shop; a stone barn backed up against one end of the corrals.

Harvey pulled the dun to a stop in the center of the yard and called out, "Hallo the house!"

The door swung open and the old rancher stepped out onto the stone stoop. "Light an' set, Mister Palmer," he said in welcome. "There's steak and biscuits ready, if you're interested."

"That's mighty kind of you, Mister Hanneman," Harvey answered. "I could eat a bite." He stepped down and looped his reins over the rail in front of the small porch. He lifted the stirrup, loosened the dun's cinch, then stepped forward with his hand out. The two men shook hands, and the older man motioned for Harvey to enter his home.

The house appeared tidy, but showed the lack of a woman's care. Dust covered the windowsills, and a haphazard stack of old newspapers and magazines lay toppled beside a tattered horsehide chair near the fireplace across the room. A semi-enclosed kitchen situated to one side housed a cast iron cook stove, cupboards, and--unusual for this country--a sink and pump. *Water in the house, of all things!* A trestle table and six chairs stood in the center of the kitchen, and on its top, a frying pan holding a pair of steaming steaks sat beside a pan of biscuits near two places neatly set with clean flatware. "Sit down, Harvey," Hanneman said. "We can talk when we're finished eating."

The meal went quickly. Harvey was impatient to get down to business so he could continue his search for Jesse, but he knew he needed to be sociable. Besides, he wanted a good look at the ranch before they finalized the deal he had offered earlier.

The two men left the ranch yard, their horses moving briskly across the grass to climb the hill at the back of the hollow. Hanneman was a conscientious sort, and it was obvious that he'd taken good care of the range. Dropping down the side of the hill to the grasslands beyond, they passed several developed springs, and the summer grass showed no sign of being overgrazed. With an effort, Harvey pushed his worries about his young friend to the back of his mind and looked carefully around him.

Off in the distance, a rangy bay stud stood atop a rocky bluff watching the two riders. The stallion raised his head and trumpeted his defiance; the sound drew a chuckle from Hanneman. "That old bugger thinks he's wild, but he ain't," the rancher said fondly. "I raised that horse from a baby, on a bottle, after a cougar got his momma. I could more'n likely ride up there and he'd come right up to me to git his ears scratched. He throws some damn fine colts. This horse I'm ridin' is one of his get."

Harvey had been eying the bay horse the rancher rode, admiring the horse's clean lines and intelligent eyes. "Looks like a good'un," he commented.

"That stud's colts are the best horseflesh you'll find for a long ways around!" Hanneman declared. "An' I ain't the only one sayin' so!" he finished proudly.

"Well, I think maybe you better introduce me to that hellion yonder before too long," Harvey said. "After all, if we can come to terms, I'm gonna have to be roundin' up his babies come spring, an' I'd kind of like the operation to be friendly!"

The grizzled rancher looked over at Harvey and

his eyes narrowed. "You know anything about raisin' horses?" he asked sternly. "I'd hate to think I was sellin' a damn good horse herd to some greenhorn who don't."

"Don't worry, Mister Hanneman, I know a good bit about horses," Harvey assured him. "I was born on a horse farm back east, an' I've gentle-broke a lot of horses over the years. I don't believe in just gettin' on 'em and lettin' 'em buck. It's too hard on me, and too hard on the horse. Far as I'm concerned, the best way to break a horse is from the ground up, by lettin' him think it's his own idea. Make's 'em easier to get along with in the long run."

Mollified, the rancher stuck out his hand. "That sounds good to me," he said. "I'll take your offer; the place is yours, pendin' you gettin' me your down payment."

Harvey leaned over and shook the old-timer's outstretched hand. "Then I guess we've got a deal, Mister Hanneman," he said. "As soon as I can get to the telegraph office, I'll wire for the money, and I should be back to see you in a few days. Now if you'll excuse me, a friend of mine didn't show up this morning when he should've, and I'd like to go try and find him."

"Why didn't you say somethin', 'stead of settin' here listenin' to an old man ramble on?" Hanneman queried. "Get on with you, and come back when you can. I'd like to be gone by the 15th of next month if I could, an' I still need to make some introductions for you." Harvey thanked him and touched a finger to his hat brim, reined the dun toward Watsonville and booted the big horse into a trot.

Twenty-five

Harvey stepped off of the sweat-stained dun in front of the smithy late in the afternoon. It was a hot day, and the horse stood with his sides heaving, slowly catching his breath. Harvey dropped the reins and the horse stood with his head hanging down as Harvey strode into the building. "Did Jesse ever show up?" he asked Lars.

"No, Harvey, he didn't, an' I don't unterstant it," Lars said worriedly. "He chenerally comes in shortly after noon, but he didn't today."

"Well, somethin's for sure happened to him, but I'll be damned if I can figure out what it is or where he is. I looked every place I could think of before I left for Hanneman's, but there was no sign of him. It's like he just dropped off the face of the earth." Harvey went back to the dun, loosened the cinch, and led the big horse into the barn. He pulled the saddle off the tired animal's sweaty back; he fussed over the horse, giving it a good brushing and pulling a couple of burrs from its long tail. Leading the grateful animal to the water trough, Harvey let it drink several swallows, then pulled him back from the water, saying, "Not too much, son, 'til you cool out some more. No use gettin' a bellyache." The dun pushed his nose toward the water and after a moment Harvey let him have some more. When he judged that the horse had cooled sufficiently, he let it drink its fill then turned the gelding in with Jesse's paint.

Standing for several minutes with one foot on the bottom rail of the fence and his arms crossed on the top pole, Harvey looked at the horses without seeing them. He was at a loss to know where Jesse had gotten to. The sun was disappearing over the hills to the west; shadows were growing and running together as the desert sky darkened. Harvey stood up straight and turned. Behind him, a rifle boomed and a bullet whined off the top rail where Harvey's head had been, spattering him with slivers. He dove to the ground with his Colt in his hand, looking wildly around, trying to find where the shot had come from. He saw a faint wisp of smoke drifting over a rise to the south and quickly low-crawled behind the water trough. He peered around the end of the trough trying to see the shooter, but no one was in sight. The fading thunder of running hooves came to Harvey's ears but he stayed put, waiting. "Harvey, you alright?" Lars yelled from the door of the barn.

"Yeah, whoever it was missed! And from the sound of things, he's runnin'!" Harvey called. He waited a moment longer, then stood quickly and sprinted for the door of the smithy. When he reached cover in the building, he moved to the far door and peered intently outside; the only sign anyone had been there was a faint, rapidly dissipating dust trail in the air to the south.

Harvey and Lars moved carefully toward the rise, separating and coming around it from different sides; as they'd expected, no one was there. It was easy to see where the shooter had fired from; a notch had been dug in the top of the rise, and the pressed down dust showed where the shooter had lain to make his play. Only Harvey's sudden turn had saved his life. It was impossible to read tracks in the deep dust, but the dimpled remains pointed the way that the shooter had gone. "You better go on back, Lars," Harvey told his friend. "I'm gonna see if I can trail this character and maybe find out where he's headed, if not who he is."

"At least come back and get a rifle, Harvey," Lars told him. "You might need a few more options."

"Good idea." Harvey went at a fast walk into the barn and headed for the rack where his saddle hung. He took the Winchester out of the scabbard and levered a round into the chamber, then let the hammer down to half-cock. It wasn't the safest thing to do, he knew, but it would speed things up if he did suddenly need it.

Rule Carson trotted his horse through the brush, looking back over his shoulder as he went. *Damn that Palmer!* If the man had stood still for another two seconds, he'd be dead and one of their problems would be solved. Instead, Palmer was now gonna be lookin' back over his shoulder even more than normal. *Damn!*

Carson's horse shied sideways as it came around a clump of mesquite. Looking behind him like he was, the outlaw nearly left his saddle when the horse jumped; only the saddle horn saved him. He grabbed at the horn, sawing on the reins at the same time. A chorus of clicking noises brought his head around to see Howdy Baxter, Marty Bannon, Cholo Montez, and Hank Jenkins all pointing guns at his chest. "Whoa, now, boys, it's just me," Carson quickly said as he lifted his hands to shoulder level. "Just steady down there."

"You idiot!" Howdy Baxter growled, holstering his Colt in disgust. "You came a hair away from getting blown loose from your boots. What in hell are you in such a hurry about?"

Carson quickly related the tale of his botched attempt to drygulch Harvey Palmer; he made sure he kept his hands raised the whole time. When he had heard all that Carson had to say, Baxter stood examining the toes of his boots for a full minute, then quietly said, "Step down and rest a bit, Rule. You seem a bit shook up." Carson looked quickly at Baxter, who continued to look down at the ground. He stepped down from his horse and turned toward Baxter just in time to meet a rock-hard fist that knocked him tail-over-teakettle into the dust.

"You ignorant excuse for a coyote!" Baxter snarled. "If it wasn't for the noise, I'd shoot you right here and now! All I told you to do was look around town a bit without being seen. I said absolutely nothing about shooting anybody. And now you've tipped Palmer off that somebody's here gunning for him!" The venom in Baxter's voice was deadly as he glared at Carson where he cowered in the dirt. Turning to the others, Baxter grated, "All of you get mounted. Palmer is probably trailing this idiot right now. We'll scatter and meet up at that spring we passed a couple of hours back. And I'm planning on shooting whoever's late." The men scrambled for their horses as Baxter stepped up on his own mount and booted it into the rapidly thickening darkness.

Harvey came into the clearing in time to hear the sound of hoofbeats fading into the distance. The smell of dust still lingered in the air. He let out a rather ugly string of words, then settled down and smiled to himself in the darkness. "What were you gonna do, take on the whole bunch of 'em alone?" he asked himself. He strode quickly back in the direction of the smithy to let Lars know what was going on.

Twenty-six

Dennis Moynahan was up late working on accounts at his desk in his office at the rear of the house. He sat back and laid down his pencil, rubbing his eyes. Lately it seemed that his eyes had taken to hurting a bit. Pretty soon he'd be putting on a pair of those spectacles the doc kept after him to buy and start wearing. Outside, his mongrel border collie-cross dog, Buster, began to bark. He was probably barking at howling coyotes again, but it didn't pay to ignore the noise. Old Buster had saved a herd for him once, and Dennis was reluctant to take a chance. He left the lamp turned low on his desk and moved toward the front of the house, going slowly, allowing his vision to adjust to the darkness away from his desk. As he entered the main room a muffled thump on the outside door suddenly brought his senses to full alert. Striding silently to a rack on the wall, he took down a pistol from a peg and moved toward the door.

Dennis pressed himself against the wall on the

hinge-side of the door and called out, "Who's there? Sing out, or I'll shoot!" Another thump met his ears, and he quickly moved to the other side of the door. He'd just recently had those new-fangled latches with knobs freighted in and installed, and he reached out to slowly turn the cut-glass doorknob. He cracked open the door slightly and peered out. Pressure from the outside kept trying to force the panel open but he kept his booted foot pressed firmly against the bottom and held it nearly closed.

The dim lamp hanging from the porch post revealed just enough of the dark figure leaning against the door to cause Dennis to sense that whoever it was needed help. Leery of an ambush, Dennis moved his foot, letting the door swing open. The stranger nearly fell into the room, but caught himself on the doorframe as he began to speak.

"Howdy, Mister Moynahan," Jesse rasped, his voice hardly above a whisper.

"Jesse Thompson? Is that you?"

"Yes sir, it's me," Jesse replied. "I'm sorry, I'm a little late for dinner."

"Boy, you look like hell," Dennis said truthfully, tucking the pistol behind his belt.

"Right at the moment, sir, I feel like hell," Jesse muttered as he passed out and fell into the room. Dennis lowered him to the flagstone floor, then turned back to his office for the lamp from his desk.

A small fire flickering in the dark led Marty Bannon to the spring where the four outlaws were to meet their boss. As he approached, leading his horse the last fifty yards, he couldn't see the fire--only the reflection of the flames on the underside of the trees around the spring. Knowing Howdy Baxter's moods, Bannon stepped out of the brush carefully. His eyes swept the small clearing; he saw nothing but the fire and Howdy's saddle. He was about to turn away when a fourfold clicking sound brought him to a halt as a cold, hard object was inserted into his right ear. "Hello, Marty," Baxter hissed, withdrawing the muzzle of his Colt from its resting place. "Good to see you." An undertone of madness lay beneath the seemingly benevolent words, and Bannon shivered. For as long as he had known Howdy, the man had never seemed to be especially tightly-wrapped, but lately it seemed like the wrappings had been getting progressively looser. Losing his brother had apparently unhinged him a bit more, and Rule's missed shot at Palmer hadn't improved things any.

Howdy moved toward the fire, leaned down to stir the flames and added a few small branches. The sound of a hoof striking rock and the jangle of a bit chain brought him upright; once more, he faded into the night. He stayed well back in the shadows and watched as Montez, Carson and Jenkins came slipping out of the darkness into the circle of firelight. Bannon was in the process of unsaddling his horse; he stopped long enough to watch the three come in, then went on with his business.

"Where's Howdy?" Hank Jenkins called toward Bannon's back. Bannon just shrugged and carried his saddle to the far edge of the clearing, as far away from Howdy's gear as he could get. Like a wraith, Baxter suddenly appeared in the firelight, causing Hank to jump back, nearly tripping over his own feet.

"What's the matter with you, Hank?" Howdy asked sarcastically. "You'd think you'd seen a ghost."

Baxter grinned evilly. *We mighta been better off with the ghost*, Hank thought to himself. Baxter looked around the clearing. "You boys're right on time. Good for you. I really hated the thought of shooting one of you. It might have tipped the law off that we were here." He sauntered over to his saddle and blankets and sat down on a small patch of grass. "Rule, why don't you boys start some grub? I'm getting hungry."

The men scurried around the clearing, slicing bacon and stirring up fry bread; soon the aroma of boiling coffee permeated the air. The men speared the bacon out of the pan as it finished cooking, then fried their bread in the grease. They finished up with coffee strong enough to stand a spoon in, if they'd had a spoon. By the time the moon was down, all but Baxter were in their blankets. Snores and an occasional less socially-acceptable noise were the only sounds in the clearing. Baxter didn't sleep: he sat through the night, brooding, with a blanket over his shoulders.

Twenty-seven

Jesse woke suddenly; bright sunlight on his eyelids brought him to the realization that he hadn't a clue where he was. He kept his breathing regular as he listened for any sound that might indicate the presence of another person nearby. Hearing nothing but birdsong through an open window, he cautiously cracked one eye open. The bright light streaming through the window sent a lance of pain through his head. Jesse turned away from the source of the light and gradually opened both eyes, squinting until his eyesight adjusted to the brightness. He found himself in a strange bed in a strange room. He lay on crisp sheets, with another over him. A bandage was wrapped around his head. A mild breeze rustled the curtains at the open window. He looked around as best he could without raising his head, and found his clothes folded neatly on a chair near the bed. His boots stood nearby, and his gunbelt, with its empty holsters, hung on the back of the chair. He reached a hand under the covers and found to his immense relief that he at least still had his long-handles on.

The feather tick he lay on was suspended by ropes in a rough-hewn frame. He could feel the crisscross of the strands under his back. Across the room stood a bureau where a bowl and pitcher sat atop a gingham cloth. A door leading to what appeared to be a small closet stood ajar to his right. A small landscape painting on the wall next to another door stood in sharp contrast to the whitewashed walls of the room.

Jesse threw the covers back and swung his feet onto a rag rug covering the smoothly sanded puncheon floor. He sat on the edge of the bed while the room appeared to spin around him; when at last the walls stayed in place, Jesse reached for his socks and carefully, so as not to jar his aching head, slipped them on his feet. Next came his shirt, which he gingerly slipped over his head, trying mightily to avoid the large knot on the back of it. He picked up his pants and carefully stepped into them. He buttoned the fly, then pulled his suspenders over his shoulders. He picked up his vest and slipped it over his arms. Now came the fun part-- getting his boots on. It took a while, but eventually he was ready to greet the world. He picked up the gun belt and hung it from his shoulder; he'd need to see about replacing the Remingtons as soon as possible. While he'd been dressing, Jesse had been working out where he was, and with a rush it came to him; he was at the Moynahan's ranch. He vaguely remembered falling against the door while a dog raised a ruckus about his presence, and Dennis catching him when he fell into the room. But how he got from there to this pleasant bedroom was still a mystery.

Jesse picked up his hat from where it hung on the back of a chair. He opened the door and stepped out into the hall. His sudden appearance startled a small dark-haired woman who had been about to open the door to his room. She let out a squeak and fled down the hall, shouting *"Señorita! Señorita!* He ees awake!"

Kitty appeared at the far end of the hall. Her hands reached out to take hold of the upper arms of the small woman. "It's alright, Maria," she laughed. "I'll take it from here." Maria dashed out of sight, and Kitty stood waiting for Jesse to make his way to her. Her hands were clasped at her waist. "Well, you certainly gave us a scare, Mister Thompson," she said. "We weren't sure for a while whether you were going to live or die. We were beginning to wonder if we should notify your next of kin." A smile curved her generous lips as she spoke.

Jesse looked at her for a moment, then decided that she was teasing. "I truly appreciate your concern, Miss Moynahan," he jokingly replied. "I wasn't too sure myself, for a while."

Kitty's demeanor became instantly serious, and she gazed intently up at Jesse. "Are you sure you're alright, Jesse? Dad said you collapsed in our front room."

"I'll be fine as soon as I get something to eat," Jesse replied. His gray eyes locked on her sapphire blue ones. "I feel like I could eat a whole buffalo by myself!"

"We haven't a whole buffalo, but we do have ham, eggs and biscuits," Dennis rumbled from the doorway behind Kitty. "That is, if you two can stop making eyes at each other long enough to eat!" He chuckled as the two young people turned toward him, their embarrassed faces glowing red. "Come on with ye." Dennis stepped out of the doorway and gestured for his daughter to lead the way.

Jesse hung his hat and gun belt on pegs near the door, seated Kitty, and went to the remaining vacant chair. Maria bustled about, pouring coffee and placing plates heaped with hot food in front of each of them. For the next several minutes, the only sound was that of cutlery on plates and the occasional muted thump of a coffee cup on the table. When they had finished eating and Maria had removed the plates and flatware, Dennis and the two young people remained at the table with their coffee. "What day is it?" Jesse inquired uncertainly.

The answer came as a shock. It had been Tuesday night when he'd been thumped on the head and dropped down the mineshaft. He'd assumed it was Wednesday when he climbed back up to the surface. If he was right, then as near as he could figure today should be Thursday. "It's Saturday, son," Dennis answered. "We were tryin' t' decide whether or not we should try wakin' ye when ye showed up on yer own."

Jesse stared at Dennis, until he realized that his mouth was actually hanging open. He closed it with a snap and said, "You can't be serious, sir. How could it be Saturday? That means I've been unconscious for..."

"About two days, young man," Dennis interrupted. "That's why Kitty told you we were gettin' a wee bit worried about you."

Stunned, Jesse leaned back in his chair, then sat bolt upright. "Sir, if I could borrow a horse, I need to get back to town. Harvey Palmer's expecting me to go with him to look at a ranch, and I'm way late." He pushed himself to his feet and the room swam again for a moment. He grabbed the edge of the table to steady himself. He didn't see Kitty start to reach for him, only to stop when she saw her father's frown.

"Are ye sure ye're up to it, Jesse?" Dennis asked.

"Doesn't matter whether I'm up to it or not, sir; I have to go. I'll be fine once I get on a horse."

Kitty looked at him then shook her head. She suddenly realized what she should already have known: western men were made of whalebone and rawhide, and would sooner take a whipping than admit weakness. Her father was cut from the same cloth. Dennis rose and reached for his hat as Jesse turned toward Kitty. He gave her a smile and picked up his own hat and empty gun belt.

"Kitty, I'm very sorry about breaking our dinner date," he said. "I will try to make it up to you. And I appreciate your hospitality. Thank you." Kitty nodded demurely as he turned toward the door. The two men left the kitchen, headed for the horse barn.

As the morning sun gleamed in the branches of the surrounding cottonwood trees, Howdy Baxter stirred and dropped the blanket from his shoulders. He'd spent the night staring into the dying embers of the fire, thinking about the two men he was planning to kill. He didn't have a concrete plan at the moment, other than to kill the two nuisances who had been more trouble than any twenty lawmen had ever been and ride away. The outlaw leader stood and stretched the kinks out of his back and shoulders. Moving to the closest of the piles of blankets that lay scattered around the nearly dead fire, Baxter kicked one end of the pile. He grumbled, "Get your butt up, and get the fire stirred up. I'm hungry, and I need some coffee." Baxter continued around the camp, kicking piles of blankets, until finally heading into the brush for his morning constitutional.

Harvey awoke as pale sunlight beamed through his bedroom window. He lay for a while on his back with his hands behind his head, staring at the ceiling. Somehow he had to find Jesse, and keep himself alive at the same time; that shot last night had nearly taken his head off, and it had been his own damned fault. Hanging around town had apparently made him a little less careful than what he ought to be if he wanted to stay alive. He rolled out of his bunk and dropped his feet to the floor, still ruminating. Something he'd overheard in the saloon last night made him wonder; he'd overheard a big stranger talking to the man alongside him about a mine shaft, and "...checkin' on that kid in the mornin'." From the looks of the two men, they weren't in the habit of rising early. Harvey thought it might be a good idea to follow them and find out just who the kid in question might be. Although he didn't have anything concrete to go on, his every instinct told him they were talking about Jesse. Harvey stepped into his britches and pulled up his suspenders, stepped into his boots and swung his pistol belt into place. He picked up his hat and stepped outside, after checking for ambushers and seeing none. He strode quickly across the street and down to the Bluebonnet Café. At the café, he talked the cook out of a handful of biscuits and headed for the smithy to saddle his horse, munching as he went.

Lars was just building up the fire in the forge when Harvey came in. "Ye're out an' about early, ain't ya Harvey?" the 'smith asked.

"Did a big fella wearin' a black hat with a Montana peak on it, an' packin' a fancy carved cross-draw, leave a horse here in the last day or two, Lars?" Harvey queried.

"Yah, him and a couple of second-rate, vannabe

gunslicks came in Tuesday, an' paid for a veek. Dey vere ridin' a buckskin, a paint, an' a blaze-faced chestnut. Dey're out yonder. Vhy do ye ask?"

"Well, last night in the saloon I heard that big guy sayin' somethin' about a mineshaft and a kid, an' I'm thinkin' it might be in Jesse's best interest for me to follow 'em."

Startled, Johansen looked up at Harvey. "You t'ink dey might've been talkin' about Jesse?"

"I don't know, but I aim to find out," Harvey answered. "I'm gonna saddle the dun an' sit out yonder in the brush an' watch where those fellas go. The only mineshafts I know about are north of here, so it seems to me that's the way they gotta be headin'." Harvey headed for the pen where his dun was, roped the big horse, led it out and cinched the saddle in place. While he was there he checked the horses Lars had told him about; he wanted to recognize the tracks if he saw them, just in case he lost sight of the riders.

Leading the dun around the corral, Harvey took the big horse into the brush on the north side of the wagon yard. There he tethered it to a stout bush and settled down to wait. Fifteen minutes later, the two men Harvey had seen in the saloon came down the street, followed by a small, rat-faced individual with a bedraggled mustache hanging under his large nose. *So, Mort Bales is in town. I should've known,* Harvey thought. *If anybody's gonna be stirrin' up trouble, it's Mort.*

Harvey had known Mort Bales for at least five years. Lars had referred to him as a "wannabe gunslick", but Mort was actually pretty fast with a gun, though he didn't look it. He and Harvey met on a ranch in southern Idaho when Harvey hired on to help at roundup time. Mort slacked off during the entire endeavor, and was quite possibly even doing some high-grading on the side, and Harvey called him on it. Rather than calling Harvey a liar, and getting himself shot for his troubles, Bales rode out, cussing Harvey all the way. Since that time the two men had each held a less than cordial dislike for the other, and avoided each other as much as possible. And now Mort was in Watsonville.

The three men got their horses out, saddled up and started north. Harvey let their dust settle some then moved out, paralleling their route and keeping out of sight. Every so often he would move up until he could see them and make sure that they hadn't turned off; on the contrary, the trio was making a beeline for Badger Mountain.

Harvey wracked his brain, trying to remember whether or not he knew the whereabouts of any mineshafts on Badger Mountain. Then it came to him; thirty years or so ago, a sourdough named Barton had hit a rich gold pocket on Badger Mountain. He'd made enough money off of the first strike to buy enough supplies to sink a shaft before the pocket had petered out; at roughly the same time, he'd hit water and abandoned the mine. It looked like Mort and his *compadres* were headed for that mine.

Deciding to take a chance at beating the three gun-hands to their destination, Harvey turned the dun away from the trail and nudged him into a trot, rapidly pulling ahead of the leisurely pace maintained by Mort and his companions. He came to the mine some time later and reined up out of sight, ground tying the dun behind a rock outcropping. He shucked his rifle from the scabbard and eased forward until he could see the opening of the shaft. The sand and broken rock around the opening looked to have been disturbed recently, so Harvey settled down behind a clump of brush in the shade to wait.

Twenty-eight

The first voice Harvey heard was Mort Bale's nasal squeak. "Yeah Grant, I'm sure he's still there. There ain't no way he got out of that hole. It's sixty or eighty feet deep if'n it's an inch, an' that whack on the noggin probly killed him anyway. Don't worry."

A rumbling bass voice that Harvey assumed belonged to the aforementioned Grant muttered something unintelligible then the three came into sight. The men stepped down from their horses and moved to the mouth of the shaft, each grabbing the rock around the hole for support so they could lean in to look over the edge.

"No way he could get outta there, huh?" Grant growled. "I sure as hell don't see no body down there, do you? I oughta throw your skinny butt down there!" Grant grabbed Mort by the front of his shirt and held him out over the edge of the shaft with just his toes holding him up.

"H-h-honest, Grant, I was s-s-sure he'd be here," Mort stammered. "I don't see h-h-how he got out! Somebody musta helped him!"

"He didn't come back to town, if they did," Grant growled. "So either he got himself out, or he crawled off and died down there. I'm thinkin' you need to go down there and find out." Grant flung Mort toward his horse. "Git yer rope. We're gonna lower you down there to check."

Mort made a beeline for his saddle and the coiled lariat tied there. He slipped the rope strap loose and practically ran back to where Grant waited impatiently with his arms crossed on his chest and a black look on his face. Grant yanked the rope from Mort's hand, shook out a loop, and dropped the loop over the smaller man's head. "Lift yer arms up, ya dummy, unless ya want me to drop ya down there with yer arms pinned to yer sides. Right at the moment, I ain't particular."

The loop came tight around Mort's scrawny chest under his arms and he stepped to the edge of the shaft. "You ain't gonna drop me, are ya Grant?" he squeaked with a tremor in his voice. Mort was afraid of heights, and hanging by a lariat over a hole as deep as this one wasn't exactly his idea of a good time. He'd face up to charging Indians or stampeding cattle, but what he was about to be subjected to was almost more than he could take.

"No, I ain't gonna drop ya, ya little weasel," Grant snapped. "Now git goin'."

Mort turned his back to the black hole yawning below his feet, and leaned back on the rope. Grant set himself, the rope passed around his back, and Bales slowly disappeared from sight. The third man, a chunky sort called Jode Benson, sat down on a nearby rock. His hand was on the butt of the crossdraw-holstered pistol that hung on his belt just in front of his left hip. The movement of Benson's hand called Harvey's attention to the gun that Benson's hand rested on. He got a glimpse of creamy yellow color from the grips of the pistol; if he wasn't mistaken, at least one of the pistols Benson was packing was one of Jesse Thompson's Remingtons. After a few seconds scrutiny, Harvey was sure that the pistol on Benson's belt was indeed a Remington; a moment later, when the man lifted his hand to scratch his ear, Harvey knew that the pistol was Jesse's. Its mate hung on the man's right hip.

The rope Grant was belaying went slack as Mort reached the bottom of the shaft. "I'm down, Grant," the squeaky voice drifted up. "There's a puddle of dried blood here, but I don't see no body." Mort immediately realized what he'd said and quickly shut his mouth before Grant decided to leave him there in Jesse's place. He stepped out of the loop of rope and fastened it to a large rock, in hopes that he could keep his ride back to the surface intact. He reached into his pocket and drew out a stub of candle. Mort struck a match on a rock, touched the flame to the candlewick, and soon a yellowish light began to push the shadows back. He bent to peer at the floor of the shaft, and saw where Jesse had crawled to the tunnel that opened in the rock wall. He followed the scuff marks to the pool of water and around its sandy edge, until he ran out of sand at a rock wall.

It was obvious that unless Jesse's body was submerged in the pool, Mort was alone as alone could be down here. He returned to the rope and blew out the candle. He waited a moment for the wick to cool, dropped the stub of candle back in his pocket, and quickly looped the rope back around himself. He checked the rope to make sure it was secure and hollered up at Grant to pull him back to the surface. But the rope stayed slack, and a mutter of voices drifted down to where Mort stood, uncomfortably aware of how far he was from daylight.

When he heard Mort call that he was ready to come back up, Harvey decided it was time to take a hand in the proceedings. With odds of only two-to-one, and with the big guy staring intently down into the hole at his feet, Harvey figured it was now or never. He worked his way quietly through the brush to a position behind Benson, then reached out with the barrel of his Winchester and nudged the man on the back of the neck. Benson stiffened and his hand tightened on the grips of the Remington at his side. Harvey whispered quietly, "Don't even think about it. I could have you dead before you got it halfway out. Just lift your hands up and put 'em on the back of your neck." Benson wasn't exceptionally bright, but he knew a cold deck when he saw it, so he did as Harvey said. "Now tell your pard there to turn around."

"Grant, would you mind turnin' around here just for a minute?" Grant turned his head far enough to see Harvey standing behind Benson with the muzzle of his rifle tucked under the man's ear. The hammer was back and Harvey's finger was white on the trigger.

"Who the hell are you, and what business have you got holdin' up my man there?" Grant demanded as he turned to face Harvey.

"I don't really think you're in any position to be asking questions," Harvey replied. "You seem to have your hands full with your pard's tether, so I'll do the asking." Benson's hands started to drift downward and Harvey nudged him with the rifle barrel again. "Ah-ah-ah, we'll have none of that, my friend. You just keep those grubby paws where I can see 'em." He turned his attention back to Grant. "So, here's my question. Who did you come out here to check on, and what is your friend here doin' with Jesse Thompson's guns?"

"We don't have to answer anything, mister," Grant growled. "It's none of your business."

"Now that's where you're wrong, friend!" Harvey shot back. "Jesse Thompson's a friend of mine, and I'm making it my business."

Jode Benson liked to think of himself as a tough man, and the way Harvey was treating him was galling. Frustrated and silently fuming, he came to the conclusion that he should do something about the man with the gun. Jode figured that maybe if he acted scared, the man holding him at gunpoint would relax, and he could get the jump on him. "Just tell him, Grant," Jode quavered. "He'll kill us both if you don't."

"Shut up, Jode!" Grant snapped. "I ain't tellin' him nothin'!"

Jode started to swivel his head to look at Harvey and Harvey let him. Jode's words came out in a rush. "Then I'll tell him. Grant had us thump some young feller on the head a couple nights ago, and we brung him out here for safekeepin', but it don't sound like maybe he's here no more, an' I took his guns, 'cause my horse fell with me the other day an' I lost my pistol, an' these here Remingtons are some of the best guns goin', an' I needed a gun an' he," he forced his chin to quiver as he indicated Grant, "said I could have 'em. An' that's the sum of that, mister. Now can I let my arms down? I don't think I can hold 'em up here much longer."

Harvey took a step back so he could watch Grant and Jode at the same time. "All right, Jode, or whatever your name is, you can put your poor arms down far enough to unbuckle that belt and hand me those guns. And if you so much as think about pullin' one of 'em, I'll put a hole through the middle of you and leave you for the ants. I might even go get the ants myself." Jode stood up carefully and reached down to the buckle of the belt. He pulled the tongue of the belt through as if to pull the buckle loose, then his right hand streaked to the Remington in the crossdraw. Amazed, Harvey stood, entranced, as Jode Benson made the fastest grab of his life--on a tied-down pistol.

The would-be gunman yanked, but the pistol didn't move. Stunned, Jode glanced down, then for some reason known only to him, he yanked at the pistol again. Suddenly the lights went out as Harvey stepped forward and clubbed him with the stock of the Winchester. It seemed like a better idea than shooting the man, even if he was too stupid for words. Grant stood watching the scene, unmoving, with both hands on the rope he'd used to lower Mort into the mineshaft.

Jode went down like his legs had been scythed out from under him, and hit the dirt on his face, raising a momentary puff of dust. Grant then started to move, but the muzzle of Harvey's Winchester swung to cover him; the black hole of the muzzle looked as wide as the mineshaft from Grant's perspective. "Now don't get antsy, Grant. That is what your sleeping friend called you, wasn't it? Grant?"

"Yeah, that's my name," Grant answered in a surly tone. "Now what the hell do you want?"

"I already told you that, Grant," Harvey said conversationally. The muzzle of the rifle was rock-steady, pointed at Grant's belt buckle. "I want to know where Jesse Thompson is."

"I guess there ain't no percentage in tryin' to

pull a fast one now," Grant conceded. "He was sposed ta be down in that hole, but he don't seem to be there."

"Why don't you pull ol' Mort up outta there before he panics and does something stupid, and let's find out for sure?" Harvey asked reasonably. "I would imagine that by now he's startin' to get a little worried. Before you pull him up, though, why don't you toss that Colt over this way? With two fingers." Grant gingerly fished his pistol out of the fancy crossdraw holster he carried it in, using two fingers. Harvey could see the thought slide behind Grant's eyes, just for a moment, that maybe, just maybe, he should take a chance. Discretion overcame valor, however, and the big outlaw tossed his gun toward Harvey.

Mort's voice drifted up from below. "Who ya talkin' to, Grant? An' when do I get outta here?"

"Hold yer horses, Mort," Grant growled. "Get the rope set, an' I'll pull ya up." The rope tightened and Mort's squeak came out of the darkness. "Ready, Grant. Hoist away." Grant leaned into the rope, and with seemingly little effort began to drag Mort up toward the daylight. As soon as his head cleared the ground Mort began to talk. "That kid ain't down there, Grant. I looked all over the place, an' there ain't no sign..." His eyes widened and he went silent as he took in the sight of Jode stretched out on the ground, not moving, and Harvey standing with his Winchester pointed at Grant. "What the hell is..." he began, but Grant cut him off.

"Shut up, Mort!" Grant snapped. "An' get your scrawny butt up here."

"And don't even think about tryin' to draw, Mort. At this distance, with this rifle, I don't think you're gonna make it." A familiar voice cut in.

"Harvey! What're you doin' here?" Mort's

incredulous squeak rose to an irritating pitch.

"I was just askin' your friends here the same question, Mort," Harvey replied. "But I think I know the answer. You boys bushwhacked Jesse Thompson an' brought him out here an' dumped him, an' now he's gone. The question now is, where'd he go? You sure you don't have any idea?"

Mort scrambled the rest of the way up to the surface, his pistol forgotten. "Honest, Harvey, he ain't down there. If he's gone somewhere, he musta did it himself, 'cause we didn't have nothin' to do with it."

Studying Mort's face, Harvey considered whether the smaller man was lying or not. "Well then, how 'bout you shuckin' that pistol and throwin' it over here, and we'll figure out what's gonna transpire next."

"Sure, Harvey, sure. Don't get antsy." Mort gingerly unhooked the tiedown from the hammer of his Colt, slid the gun from the holster, and tossed it toward Harvey. "Uh, what happened to Jode?"

"He tried to draw after I told him not to," Harvey smirked.

"I didn't hear a shot. Is he dead?"

"I don't think so. I didn't hit him that hard." Harvey motioned with the rifle barrel. "You boys move away from that hole and sit down while I contemplate on what to do with you."

The two men did as they were told, sitting down and sharing a large, half-buried rock that protruded from the sand near the mouth of the shaft. Harvey stood for a moment as if deep in thought, but he already knew what he was going to do. He started to speak and noticed that Benson was beginning to stir. He lifted his foot and let it rest on the back of Jode's neck. "You just lay still there, pard. I'll let you up in a minute."

Jode went still. "Here's what's gonna happen, boys," Harvey continued. "Mort, you're gonna unsaddle your horses, then you're all gonna shuck your boots and your britches. I'm gonna lead your horses off a ways, then let 'em go. I'll leave your guns an' some water with the horses. Never let it be said that Harvey Palmer left a man defenseless and dyin' of thirst. I'll be takin' this feller's misappropriated pistols with me, so I can return them to their rightful owner."

Mort and Grant just sat glaring at Harvey. As far as he was concerned, it was about time somebody else's life got complicated. He was getting tired of it constantly happening to him. "Move, Mort!" Harvey suddenly snarled. "Unless you want me to shoot you and dump you down that hole."

Mort jumped up and scurried to where the three men's horses were tethered to a bushy mahogany tree. Their saddles and blankets soon lay in an untidy heap on the ground, and Mort led the three mounts to where Harvey stood with his foot still on the back of Jode's neck. Mort held out the reins to Harvey.

"Here ya go, Harvey."

Harvey took the reins and motioned for Mort to move back to his place on the boulder next to Grant. "Now you boys get outta those boots and pants! You too, sleeping beauty!" This last comman was aimed at Jode as Harvey stepped back, pushing the horses behind him. The prone man rolled to a sitting position with a groan.

"I think ya broke something, ya son of a..."

"I'll break it worse if you don't shut up and do what you're told!" Harvey growled impatiently. "Now shuck 'em!" A few short minutes later, the three men sat in their dirty, holey drawers glaring at Harvey as he made a bundle of their gear, including their canteens. He hung Jesse's holstered guns over his shoulder and slung the bundle of the men's gear over the back of one of the horses. He pulled a long string out of his pocket, bundled up the rifles that were on the saddles and hung them with the rest of the gear. "You boys just stay put until you can't hear the horses anymore. After that, I don't care what you do. But remember this: if I see any of you on my back trail, I'll blow a hole through you and leave you for the buzzards. Mort'll tell you that I'm a man of my word."

Keeping the rifle trained on his three captives, Harvey backed away. Once he was out of sight, he yanked the three horses into a trot, heading toward where he'd left the dun. He shoved the Winchester into the boot, quickly tightened the cinch, leapt aboard the big horse and booted him into the brush, leading the extra horses. A couple of miles toward the south, he dropped the reins of the led horses and the three stopped in the shade of a clump of junipers. Well-trained as they were, the animals would stand pat until either someone found them or they got thirsty enough to wander off. Either way Harvey was done with them. He hung Jesse's Remingtons on his own saddle horn and moved out on the trail toward Watsonville. At least now he could be fairly sure that Jesse was still alive.

Twenty-nine

Dennis was closing the door behind Jesse and himself when he noticed the empty holsters Jesse wore. "It's none o' me business, I'm sure," he said quietly, "But those holsters are lookin' a tad bit on the light side. If ye've got enemies, don't ye think ye might want to go heeled?"

Jesse stopped and mumbled an unkind word about Grant Morgan under his breath, then turned toward Dennis. "Do you think I could trouble you for the loan of a couple of shooters, sir?" he asked.

"I think I might have somethin' I can let go of for a day or two. Come on back in the house, and we'll see what we can find." The two men reentered the house, startling Kitty. "Sorry, daughter," Dennis rumbled, "but this fellow doesn't appear to be armed, and methinks that's a state that needs to be remedied."

Kitty sat and watched pensively as the two men sorted through the guns in the cabinet near the door until Jesse found a pair of long-barreled, walnut-stocked Colts whose balance suited him. The Colts were fine weapons, but didn't feel as good in his hands as his Remingtons; still, they had the best feel of all the pistols he handled. He worked the action of each gun several times, careful to draw the hammer back all the way before letting it down each time, then pulled rounds from his belt and loaded them. Letting the hammer down on an empty chamber on each gun, he slipped them into the holsters. The weight was different than that of his own guns--the Colts didn't have the under-barrel web as did his Remingtons--but the difference was barely noticeable. "I think these will work, sir. I'll return them as soon as possible."

"Not to worry, Jesse," Dennis assured him. "Return 'em when ye can. Now let's go find ye a horse." Jesse tipped his hat to Kitty and the two men headed back outside.

The horse corral lay across the yard. The gaps between the poles showed a milling mass of multicolored hide as the Bar M horse-breaking crew roped out their next mounts to take to the round pen by the main corral. All the horses had been ridden at some time but some needed a little more work than others. Dennis leaned on the top rail of the fence with one foot on a lower pole. "Well, see anything ye like, Jesse?"

"They all look fine, sir. But I do believe I like that gray over yonder." Jesse pointed at a stoutly-built dapple gray that stood warily watching the men. Dennis nodded his approval and reached up to a rope hanging on the gatepost.

"Rope him out, and let's get him to the barn and find you a saddle." Jesse slipped the gate latch and stepped inside, shaking out a loop. The gray seemed to know that he was the target, and ducked into the middle of the milling mass of horses. Jesse strolled across the corral nonchalantly, the loop dragging behind him in the dust. He was looking anywhere but at the gray when the loop suddenly snaked out and dropped over the horse's head. The green-broke mustang made a half-hearted attempt to escape, but gave up when it felt Jesse lean into the rope. The young horse stood with its ears up, facing its captor, as Jesse walked, hand-over-hand, towards the horse, coiling the rope. The horse snorted but stood fast as Jesse flipped a loop over its nose to make a halter then turned to lead the gray out of the corral. It was the work of only a few short minutes to get a borrowed saddle cinched in place and a hackamore settled on the gray's head. The horse stood fast throughout the entire operation, never once offering to fight. *This is one smart horse*, Jesse thought. Somehow he knew the gray was just readying itself for what was coming next.

Jesse led the gray into a small corral near the barn and stepped into the saddle. He kept one hand on the horn, and with the other he pulled the gray's nose around to the left. He figured on at least getting seated before the horse blew into the air. The gray's ears were back and its eyes rolled to look at Jesse. Jesse could feel the gelding tense, and just as the short-coupled horse's muscles started to bunch in preparation for its first jump, Jesse sunk his heel into its short ribs just ahead of the flank. The horse huffed out the deep breath it had sucked in, and its hindquarters shifted away from Jesse's boot. Jesse made sure that the horse's nose followed. The gray spun in a tight circle, fighting half-heartedly to get its nose down to buck; Jesse never gave it the chance.

After making several circles in the dusty corral,

with its nose nearly touching its shoulder, the gray's muscles relaxed, its ears tipped forward, and Jesse settled back in the saddle. He was still ready for any shenanigans the horse might try, but the mustang stood calmly with its sides heaving and a few small rivulets of sweat darkening the light-colored hide. Jesse gave the gray its head and booted it into a trot, then a lope, around the inside of the corral fence.

A few circuits around the corral later, Jesse pulled up on the hackamore rein. He brought the horse to a sliding stop then lifted the rein again until the gray backed a step. Jesse immediately relaxed the pressure on the rein and the horse stopped, switching his tail at an errant fly. The animal sensed its rider's confidence, submitting to Jesse's quiet manner. The gray accepted Jesse's mastery and stood quietly, waiting for further instructions.

"I believe you can open the gate now, sir. I don't think he's gonna try anything," Jesse said to Dennis, who stood with one hand on the gate latch. Dennis slid the bar and swung the gate open. Jesse trotted the gray out the gate then slid him to a stop just outside the corral.

"I think young Dapple's ready to be a real horse, Jesse," Dennis remarked. "But he's still pretty green. Ye'd best be careful on the way into town."

"I will sir, and thank you," Jesse assured him. "I'll get him back to you as soon as I can."

"No hurry, Jesse. As y'can see, we've no shortage of horseflesh hereabouts." Dennis grinned and raised a hand. "Adios, Jesse."

"Adios, sir. Take care." Jesse nudged the gray with his heels and left the ranch yard.

Behind Dennis, the house door closed with

a click that echoed across the yard. He turned his attention toward the house, where Kitty stood with one hand on a porch post and the other shading her eyes as she watched Jesse disappear into the morning heat waves. Dennis walked to his daughter and slipped his arm around her shoulders. "Yonder's a good man, daughter. He'll do to ride the river with, I'm thinkin'," he said softly.

"I think so too, Daddy." Kitty returned to the house to change into her riding clothes. It was time to check the cattle in the west pasture.

Thirty

The dun's ground-eating trot carried Harvey back down the trail toward Watsonville. There'd been enough movement at the mineshaft and the sand was loose enough that he'd never be able to find Jesse's tracks. By now, those three owlhoots would be hot-footing it down the trail after him. Mad as they were, they'd more than likely be flat out chasing him once they got to their horses unless Mort could convince them to wait. Harvey hoped Mort could do it; he still had to find Jesse.

A few miles to the west, Rule Carson got down from his horse to kneel and finger a track in a patch of clay near a seep. "Somebody's been here recently, Howdy," he said over his shoulder. "But it's been a few hours. I don't know for sure if it's him or not. Could be."

Howdy Baxter sat still for a moment then pulled his horse to the east. "We'll hit the trail to Watsonville. Maybe whoever it is will show himself, and then we'll know for sure." He kicked his horse into a trot and led off.

Behind him, Hank Jenkins pulled alongside of Carson. "Ain't this the way to that mine of old man Barton's?" he whispered. Carson nodded and Hank went on. "You think there's any gold left up there?"

"Not hardly," Carson told him. "If there was, somebody'd be workin' it and we'd've heard about it. Now shut up and ride." The men rode in silence, not missing anything around them.

As they neared the trail to Watsonville, Baxter lifted a hand and stopped his horse. "I hear voices," he muttered. "Marty, go check it out."

Just then, on the other side of a screen of high brush, a voice commanded loudly, "Stand still, you stupid bag of bones, or I'll shoot ya and pack my saddle outta here myself!" The clatter of hooves on gravel signified that maybe the horse still wasn't cooperating. Baxter and his men looked at each other in amazement. What kind of circus had they stumbled onto?

The five outlaws rode out of the brush and sat their horses silently, watching the three men in front of them. Grant Morgan had finally succeeded in getting his horse to stand still, and was engrossed in the saddling operation. Mort Bales looked up from pulling on his left boot, directly into the glacial eyes of Howdy Baxter. He swallowed convulsively, his mustache twitching. "Uh, Grant, uh, you might wanna stop what yer doin' for a minute."

"What in hell are you stutterin' about, Mort?" Grant demanded without looking around. "Can't you see I'm busy?"

"Grant, I really think you oughta let that horse be a minute." Bales' voice was unusually husky; his throat had suddenly gone dry.

Grant turned from his horse, and for the first time saw the five men who sat side by side looking amusedly down at him. "Who are you, and what the hell do you want?" he demanded, on the verge of totally losing his temper. Grant had really not been having a good day so far.

Baxter leaned his forearms on his saddle horn and said mildly, "My name's Baxter. And I had given thought to asking you the same questions." A strange, unstable undercurrent twitched beneath his deceptively calm demeanor.

Grant paused. If this was the Baxter he thought it was, the wrong word could get them all killed. And the five men in front of him had the high ground, in a manner of speaking. He felt, more than saw, Mort and Jode step up on either side of him, and he devoutly hoped that neither of them would do anything stupid. Five against three wasn't very good odds; especially these particular five, if the man in front of him was Howdy Baxter.

"Howdy Baxter?" Morgan asked diffidently.

Baxter nodded. "Yessir."

"What can we do for you, Baxter?" Grant queried cautiously. "If you don't mind, we've got a man to take after."

"And who might that be?" Baxter wondered. The mild tone of his voice continued and the answer surprised him not one whit.

"It ain't none of your business, but it happens to be a gent name of Harvey Palmer," Grant answered. "He got the drop on us an' took our horses an' guns, an' we aim to take it out of his hide." He deliberately didn't mention the fact that they had just now gotten their clothes and boots back as well.

"And you are?"

"Name's Grant Morgan. Now if you don't mind, we'll be on our way."

"Don't be so hasty, Mister Morgan," Baxter replied. "We may have a common interest. Why exactly did this Palmer perpetrate such a heinous prank on you fine fellows?"

"I don't think that's none of your never mind, Baxter," Morgan began roughly. He wasn't exactly sure what Baxter had asked him, but he was nonetheless pretty sure it wasn't Baxter's business anyway. And his temper was making him forget who he was talking to. The sudden appearance of Baxter's Colt with the hammer eared back stopped Grant in mid-growl.

"I believe it is my business, Morgan!" Baxter hissed. "We were trailing that same gentleman when we heard you making a fool of yourself."

Grant bristled up and his hand hovered over the butt of his holstered pistol, but only a fool bucks a stacked deck. After a tense minute, he relaxed and hooked his thumb in his belt as he stood looking at Baxter. He visibly made up his mind that he probably ought to offer more detail if he wanted to live to chase down Harvey Palmer. "I still don't see where it's any of your business, but we come out to check on a fella we had cached out yonder. Palmer took exception to us bein' there. Said that boy's a friend of his."

Bannon spoke up. "Is this friend of Palmer's a tall drink of water with a mustache, wears a pair of tied-down Remingtons an' a flat-crowned hat?"

Grant looked around at Bannon. "Yeah, as a matter of fact he is. Name's Jesse Thompson. Why, you know him?"

Carson snickered and got a withering glare from

Bannon in return. "You might say that," Carson said, mirth evident behind his words. "That fella you're callin' Jesse Thompson sounds like the same one that whipped Marty's butt in Watsonville not too long back."

"And I plan on stompin' him into the ground!" Bannon growled.

"That's enough!" Baxter barked. "You didn't do so well the first time; what makes you think you can do it a second?" The silky tone returned to his voice and he said, "Morgan, I think we need to work together. We seem to have enemies in common."

Grant stood for a moment with a thoughtful look on his face, looking up at Baxter. It was easy to see that he was contemplating his future. "What exactly are you talkin' about, Baxter?"

"I owe Harvey Palmer for the untimely death of my brother. And you seem to owe that young man you mentioned something, or you wouldn't have "cached" him out here, as you so eloquently put it. It might benefit us both to combine our forces and deal with these two fellows at the same time. You did say they were friends, did you not?"

Grant stared at Baxter in slack-jawed confusion. He suddenly came back to himself and closed his mouth with a snap. "What in hell are you spoutin' off about, Baxter?" he demanded.

"I'm talking about us working together to kill Harvey Palmer and his friend, you idiot!" Baxter snapped. "Is that plain enough for you?" Morgan started to bristle up again, but Baxter tilted the muzzle of his pistol toward Grant's belt buckle. "Think before you leap, my intemperate friend. I am more than capable of killing you and your companions and going after Palmer and his friend myself."

Grant slowly steadied down as a cool breeze of reason wafted through his heated brain. In spite of his sometimes-flowery speech, Baxter had a point. Surely two men couldn't take on eight and win, could they? "Alright, we can ride together," he conceded. "But Jesse Thompson's mine. You can have Harvey Palmer. I really don't care who kills him, as long as somebody does. But I owe Thompson." Grant took a calculated risk and turned back to his horse. He pulled up the cinch, stepped into the leather, and glared down at Mort and Jode. He snarled, "Are you two comin', or stayin' here?" The two men scrambled aboard their horses as Grant turned to Baxter. "So what are you plannin' on doin' about killin' those boys?"

"How much do you know about their day-to-day activities?" Baxter queried. "Do they follow a routine? Are there women involved? Have you watched them at all?"

Harvey rode into Watsonville with the dun at a long trot. The first person he saw was Jesse, sitting on the porch fronting the Desert Inn in a chair with its back leaning against the hotel wall. Harvey stopped the dun in front of Jesse and exclaimed, "Just where the hell have you been? I've been lookin' all over for you! According to some pals of yours, and I use the term loosely, you should be in the bottom of Sidemeat Barton's mineshaft on Badger Mountain! And here I find you sittin' on the hotel porch like you've never been gone!"

Jesse tipped his hat back from his eyes and grinned up at Harvey, unperturbed. "If one of my pals, as you called 'em, is Grant Morgan, he was right. I should've been down in that hole. The only thing that saved me is that I've got a hard head and the bottom of that hole's got some soft sand in it. They hit me on the head, threw me across a horse, hauled me out there and dumped me down that mineshaft. That was Tuesday night. When I came to, my guns and knife were gone and I had one hell of a headache." He took off his hat and showed Harvey the knot on the back of his head. "I found some water, and kind of got myself organized, then managed to drag my carcass up out of there. I kept passin' out, and I don't mind tellin' you I was plenty scared. But I made it out and stumbled across the country and ended up passin' out for good in Dennis Moynahan's front room. I woke up at Moynahan's this morning an' here I am. I sure do miss my Remingtons, though. These Colts of Moynahan's are pretty good guns, but they just don't fit my hand like those 75's."

"My friend, have I got a deal for you." Harvey grinned and lifted Jode's gun belt from around his saddle horn. "I took these junky old pistols from a gentleman whom his traveling companions called Jode just this morning. I realize that they're a poor substitute for a fine Colt, but maybe you can use them."

Jesse's eyes lit up when he saw his Remingtons dangling from Harvey's hand. He tipped his chair down, wincing slightly as he stood and stepped down into the street. He walked up to the dun. "Thanks, Harvey," he said appreciatively. "I owe you one."

"You're damn right you do!" Harvey declared. "Those boys woulda willingly left me for buzzard bait if they'd got the chance." He handed Jesse the guns and watched as Jesse switched Dennis Moynahan's Colts for his own perfectly balanced Remingtons.

Jesse took Benson's belt, with the Colts in the holsters, to the hotel porch and laid them on the chair.

He stepped back down into the street with his hands on the scuffed ivory grips of his pistols. Making sure there was no one in the line of fire, Jesse drew first one, then the other, then both pistols at the same time. Harvey watched and was a little overwhelmed; that boy was fast! Jesse's hands were a blur as he drew both guns then slipped them back into the leather. "That's just like comin' home," Jesse sighed. "I've had these shooters for long enough that I sure missed 'em while they were gone."

Harvey stepped down from the dun and let his reins trail in the dust. He moved to the shade of the hotel porch, wrapping the Colts up in the belts and placing them on the floor. He seated himself on the empty chair and tipped it back against the wall. "Now that you've got your babies back," Harvey snorted, "Why don't you tell me why Grant Morgan is so upset at you?"

"Hey, the last thing I knew, Grant was in jail," Jesse protested. "I arrested him about a year and a half ago, and hauled him and his dead saddle partner into Laramie and…"

"Dead saddle partner?" Harvey's eyebrows were climbing toward the tipped back brim of his hat. "Do tell."

Thirty-one

Jesse launched into the story of how he had come into Morgan and Davis' camp; he told how Cutter Davis had decided he could beat a pat hand and had gotten himself shot for his troubles. "So anyway, I hauled Morgan and Davis into Laramie, and right now Morgan should be in the territorial prison; or at least the Laramie County jail. I'd be interested in finding out just why he's out here whackin' poor innocent deputies on the noggin and dropping them down mineshafts."

Harvey sat for a moment, thinking. "I'll tell you what, my friend. I need to go on over to Mason and wire for some money to pay Orville Hanneman the down payment for his place. What say we both go on over there and you can wire Laramie, an' see if you can find out anything about Mister Morgan."

"Good plan. Are you ready to leave now or do you wanna wait for morning?"

"There's no time like the present," Harvey said. He tipped the chair down and got to his feet. "You get your horse, an' I'll meet you at the Emporium; we'll pick up some grub for the trip. If we leave, now we can be there by noon or somewhere thereabouts tomorrow. I'll go tell Lila where I'm goin' and I'll meet you at the Emporium."

Jesse nodded and picked up the Colts. As he turned toward the smithy to saddle the gray, he thought about how much he liked that horse, and it was in his mind to make Dennis Moynahan an offer to buy him. That was pretty much of a horse. The pistols he'd leave with Lars.

Harvey stepped inside the hotel. Seeing no sign of Lila Foster, he reached over and rang the bell. Apparently she was out somewhere; he scrawled a quick note on a scrap of paper and put it under the bell so an errant breeze wouldn't carry it away. Stepping outside, he picked up the dun's reins and led the horse the short distance to the Emporium, where he tied it to the hitchrail after letting it drink from a nearby water trough. He stepped up onto the porch and strode through the door, stopping for a moment to let his eyes adjust to the dimness inside.

The pretty young lady behind the counter glanced up from the magazine she was reading. "May I help...oh, hello," she said cheerfully. "You're the man who rented the shotgun from me the day of that fight in the saloon, aren't you?" Melody Hoskins smiled at him as Harvey tipped his hat. His face reddened. After the fight, he'd returned the Greener to her, and asked for part of his money back. When he'd explained to Melody why he'd needed the shotgun, she'd taken pity on him and taken the gun back.

"Guilty as charged, miss. My name's Harvey Palmer. I do hope you were able to sell it."

"As a matter of fact I still have it if you'd like to actually purchase it this time," Melody answered. "And I still have the box of ammunition you borrowed, as well."

"I think I'll just pick up some supplies, if it's all the same to you," Harvey said sheepishly. He nodded toward the ranks of shelves containing jars of dried fruit and other food that would work well for travel. "I'd like a pound of dried apples, a couple of pounds of jerky, and a pound of coffee, please." He thought for a moment. "And a small sack of horehound candy." Melody bustled about gathering the things that Harvey had requested.

Harvey went to the wheel of cheese on the counter and cut off a small wedge to munch on while Melody gathered his order. He turned to lean on the counter as footsteps sounded on the boardwalk out front. Jesse came through the door and, like Harvey had done, stepped to one side to let his eyes adjust for a moment before coming further into the store. "I've got our supplies coming," Harvey said. "I hope you don't mind jerky and dried apples."

"Sounds good to me," Jesse replied. "Better get some sweets for the trail, though."

"Got it covered," Harvey said as Melody handed him the bag of candy. Harvey held it out to Jesse with the top open. "Horehound?"

Jesse laughed and reached into the bag. He brought his hand out and popped a piece of the brown candy into his mouth. "Miss, I could use a box of .44's, if you have them."

"I certainly do. It'll be just one moment." Melody gathered Harvey's order together and bound everything up in brown paper, wrapping the bundle neatly with string. Harvey paid her and she reached below the counter for Jesse's ammunition. Jesse handed her the payment for the cartridges and she said, "Have a nice day, gentlemen." The two tipped their hats and walked toward the door. As they left Melody watched them, musing, *I can see what Kitty likes about him. He's very good looking.* With a sigh, and a wistful little smile, she returned to her magazine.

Harvey strode to the dun, stashed the supplies in his saddlebags then checked his cinch. Jesse gave the young gray horse a reassuring pat as he tugged on his cinch one last time. The two men mounted and reined their horses toward Mason. They had a fair ride ahead of them.

Thirty-two

The outlaws, led by Howdy Baxter and--in his own mind at least--Grant Morgan, returned to the spring where Baxter and his men had camped earlier in the week. They reached the campground at dusk, carefully looking and listening for any sign that there was anyone around, but all was still.

With his Colt drawn, Baxter walked his horse forward and stopped at the edge of the clearing. "It's all clear, you can come in," he called. The rest of the men walked their horses forward, holstering their guns as they came. Carson stepped down, handed his reins to Montez, and started gathering wood for a fire. Montez led both horses to water; after they had drunk their fill, he turned away to string a picket line.

Baxter unsaddled his horse, tied him to the picket line, and moved to where Carson had gotten the first glimmerings of a fire going. Standing near the fire, Baxter called, "Come here, Morgan. We need to come up with some kind of a plan other than your 'let's just kill 'em'. That one's all well and good, but I'd just as soon not get any of my own men killed in the process--although from the look of your traveling companions, it would be a service to the human race to get rid of them."

Grant, who still thought of himself as the bull-of-the-woods, so to speak, began to bristle once again at Baxter's tone. "Who died and left you in charge of this bunch, Baxter?" he grated. His hand was hovering near his gun; Grant had never been exceptionally smart.

Before Grant could even think about drawing, Baxter's Colt was in his face. "No one has died yet, Morgan," Baxter said mildly. "Would you like to be the first, or would you like to shut up, sit down, and see what kind of plan we can come up with?"

Grant swallowed the sudden lump in his throat and visibly relaxed. The crazed light in Baxter's eyes convinced him to start looking at his options. Trying to save face he blustered, "I just wanta make sure I get Jesse Thompson..."

Baxter's Colt vanished as quickly as it had appeared, and so did the madness lurking behind the outlaw's calm facade. "Fine." Baxter dropped to the ground and sat with his legs crossed under him. He looked relaxed as he waited for Morgan to join him.

When Grant finally managed to deposit himself on the packed dirt nearby he looked over at Baxter. "So, what's your plan?" he questioned.

"I asked you earlier if you'd been observing your quarry," Baxter replied. "Do either of them have a particular female they are interested in? A regular girl? If so, do you know who it is?"

"What the hell are you goin' on about, Baxter?"

Grant asked, confused again.

"All right, you simple minded ape, I'll spell it out for you!" Baxter snapped. "We are going to watch Thompson and Palmer from a distance, without them knowing. And we are going to see if they have any women in their lives. If so, we will kidnap those women, and when Thompson and Palmer come for them, we will kill them both, without being killed ourselves. Is that plain enough for you?" Morgan wasn't exactly sure what an ape was, and he didn't like being called simple-minded; but he did like living, and he knew that if he braced Baxter in the position he was in, he'd more than likely end up dead. With an effort, he reined his temper in. He could get even for the insult later.

"No, we ain't done any observin' of anybody," he said sarcastically. Baxter chose to ignore his tone. "I didn't even know there was a Harvey Palmer until he threw down on us up yonder at that mine. An' I had no idea Jesse Thompson was anywhere around these parts until I seen him through the cafe window. I seen him, and Mort knew about the mineshaft, so we waited around until he come outta the beanery, whopped him on the head, and hauled him off."

"All right then. Now we have to decide who we can send where. Jesse Thompson knows all of my men, because of the butt-kicking he gave Marty. And it appears that Harvey Palmer knows all of yours. This will take some planning. But first, we're going to check the livery and see if their horses are there. Then we'll plan from that point."

Baxter rose gracefully and reached back to dust off the seat of his wool pants. Carson chuckled to himself at the sight of Grant clambering awkwardly to his feet. The sound drew a glare from Grant as he moved over to where Mort and Jode stood watching Baxter's hard case crew uneasily. "What'd he want..." Mort began.

"Quiet, you little weasel," Grant snapped. "We'll talk later."

Thirty-three

The sun dropped below the horizon and the moon rose high as the gray and the dun jogged comfortably along the trail to Mason. Their riders lounged easily in the saddle, looking for all the world like they hadn't a care. Both men were used to long miles on the hurricane deck of a bronc. Conversation was light as the two went along, sometimes side-by-side, sometimes single file. They had been silent for a few miles when Jesse suddenly asked, "Harvey, you ever been married?"

"No, I haven't," Harvey replied. "I had the chance once and turned tail and ran, an' I've been kickin' myself ever since. She's a good woman. Why, are you thinkin' about gettin' hitched?"

Jesse answered Harvey's question with one of his own. "Have you seen Kitty Moynahan in town?"

"The black-haired gal with the big spotted horse?" Jesse nodded. "Yeah, I've seen her. Why?" Jesse's silence spoke volumes. "You've got a case on that gal, haven't you?"

"I reckon," Jesse acknowledged. "She's pretty,

and she's smart. She helps her pa run the ranch, an' according to him she can do a day's work with the best of 'em."

"But mostly she's pretty, eh?" Harvey commented wryly. "You know what they say--pretty is as pretty does. The way it sounds, that pretty does pretty well. I think a man could do a lot worse." Jesse settled back in his saddle and let out a breath he didn't know he'd been holding. He didn't know for sure why, but it had been important to him that Harvey approve of Kitty.

The two men pulled their horses to a halt where a small creek crossed the trail. The dun and the gray dipped their noses into the cool water and slurped noisily as the two men sat quietly. "'S'pose we oughta get some sleep, Jesse?" Harvey asked, yawning. "It feels like I've been up for a couple of days."

"Might be a good idea," Jesse answered with a yawn of his own. "Soon's the horses drink, why don't we find a place to catch a few winks?" As if on cue, the horses lifted their heads, water droplets from their muzzles falling and catching the last beams of pale light as the moon dipped below the western horizon. The two animals shook themselves, as horses are occasionally wont to do, then stood with their tails switching, patiently waiting for their riders to tell them which way to go. Jesse stood high in his stirrups, stretching and looking around for a likely campsite. Off to the right a small grass-covered clearing caught his eye. He settled back in his saddle and heeled the gray into motion toward the clearing. The grass was knee high, and appeared to have never been grazed. The stocky horse dropped its head and nipped off a mouthful of greenery as soon as Jesse stopped and let the rein go slack.

Jesse stepped down as Harvey and the dun

followed him into the clearing. "Look okay?"

"Looks good to me," Harvey replied. "Let's picket these critters and hit the sack." The gray was obviously enjoying the lush grass. Jesse hobbled him right there and removed the saddle and hackamore. He carried his tack and the saddle blankets to a small tree at the edge of the clearing. Jesse set the saddle nose-down, untied his bedroll and saddlebags, and turned the saddle blankets horse-side-up on top of the saddle to dry. He rolled out his bed while Harvey did the same a short distance away. Jesse slipped off his boots and hat, pulled a blanket over himself, and was soon deep in slumber.

Jesse woke from a sound sleep to the sound of scratching and whining. He stayed motionless and kept his breathing steady while he peered out through his eyelashes. The sound came from his left, near where his saddlebags lay. He slowly turned his head to see some kind of dog trying to get at whatever food might be in the bags. From what Jesse could see in the silvery starlight, that critter had been missing a lot of meals lately. Its coat was scruffy and full of burrs, and its ribs stood out starkly under its hide. Its flag of a tail was tattered; it was hard to tell what color the mongrel was, but it appeared to be some sort of shepherd. Breed was difficult to distinguish through the dirt that matted the dog's scraggly hair.

Jesse squeaked his lips at the dog and whispered softly, "Hey boy. What ya doin'?" The dog jumped away with its tail tucked, and streaked toward the brush at the far side of the clearing. "Now where'd that critter come from?" Jesse asked the stars.

"Who, or what, are you talkin' to, if you don't

mind my askin'?" Harvey grumbled from his bed. "I was sleepin' just fine 'til you started chatterin'."

"There was some kind of dog trying to get into my saddlebags. It looked kinda hungry," Jesse answered. The sun was turning the horizon to pink by now, so Jesse threw back the blankets and shook out his boots. When no stray beasties fell out of either boot, he put them on and rolled to his feet. "How about some coffee?" he asked.

"I reckon, since you don't seem to be plannin' on goin' back to sleep, that I might's well get up too," Harvey said. "An' if I'm gonna be up, I might 's well have some coffee."

Jesse started breaking twigs for a fire and shortly a cheery blaze was crackling. Jesse went to the spring, filled his small coffeepot with water, dumped in a handful of ground Arbuckle's, and set the pot in the edge of the fire to boil. The flickering flames lit the edges of the clearing indistinctly, and some of the shadows seemed to move. As Jesse glanced around, one of the shadows did indeed move.

A faint whining sound came to Jesse's keen ears. The dog lay in the shadows on its belly, ears drooping as it stared at Jesse. Again Jesse squeaked his lips and held out his hand. "C'mere, boy. I ain't gonna hurt ya. Come on" he said softly. The dog crept warily from its hiding place. Its belly was close to the ground as it came forward, cringing as if expecting a beating. As the dog crept closer, Jesse could see the marks and scars of past whippings on its coat. Harvey started to say something and Jesse shook his head slowly. Harvey remained still, watching. After what seemed like forever--but could only have been a minute or two--the dog was at Jesse's knee. Jesse reached out to pet it, but the dog started to draw back. Jesse lowered his hand for the dog to sniff; a few snuffles later Jesse felt the dog's tongue touch his palm.

"Harvey, reach me over a piece of that jerky, would ya?" Jesse asked quietly. "An' don't throw it, just hand it to me, okay?" Jesse held his hand behind his back and felt the piece of dried beef touch his palm. He brought the hand to the front and handed the meat to the dog, who gave it a quick sniff; with a slurp, the jerky disappeared. Harvey touched Jesse's shoulder and Jesse reached back for another piece. After the second morsel, the dog's tail wagged, once. Jesse dropped his hand and rubbed the dog's ears. The poor creature didn't seem to understand affection but finally relaxed under Jesse's calm handling.

"This dog's had the crap kicked out of him by somebody!" Jesse declared angrily. "And if I find out who it was I intend to do a little kickin' of my own! Did you ever see such a thing?" The coffeepot suddenly boiled over with a hiss and a splash; the dog jumped away from Jesse, the hair on the back of its neck standing up and its teeth bared. A low growl rumbled in its throat. Jesse said, "What's the matter with you, dog? It's just a dang coffeepot." He reached his hand toward the dog again as Harvey wrapped a bandanna around his own hand and lifted the hissing pot from the flames.

"You and your buddy ready for some of this mud, or are you still kissin' an' makin' up?" Harvey asked dryly.

When the hissing subsided the dog relaxed, came back to Jesse, and laid its head on his knee. "Yeah, pour me a cup, would ya?" he replied. "I don't wanna move from here right at the moment." He laid his hand on the dog's neck. A tattered strand of rope drug the ground next to the dog; Jesse dug his fingers into the matted fur on its neck and felt, deep under the hair, a tough band that had practically worked its way into the skin.

"I think this critter's got a collar of some sort on, but it's been there awhile," Jesse commented. "There doesn't seem to be any slack under it anywhere." He kept working it with his fingers and felt it loosen a little. He reached to the back of his belt for his knife, forgetting that Grant Morgan and his cohorts had taken it and he hadn't replaced it.

"Hand me a knife, would ya, Harve?" Harvey handed Jesse a thin-bladed sheath knife, then watched closely as Jesse slipped it under the leather strap on the dog's neck. When Jesse turned the edge of the blade up to cut the strap, the dog started to choke and struggle; the keen edge quickly parted the strap and immediately the dog stopped struggling. Jesse pulled the strap free and cursed.

"Dammit, this is rawhide!" Jesse snapped. "No wonder this critter's so skinny. The rawhide must've shrunk, and she probably hasn't been able to eat much for quite awhile. Somebody must've really had it in for dogs in general, and this one in particular."

Harvey looked quizzically at Jesse. "How can anyone not like dogs?"

"I don't have any idea, but if I find the fella that apparently didn't like this one, he's gonna wish to hell he had. This is nonsense!" Jesse sat for a minute while his temper cooled. He was usually slow to anger, but seeing the sorry condition of the much-abused dog was more than he could take. He reached over to his saddlebags and brought out a currycomb.

Jesse let the dog sniff the comb, then carefully started working the tangles out of its hair. At first, when the comb pulled, the dog would flinch and start to run, but Jesse's voice and quiet touch calmed it; slowly the coat began to smooth and the burrs let go their grip. After a half hour or so, Jesse sat back and looked at Harvey, who sat with a cup of coffee in his hand and a smile on his face. "You plannin' on keepin' that critter, or what?" Harvey asked. "An' how do you know it's a she?"

"Depends on what the dog wants to do," Jesse replied reasonably. "I reckon we'll see when we start on into Mason. An' I looked. That's how I know it's a she." Jesse pulled the last of the matted, filthy hair out of the currycomb and looked around. It had been almost dark when he started fussing over the dog; it was now full daylight. "I reckon we probably oughta get headed that way, eh?"

"I've just been waitin' for you to say the word," Harvey answered. While Jesse had been working over the dog, Harvey had picked up the camp. He'd rolled both sets of blankets and cleaned out the coffeepot.

The two men saddled their horses and stepped aboard. "C'mon, dog," Jesse said as he gigged the gray into motion. Obediently the dog fell in behind the horse and the two men and the stray headed for Mason.

Thirty-four

The three travelers trotted down the west end of the main street of Mason shortly after noon. They pulled up in front of the Longhorn Café and the two men stepped down from their horses. A trough stood at the corner of the building and the men led their horses to water. They watched as the horses plunged their muzzles deep, their throats working as they drank. The dog put its front feet up on the edge of the trough and lapped up the cool water then sat down. Its gently waving tail stirred up a small dust storm.

The horses lifted their heads. Bit chains, stirrups and loose gear rattled, and drops of water flew from their muzzles, as the two horses shook themselves. The droplets spattered in a wide spray across the café wall. The two men ducked away from moisture, grinning, then led the horses to the hitch rail in front of the building. Jesse tied the gray, then told the dog, "Stay. And watch." He hadn't a clue that the dog knew any such commands, but he figured it was worth a shot. Almost as if it knew exactly what he'd said, the dog sat down in the shade of the gray horse with its tail curled around its hindquarters.

Jesse and Harvey stepped into the café and looked around. Two vacant places at one of the long oilcloth-covered tables beckoned; soon both men were digging hungrily into the food placed before them. The fare was venison stew accompanied by strong black coffee; that was perfectly fine with them after cold meals of jerky and dried apples. Jesse sat back from the table with a quiet belch of satisfaction and lifted his cup for one last long swallow. "Dang, I think I ate more than's good for me--guess I was hungry."

"Me too," Harvey replied, easing the waistband of his pants as best he could. "What're ya gonna take to the dog?"

Jesse raised a hand to the harried waitress who was scurrying around picking up plates and coins from the tables. She was dropping the coins in the pocket of her apron, then slinging the dirty plates and flatware into the wreck pan near the kitchen door. Jesse called politely, "Ma'am, could I trouble you for some scraps from the kitchen? Got a hungry hound outside, an' I'm sure she'd appreciate bein' fed. I'll pay, of course."

The frazzled-looking woman glared at him irritably, ready to bite him in two. Instead, she took in his innocent look and decided to leave him intact. Brushing a loose strand of hair away from her damp brow, she answered, "Hang on a minute, there, cowboy, and I'll see what I can rustle up. Never let it be said I let a dog go hungry." She hurried into the kitchen and came out a few minutes later with a pie pan heaped with stew and meat trimmings. "There you go, cowboy." She slapped the pie plate onto the table in front of Jesse. "Just leave the plate on the table by the door when the critter's done. The boss says no charge."

"Much obliged, ma'am," Jesse said and touched the brim of his hat. "I'll do that." Jesse got up, dropped some coins on the table, and stepped over the bench he had occupied. Harvey made no move to leave and Jesse said sarcastically, "Don't get up, Harve. I'll take care of this."

Harvey smiled, reaching for the coffeepot. "I had no intention of gettin' up, Jesse. This coffee's pretty good, especially compared to mine."

Jesse opened the door to find the dog standing under the gray, braced against the horse's front legs. A growl was rumbling deep in her throat and her lips were drawn back in a vicious snarl. A large, unkempt fellow in tattered range garb was standing a few feet away, cursing and holding his left wrist. "I'll kill ya for that, ya cur! I shoulda killed ya a long time ago!"

"Excuse me, sir," Jesse said mildly. "Are you addressing my dog?"

"Yer dog, my eye!" the man growled. "That dog's been mine for a long time! An' she's gonna be mine again, soon's I get ahold of her!"

"I take it you're the one who's been whipping her?" Jesse asked, his demeanor mild; but if the angry man had been paying attention, he would have heard the threatening scrape of steel on granite that underlay the words, and seen the resulting sparks of fury in Jesse's gray eyes.

"Yer damn right I have!" the oblivious ruffian snapped. "That cur's taken a chunk outta me one too many times!" Turning his back on Jesse, the cowboy leaned down again to grab the dog; her jaws snapped together like a steel trap, hardly a hair's breadth from his fingers. With another curse the man straightened and reached for the pistol high on his right hip. His fingers had no sooner touched the worn walnut of the Colt's grips than he heard a clicking noise behind his head and felt a cold ring of steel touch the base of his skull.

"You just go right ahead and draw that gun, mister," Jesse said softly, menacingly. "But if you do, I will spread what few brains you have all over the street. That dog's been mistreated enough."

The man stiffened and his hands moved up to shoulder height. "Stranger, I don't know who you are, an' it's fer damn sure you don't know me, or you wouldn't be buttin' in like you are," he said roughly. "I'll kill you for this. You put down that gun an' I'll tear you in two with my hands. Nobody pulls a gun on Buster McLanahan and lives ta spread the story."

Jesse kept the muzzle of the Remington tucked behind McLanahan's ear as he reached down to set the plate of dog food, which he still held, on the boardwalk. "Then I'd be a fool to put down my gun if that's the case, wouldn't I?" Jesse asked mildly. "But just to show you that I'm a fair man, Mister McLanahan, I'll put my gun away. And we'll just see what happens to who."

In one smooth motion, Jesse stepped away from McLanahan and holstered the Remington, keeping his eyes on the burly cowboy's hands. His own hand remained near his belt while he waited for McLanahan's next move. The last thing he needed was to get into a fight, but he wasn't going to stand by and let that dog be mistreated anymore--it had suffered enough. Sometimes a man just had to draw a line and stand his ground, no matter how much it complicated things.

McLanahan reached for his belt buckle. "Shed that pistol belt, stranger, an' come on down here. I'm gonna hurt you bad!" He unbuckled his pistol belt, swung it from around his waist, and hung it on the end of the hitch rail.

At that moment, the screen door behind Jesse scraped open. "Want me ta hang on t' your hoglegs, partner?" Harvey offered.

"Sure thing, friend," Jesse replied. He unbuckled his gun belt, handing it to Harvey without looking away from Buster McLanahan. "Take good care of 'em, friend. I'd hate to lose 'em again."

Buster stood flexing his hands, the dog bite on his wrist forgotten. His shirt buttons strained at the cloth as he drew in a deep breath and raised his hands. He had been the cock-of-the-walk in this burg for a good long time, and he couldn't see any reason why this fight should be any different than usual. Generally, a couple of punches persuaded whoever Buster was facing that he had bitten off more than he could chew.

Jesse stepped down into the dust of the street and raised his own hands. A jarring right hand suddenly thumped into Jesse's chest and he staggered. He hadn't even seen McLanahan move. The cowboy was fast, but Jesse was pretty sure he wouldn't last long. Still, this could be a seriously painful fight unless Jesse took it seriously. He set himself again and began to circle, keeping a steady stream of jabs going, stinging and moving away while the bully tried to counter. Buster snarled, "Dammit, quit yer runnin' an' stand still an' fight like a man!"

Buster could hardly believe what was happening. This kid had taken one of his best shots and had come back swinging like he hadn't felt a thing. A cut appeared at the corner of Buster's mouth; he raised a hand to wipe away the blood that began to trickle down his chin. As he did, Jesse's hard right fist pounded him under the short ribs with a punch that had started somewhere down around Jesse's knees. The force of the blow took Buster's wind, and the burly cowboy's knees buckled before he forced himself back up and tucked his arms in to protect his now tender ribcage. Covering his belly left his face wide-open and unguarded, and Jesse pounded McLanahan's nose and lips. A cascade of blood began running down McLanahan's chin and chest.

Buster raised his guard to protect his face and tried to counter-punch, but he was hopelessly outclassed. And that punch to the belly had taken a lot out of him; a few feeble blows hit Jesse's shoulder, where his chin was tucked, but there was little force in them. McLanahan just couldn't seem to get himself set. Ready to finish the bully off, Jesse suddenly slammed a flurry of blows into McLanahan's ribs and belly. He danced away from the man's attempts to fight back, and each counter by McLanahan was a little slower than the last. Jesse's rain of punches quickly sapped Buster's strength.

It wasn't a fair fight by any stretch of the imagination, in spite of the size difference between the two men. Despite his recent ordeal, Jesse was in much better physical condition than McLanahan, whose most strenuous exercise in quite a long time had probably been lifting a beer mug. Jesse would have long since stopped the fight if it weren't for the dog.

McLanahan's hands dropped to hang at his sides as his strength ran out. Jesse screwed his bootsoles into the dirt of the street and brought a right-handed uppercut from waist level that thumped into McLanahan's jaw like an axe hitting the butt of a log; Buster staggered back from the force of the blow, and his eyes rolled back in his head. He slammed against the café wall; the impact jarred the building, knocking dishware on the shelves inside to the floor with a crash. Buster stood for a moment as if leaning against the wall to catch his breath, then collapsed onto his face in the dirt like a puppet whose strings had been cut.

A tiny flash of light sparked in the midst of a clump of rye grass standing on the peak of the knoll near Johansen's blacksmith shop. The thick stems made for a good observation post. Rule Carson lay on his belly behind the grass, watching through field glasses for any sign that Harvey and Jesse might be around. As near as he could tell Palmer's dun was gone, as was the kid's roan. Carson had no way of knowing that the roan was now only scattered bones and pieces of hide out in the basin west of town.

Carson had been hiding and watching since long before daylight, and it was coming on ten o'clock in the morning. The sun was hot, and a horsefly had discovered him and was buzzing around in front of his face; it had been harassing him for the better part of an hour. The insect suddenly decided to take a chunk out of the back of Carson's hand and came in for a landing. Just as the fly settled in for a snack, the sound of a slap brought its meal to an end as Carson took exception to such goings on and squashed the big fly. *That'd teach the critter.* Carson smiled smugly to himself before turning his attention to his growling belly. It'd been a long time since supper last night; like a fool he'd only had coffee for breakfast. It seemed pretty likely that if

Harvey Palmer or Jesse Thompson were in town, their horses would be in one of the corrals below and they'd have shown up at the livery by now to check on them. In Carson's mind it followed that the two men had to be gone somewhere.

Slithering on his belly down the backside of the knoll, Carson got to his feet and hiked back to where he'd left his horse. Howdy Baxter had been adamant about that. "You make damn sure nobody knows you're there, Rule. Leave your horse back at least a quarter of a mile; half a mile would be better. That way you don't raise dust and the horse can't give you away by nickering. And no shooting! You got that?"

"Yeah, Howdy, I got it. I ain't gonna do nothin' but watch." Now, however, Carson was muttering curses under his breath. It was a long walk back to his horse on an empty stomach. At last he rounded the last clump of brush and came to where his horse was tied in the shade of some small trees. He pulled the bridle rein free from where it was tied, stepped into the saddle, and turned the horse toward the outlaw camp. As he rode, he chewed on some jerky he found in his saddlebag and sipped on his canteen, thinking that the next time he went on an expedition like this one he'd be smart enough to bring some grub with him. He arrived back in their camp a few hours later, stepped down and led his horse to the spring for a drink.

"Well?" Baxter demanded from where he sat, leaning against a tree. "Are they there?"

"If they are, then somebody's done stole their horses," Carson answered. "That dun of Palmer's, and that other feller's roan, ain't nowhere to be seen. The only horses there are them plugs that blacksmith rents out an' a flashy paint. Far as I can tell, ain't neither one of them boys in town."

"Good. Get yourself something to eat, and we'll do some planning. Benson!" Baxter called loudly, "Get over here." Jode glanced uncertainly at Grant. At his aggravated nod, Jode got to his feet and walked over to Baxter.

"Yeah?"

"Nobody really knows you in that town, do they?" When Jode shook his head, Baxter continued. "I want you to ride to Watsonville and find someplace out of the way to watch from. There should be a vacant building or something of the sort where you can stay out of sight. No drinking, and no trouble. Go to the general store and get yourself some supplies, then ride out like you're leaving town; then double back, and get yourself under cover. When Thompson and Palmer show up, you ride back here and let us know, but don't let them know you're anywhere around. Understand?"

"I reckon I can handle that. But I ain't got any money for supplies."

Annoyed, Baxter dug in his vest pocket and came out with a pair of silver dollars. Irritably he tossed the coins to Benson. "There you are. Now go. We'll be waiting for word." Jode caught the coins in the air, walked over and saddled his horse. Soon the only sign of him was a dust cloud fading away in the afternoon sunshine.

Thirty-five

After riding a long circle around the town, Jode came into Watsonville from the east. He walked his horse down the street, trying to act casually. He kept his hat brim pulled down, and as his horse meandered down the street his faded blue eyes peered out from the shadows there. He kept a lookout for an empty building or anyplace else he could use as an observation post. It might be a day or more before Thompson and Palmer showed--if Carson was right about them being gone--so he might just as well be comfortable. There were two horses tied to the hitchrail in front of the Nugget, neither of which Jode recognized. Another horse stood relaxed and dozing between the shafts of a buckboard in the shade of the awning fronting the Emporium. He drew rein near the buckboard, stepped down into the dust of the street and looped the reins around the hitchrail. His worn boot heels thumped on the boardwalk as he stepped up to enter the store. When his shadow crossed the threshold, the good-looking young blond woman behind the counter raised her eyes from the account book she was perusing. The slant of the late afternoon sunlight streaming through the windows made it difficult for Melody to make out the features of the man who had just entered her father's store.

What she could see through the sun's glare was not especially encouraging. From the looks of this one, she figured that he would probably be asking for a handout as soon as his eyes had adjusted to the relatively dim light in the building, but his first words surprised her. "I'd like some jerky an' some crackers, an' a piece of that cheese yonder, if it ain't too much trouble, ma'am. I got the money ta pay."

"It won't be but just a moment," Melody replied in a friendly tone as she began to gather the man's order. "Are you just passing through, or are you going to be staying with us for a bit?"

"Just passin' through, ma'am, just passin' through," the drifter replied. He was careful not to let his annoyance at the young woman's question show on his face. He felt that his business was his business, and he resented her inquiry. In addition, Jode wasn't exactly a genius under the best of conditions, and her questioning made him nervous. He'd only come to get food, not answer questions.

"That will be one dollar and fifty cents," Melody told him. She wrapped the jerky and crackers in brown paper; the cheese went into a twist of waxed paper. Jode dug in the pocket of his torn and dirty vest and handed her the two silver dollars Howdy Baxter had given him. He took back his change, picked up his package and turned toward the door with a mumbled "Thank you". Outside, the sound of hooves and the jingle of bit chains announced the arrival of another customer.

Kitty Moynahan tied Socorro to the rail in front of the Emporium next to a blaze-faced chestnut horse with a beat-up saddle on its back. She stepped lightly into the store and greeted Melody. A medium-sized fellow who, she was sure from the looks of his clothes, belonged to the horse outside, was browsing about the store with a package under one arm. She dismissed him as just another range bum and moved to the counter. "Melody, have you seen Jesse?" she asked. She didn't see the man stiffen and start to drift closer. "The horse he got from Dad isn't at the livery."

"Jesse and that Palmer fellow came in yesterday and bought some supplies like they were going on a trip of some sort. They didn't say where they were going or when they'd be back. But they did turn like they might be going toward Mason when they left here. Why, Kitty?" Melody asked curiously.

"Oh, I just thought I might invite him out to the ranch for dinner, is all," Kitty replied absently, trying to sound unconcerned. "The last time didn't work out so well, and I was hoping to make it up to him."

Behind Kitty, Jode turned and shuffled silently toward the door. Now that he had a name for Thompson's girl, it shouldn't be all that hard to find out what ranch she lived on. There couldn't be more than one Kitty living in these parts. The more he thought about it, the more he figured that he should head on back to camp and let Howdy know what he'd found out. It sounded for sure like the two men they were after were gone and wouldn't be back for at least a day or two. Jode walked out to the hitchrail, where a flashy appaloosa was tied beside his chestnut. That big spotted horse would be easy to recognize from a distance, too. He untied his own horse, mounted, and rode out of town.

Jode trotted his horse into the outlaw camp a few hours later. The other outlaws were lounging around the clearing. When he saw Jode, Grant raised up from where he'd been lazing in the shade and snarled, "What're you doin' back here already?"

Jode stepped down and led his horse to the spring. "I found out them two boys ain't in Watsonville," he said with an air of one who knows he's done well. "They left yesterday, don't know when they'll be back. An' I found out there's a girl that's sweet on that Thompson feller. Her name's Kitty an' she lives on a ranch outside of town. She was talkin' about invitin' him to supper. She rides a big blue horse with a white blanket an' blue spots on its butt."

"It's called an Appaloosa," Howdy Baxter said from behind Jode, startling him. "Did you get a last name, or find out which ranch she lives on?"

"No, but I figger there's probly only one gal named Kitty livin' around that there town an' ridin' a flashy horse like that 'un. Can't be that hard to find out who she is."

Grant thought for a moment, then snapped his fingers. He got to his feet and walked across the clearing to where Mort Bales lay asleep in the shade. A boot toe in the ribs brought Mort snuffling and snorting to a semi-alert state. "Wha, wha…" he stammered, rubbing a hand across his unshaven face. He sat up and saw who had gouged him in the side; he was getting little bit tired of Grant's pushy nature, but he swallowed his resentment for now. "Whaddya do that for, Grant?"

Without preamble or explanation, Grant asked, "Didn't you useta work on a ranch around here somewhere's?"

"Yeah, why?"

"Never mind why. Do you remember if any of the ranchers had a gal name of Kitty?"

Bales thought for a minute, frown lines creasing his forehead. It had been a while since he'd worked around here, but that name seemed familiar. Then it came to him. "Dennis Moynahan on the Bar M's got a daughter. I do believe Kitty's her name. Right pert filly, too. Rides the range with her Pa a lot of the time. Why ya askin' about her?"

"I think she's got somethin' to do with what Baxter's plannin' for that Thompson, but I ain't sure." Morgan turned back to where Baxter waited, and related what he'd heard from Mort.

"Perfect!" Baxter chuckle, an evil smile spreading across his face. "That's one part of the puzzle solved."

"What puzzle?" Grant was confused, and it showed on his face. That had been happening more and more since he'd been around Baxter.

"Never mind," Baxter answered. "I'll fill you in when it's time. We'll send Benson back to town in a couple of days and see what else he comes up with."

Thirty-six

The cafe door slammed open as the diners rushed outside. They milled in a clump around Buster McLanahan, staring and exclaiming. Buster had been bullying the townsfolk for quite a while; nobody could believe he'd been whipped--especially by a young man who was barely breathing hard. Jesse moved to pick up the plateful of scraps and set it in front of the dog before one of the murmuring crowd stepped in it. A tentative wag of its tail as the dog dove into the food told Jesse how much the meal was appreciated. Harvey handed Jesse his gun belt; he took it from the outstretched hand of his friend and swung it around his waist. The crowd was thinning now as people went back to their meals and their business. No one offered aid to the fallen bully. "Ready to go to the telegraph office, Jesse?" Harvey asked.

"I reckon," Jesse replied cheerfully. "The dog'll be done eating in a minute; I can set the plate indoors an' we can go. You suppose we should do somethin' with that gent?" He pointed at Buster, a mischievous grin spreading across his face.

"Even if I say no, you're gonna do it anyway, aren't ya?" Harvey said resignedly.

"Yep." Jesse grinned even more broadly and headed for a nearby rain barrel. A bucket conveniently sat on the ground next to it. He dipped the bucket into the barrel and drew it out, full and dripping. He started toward the recumbent Buster with the bucket held in both hands. From a range of about three feet, he flung the contents of the bucket over the bully's head. "Looks to me like this fellow's all washed up," he said to no one in particular. Buster sat up, sputtering and coughing; his swollen eyes slowly focused on Jesse, who stood in front of him with the heavy bucket in his hand. "Had enough?" Jesse asked. Buster nodded then wished he hadn't, as the nod jostled his aching head. "An' you're gonna leave the dog alone, right?"

"Yeah," Buster grunted, unwilling to make any sudden moves that might make his headache worse.

"Okay," Jesse said. He reached down with his free hand. Buster took it and Jesse hoisted him to his feet. Buster stumbled to the hitchrail, picked up his gun belt, and meandered down the street with the belt in his hand. Jesse replaced the bucket and picked up the empty plate from in front of the dog. He set the plate on the table just inside the cafe door and called, "Come on, dog." They started after Harvey, who had already headed for the telegraph office.

Harvey waited for Jesse with one hand on the knob of the door to the telegraph office. "You don't ever give up, do ya?" he asked sarcastically.

"Who, me?" Jesse answered in an innocent-sounding voice. Harvey just snorted. He opened the door and led the way inside.

"What are you plannin' on callin' your friend there?" Harvey asked, shutting the door after the dog came in. The dog sat down to one side with her eyes fixed on Jesse, and her tail curled around her front paws.

"'Dog' seems to be workin' so far," Jesse replied dryly. "I reckon I'll just keep on callin' her that, unless she tells me she wants me to call her somethin' else." He turned toward the barred window. A man wearing an eyeshade and sleeve garters was seated behind the window with a flyswatter in his hand. "Say there, friend. You don't happen to have a wire for Jesse Thompson hidin' somewhere back in there, do you?"

"I may have," the man replied as he stood and ambled toward the window. "And what business is that of yours?"

"Well, I guess since my name's Jesse Thompson, that sorta makes it my business."

"Do you have some means of identification?" the telegrapher asked. "I can't just hand telegrams to anyone who comes along claiming to be someone, now can I?"

Jesse thought for a minute; it was easy to see that this fellow had way too much time on his hands. Jesse reached into his vest and came out with a letter he'd recently gotten from his parents. His name was on the envelope in easily recognizable script. "Will this work, friend?" He handed the letter to the telegrapher, who scrutinized the handwriting carefully.

"I suppose so," the telegrapher remarked, after looking between Jesse and the envelope several times as if comparing the envelope to Jesse's face. "I hope you do realize that this wire has been here for quite some time. This has been a heavy responsibility."

Jesse tried hard to keep a straight face as he replied solemnly, "I fully understand, my friend. I will be more than happy to relieve you of that weight." Jesse held out his hand and the fellow behind the counter placed an envelope in it. "Thanks, partner. I appreciate it." Stepping away from the counter, he quickly tore open the envelope.

Grant Morgan escaped while in transit to territorial prison. Stop. Last seen in company of two men. Stop. Apprehend if possible. Stop. Use utmost caution. Stop. Signed, Judge Randolph Martin.

Jesse reread the telegram while a number of ideas paraded through his brain. It was obvious that there were things the Judge was not saying, but those were pretty much irrelevant at this point. What was relevant was the fact that Grant Morgan was now his job for the second time, along with Howdy Baxter. Sometimes being one of the Judge's fair-haired boys was a lot of work. *Complicated work...*

Thirty-seven

"From the look on your face, I take it that wire wasn't good news, huh?" Harvey said. Wordlessly Jesse handed him the piece of paper. Harvey read the message and whistled quietly. "That Judge must figure you're one helluva lawman, dropping Morgan and Baxter both on your plate at the same time. One thing about it though--they're both around these parts somewhere, so at least you don't have to chase all over hell's half acre lookin' for 'em."

"Thanks a lot, Harve. That makes me feel a whole lot better," Jesse said morosely.

"Anything for friend, Jesse, anything for a friend." Harvey smirked, returning the telegram to Jesse. He stepped to the window and told the telegrapher, "I need to send a message to Ellsworth, if I could." The man nodded and handed Harvey a lined pad and a pencil, and Harvey wrote out the message. He had the money for the down payment on the Hanneman place in the Cattleman's Bank and Trust in Ellsworth. He just needed to have the money sent to Watsonville, and with any luck a bank draft for the amount of the payment would be coming in on the stage in a couple of days.

"I suspect that as late in the day as it is, you may have to wait until tomorrow for an answer," the telegrapher said prissily. He began to work his key. "If you'd like to check back later, I'll know for sure. And that will be fifty cents for the service." Harvey laid a half-dollar on the counter and turned back to Jesse.

"Your friend here thinks it'll be tomorrow before I get an answer. You wanna head on back, or wait? Either way, I'm stuck here in Mason unless something happens today."

"I don't have anything really pressing to do, aside from Baxter and Morgan," Jesse said wryly. "I reckon me and Dog can wait." At the sound of her new name, Dog's tail thumped on the floor where she lay with her head on her front paws. "I saw a livery sign down yonder. Why don't I go see about unsaddlin' the horses, and you can wait here and see if you get an answer?"

"If I don't show up before you get ready to come back, I reckon you'd best come find me. Yonder wire mechanic may have driven me to suicide by then." Harvey smiled and sat down in the only available chair--an old ladder-back number sitting to one side of the telegrapher's window. Near the chair was a small table holding a dusty stack of long out-of-date newspapers and magazines. Harvey picked up a six-month old copy of *Harper's* and started leafing through its tattered yellowing pages. Jesse just shook his head and departed for the livery with Dog following closely at his heels.

Jesse led the horses down the street to a ramshackle barn with "*Livery*" painted on its front above a sagging set of double doors. A man wearing tattered canvas britches held up by a rope belt sat on a backless chair in the shadow of the barn, picking his teeth and spitting. "Help you stranger?" he asked through a bushy tobacco-stained mustache.

"I'd like to feed and water these two cayuses and take the saddles off for a while, if I might," Jesse said, examining the figure in front of him. "If it's not too much trouble, that is," he continued.

The man hooked a thumb over his shoulder at a row of stalls. "Take yer pick. Ain't nothin' in the first three. There's hay up in the loft ya can fork down, an' water in the trough over t'the corral. Four bits a critter." Jesse started to lead the horses inside. "In advance." Jesse stopped and gazed steadily at the man until he smiled uneasily, showing a considerable gap in his front teeth.

"You will be doing the stall cleaning, won't you?" Jesse asked at last. The man nodded eagerly. "I was just wondering, seein' as how I'm doin' everything else." He flipped the man a dollar and led the horses on into the barn. He unsaddled them and hung bridle and hackamore on pegs in the stall posts. The saddles went up on the horizontal poles that divided the two stalls from one another. The inside of the barn didn't look a whole lot better than the outside.

"Say," the man's voice drifted inside. "Isn't that Buster McLanahan's mutt you got follerin' you, stranger?"

"Not any more," Jesse replied. "Buster and I had a little talk, and he decided he didn't need a dog any more."

The clattering of the telegraph key startled Harvey awake. The magazine he had been reading was laying open on the floor, and he had a decidedly stiff neck; apparently, he'd dozed off while sitting in the chair. He took a gander around the room as he rubbed the ache from his neck; the shadows had lengthened considerably since he'd looked around last. He stood, stretching and yawning. He looked through the barred window in front of the telegraph key just in time to see the telegrapher tear a sheet of paper from the pad next to the key and rise up out of his chair. "Humph," the man sniffed. "I really didn't expect an answer so soon, but it seems that your bank draft will be on tomorrow's stage," he huffed, handing the sheet to Harvey.

"Thanks, partner," Harvey drawled. The man just nodded curtly and turned away from the window. Harvey chuckled and watched the man's back stiffen before he stomped out of sight. Harvey grinned to himself and headed for the door. He figured that by this time, Jesse should be done at the livery. Harvey stepped outside and found Jesse sitting in a tipped back chair against the building wall, whittling. A substantial pile of shavings indicated that he'd been working on that stick for quite a while. Dog lay napping in a nearby patch of sunlight. "Been sittin' there long?"

"Oh, a while. You looked so peaceful in that chair in there that I didn't have the heart to wake you up." Jesse brought his chair's front legs back to earth and stood. The jackknife he folded and dropped into his hip pocket. Harvey snorted as Jesse went on, "I don't know about the rest of the world, but I think maybe it's time for a drink. How 'bout you?"

"Now that sounds like a plan," Harvey agreed. "An' it might be an idea to see if this town's got a decent hotel too. I'm thinkin' it's maybe a little late in the day to head back to Watsonville tonight, an' I've been sleepin' in a bed enough lately that I'm gettin' kinda spoiled."

"Works for me," Jesse answered. "There's one down yonder that don't look too bad. Come on, Dog," he directed toward the third member of their group.

"One what? Hotel or saloon?" Harvey wanted to know.

"Both," Jesse said firmly.

Thirty-eight

A crashing blast of thunder and the trident glory of lightning heralded the dawn. In the outlaw camp men sat bolt upright in their blankets, cursing. The neighing and stamping of startled horses along the picket line added to the sudden confusion. As the echoes of the thunderclap rolled across the land and began to fade, the wind came. At first, while the grumbling men reached for their boots and hats--they'd been sleeping in their clothes--the wind was merely a few prying fingers that lifted and rustled the grass in the clearing.

As the men belted on their guns and the nervous horses began to settle down, there came a howl and a splash, and the storm's full fury burst over the camp. The wall of brush to the west gave minimal shelter from the slashing rain as the men scrambled to untie oilskins from saddle strings, but in a matter of moments the camp was a shambles. Blankets fluttered and tumbled through the mud until they were too sodden for even the demon wind to pick up. The drenched bedding lay in heaps around the clearing. The fire ring was a bed of black muck with brown rivulets oozing through it from the contents of the overturned coffeepot. A sack of Arbuckle's that lay nearby rapidly became a casualty of the onslaught as its contents began to seep brown liquid through the fibers of the bag. Saddlebags, boots, and hats quickly soaked through under the torrent while the outlaws scurried about in an attempt to salvage what they could.

Another cannonade of thunder slammed a bolt of lightning into the bushy top of a tall juniper standing nearby. The tree split asunder with a shriek of tearing wood fibers that sounded almost human. The blast showered the camp and the line of terrified horses with jagged, flaming splinters. With a scream the rearing, plunging mounts tore the picket line loose from its moorings and thundered through the camp *en masse*. The stampeding beasts bowled over anything and anyone without the presence of mind to escape their path, or who was deranged enough to try to stop them. The slashing of steel-shod hooves further compounded the destruction in the camp. Howdy Baxter, with his head bare and water streaming down his face, screamed, "Stop them, you fools!" to no avail as the panicked animals disappeared beyond a curtain of rain, running with the wind.

An eternity seemed to pass as the wind screamed and the rain beat down. The outlaws had at last surrendered to the storm. They stood in a huddled mass crowded under the lee side of the brush at the edge of the clearing, taking what shelter they could from the foliage that whipped overhead. No one tried to talk over the wind's banshee howling. Each man was lost in his own thoughts as they stood dumbly, wondering if this was the end, stunned by the brute fury of the elements. None of them had ever been caught out in a storm like this.

Dog lifted an ear at the distant rumbling. She lay curled on the woven rag rug in front of the hotel-room door with her chin on the floor. Jesse stirred, rolled over, and pulled the blankets up higher as the wind rattled raindrops against the window. The storm that had inundated the outlaw camp had washed over Watsonville and was advancing on Mason.

In the cactus-fenced chicken yard behind the hotel kitchen, a scrawny rooster crowed. His hens clucked around him as they scratched in the rain-freckled dust. The raindrops soon convinced him that discretion was the better part of valor, and the rooster subsided and began herding his flock into the makeshift coop he guarded. At the sound of the rooster's voice, Jesse's eyes opened and he yawned, rolling onto his back. Dog's tail thumped on the rug and Jesse turned his head. "Mornin', Dog," he said as he reached down to scratch behind the furry ears. "Sounds like a storm's comin'." Outside the rain began to pour in earnest.

Jesse swung his feet to the floor and reached for his shirt. He pulled it over his head, picked up his pants and slipped into them. When his boots were firmly in place, he swung his gun belt around his lean waist, put on his hat and moved to the door. Dog rose and stretched, then stood patiently with her tail waving waiting for the door to open. "Let's us go find some breakfast, shall we?" Jesse inquired. Dog seemed to agree, so Jesse pulled the door open and Dog led the way out onto the worn strip of carpeting that covered the hardwood floor. The door clicked shut behind the pair as they started down the stairs.

The hotel dining room was nearly empty. The usual breakfast crowd had stayed home rather than brave the deluge outside. The telegrapher, a man in a boiled shirt and bowler hat who looked like a whiskey drummer, and an elderly ranch couple in town for supplies were the only patrons besides Harvey, who was sitting in a corner sipping coffee. "Ready to hit the trail, partner?" Harvey asked jokingly.

"Can I at least feed Dog, or are you in a big roarin' hurry to go out in that frog-strangler out there for some reason?" Jesse shot back, pulling out a chair and dropping into it.

"Well, I do need to get Old Man Hanneman his money."

"Yeah, but the stage don't get to Watsonville 'til tomorrow some time. I know that for sure. So he's gonna have to wait that long anyway. I think maybe you're just getting' tired of our company and wanna get back so you can have breakfast with your hotel lady."

"She is a good bit purtier than either one of you two. She smells better, too," Harvey grinned as he went back to his coffee.

A long, indeterminate time later light gradually spread across the camp. Mort Bales raised his head from where he had been huddled under a bushy mahogany. He cocked his head to one side and said, "Listen." The others slowly looked around, their faces dull under their sodden hats. "The wind's dyin'. An' it ain't rainin' near as hard as it was." He was right. Moments later the wind died as quickly as it had begun, and the rain subsided to a gentle pattering on felt and oilskin. The storm had at last run its course and moved on.

The rain finally stopped altogether and the outlaws began trying to restore some semblance of order to their disheveled camp. That it hadn't been especially orderly to begin with made things more difficult. Grant Morgan stomped around importantly barking orders that nobody paid much attention to as he splashed through puddles and stepped over sodden packs and bedrolls, until finally even Mort had enough of Grant and his noise. He straightened up from where he was squatting, going through the food packs to see if anything was salvageable. Mort's mustache twitched and he snapped with a trace of heat in his squeaky voice, "For God's sake, Grant, shut up and do somethin' constructive, would ya? All our fixin's are soakin' wet, an' our horses are gone, an' all you're doin' is just makin' a helluva annoyin' racket."

Grant stopped in mid-bellow and turned to face Mort. His frowning face turned red as his temper flared; Howdy Baxter's off-key laughter didn't help things any. This was the kind of fun Baxter really enjoyed. Grant's right hand dropped to the butt of his pistol and he grated through clenched teeth, "What did you say?"

Grant managed a half step toward him before Mort's voice stopped Grant dead in his tracks with one foot still in the air; that and the four distinct clicks of a Colt's hammer ratcheting back. "Don't even think about it, Grant!" Mort grated. "You heard what I said. We're all gettin' tired of your gas." Grant's foot settled back to earth as he looked down at the .44 in Mort's hand. The muzzle was pointed a little north of Grant's belt buckle, and Mort's white-knuckled finger was on the trigger. It suddenly dawned on Grant that he hadn't even seen the little sucker draw--had never seen him draw, for that matter. He'd just taken it for granted, so to speak, that he would be able to take Mort in a fight if push came to shove. Now he wasn't so sure.

Across the clearing, Baxter's eerie chuckling

erupted into full-blown laughter. "What's so damn funny?" Grant wanted to know. His eyes never left the pistol in Mort's hand as he spoke.

"You are!" Baxter exclaimed between guffaws. "The look on your face when you saw that pistol was priceless. You didn't know whether to crap, scream, or cry, and it's pretty obvious you still don't. I think if it was me, I'd back off just a little." He stopped for breath, then went on. "It seems to me like maybe your sawed-off pard there has had about all of you he wants for a while. You try to bite off a piece of him, and I think that you're gonna have more there than you can chew."

Jode chimed in with, "He's right, Grant. Whatever your sellin', Mort ain't buyin', and he's holdin' the high cards. All you got is the joker."

Grant wanted to do something--anything--other than step back. He wanted it so bad he could almost taste it. But even he could tell that he was about as close to dying as he'd ever been in a long and checkered career on the wrong side of the law. After a tense half-minute that dragged as if the seconds were slathered with January molasses, he turned on his heel and stomped off toward where his saddle lay. "All of ya can go ta hell," he muttered roughly.

"That's pretty likely," Baxter replied with the laughter still in his voice. "That's pretty likely." He looked over to where Mort still stood with his eyes on Grant, who had dropped down to sit on his saddle and sulk. "I think the party's over, Mort. You can put away the noisemaker." Mort turned his eyes toward Baxter, nodded curtly, and let the hammer down on the Colt. He dropped it back into the holster as he hooked the thong over the hammer, then wordlessly hunkered down and went back to sorting through the food supplies. Baxter eyed him appraisingly; this was a side of Mort none of the men in the clearing had seen before. Baxter's crew visibly relaxed as they went back to what they'd been doing. It looked like this storm was over, too.

As he worked, Mort was thinking. *He was trailing with Grant and Jode mainly because it was easier to get through Indian country with more guns than it was alone. He really didn't like either one of them all that much, but Benson was with Morgan when Mort first ran into them in a saloon forty miles away. Mort rode away from the saloon with them of his own accord, so he really couldn't complain too much. He'd seen Benson around and shared a fire with him a time or two, but they were far from friends. Mort was down on his luck when he ran across the two outlaws, and his luck didn't seem to have changed too much for the better since then. Grant seemed to have plenty of ready cash and he wasn't shy about sharing it so Mort let him lead; it was easier to do that than it was to fight with him. But Mort had taken water from the big blow-hard for a month now and he'd about had enough.*

Mort wasn't always completely honest with the world, but he could be honest with himself when he needed to be; and now he decided that it was time he made a change. He wasn't especially ambitious, and he occasionally played fast and loose with the law, but he never really strayed too far over the line. He really hadn't wanted to dump that young feller down the mineshaft, but again it had been easier to just go along when Benson had whacked him following Grant's orders. It had been Mort who knew about the mineshaft, and he had regretted that whole fiasco even before Harvey had made the three of them walk after their horses. And now this thing with Grant had happened. Maybe it was an omen. Maybe it was time to leave.

He caught Baxter watching him, a measuring look in his crazy eyes. Mort gazed back coolly for a moment, then went back to his sorting. Somehow, he had to find a way out of the mess he'd gotten into by going along with the plans. Mort vowed silently that if he made it out of this clearing alive, he was going to find Harvey and Jesse and do what he could to try to make amends. Until then he would have to guard his thoughts carefully and not let on that he was leaving. He was sure Baxter would gut him like a fish right on the spot if he suspected that anything was amiss. How complicated could one man's life get, anyway?

Thirty-nine

The rain gradually slowed then stopped altogether as the storm rumbled over the hills beyond Mason. The sun peeked out from behind what was left of the clouds and bedecked the trees, bushes, and even the weeds in and around Mason with a million jewels. It was almost as if each plant was determined to outshine its neighbor. Harvey and Jesse stepped out onto the boardwalk in front of the café with Dog at their heels. "It's a beautiful day for a ride!" Jesse exclaimed.

"Nothin' like a hard rain to wash everything clean," Harvey replied in admiration of Nature's work, "an' no better way to enjoy a day like this than settin' in a saddle. What say we head for home?" Without waiting for an answer, he grinned and led the way toward the livery. A short while later they were on the trail. Their horses' hooves splashed through puddles that sparkled in the morning sun; the horses' shoes picked up and threw sticky clods of wet clay in their wake. Dog ran ahead, sniffing and prospecting, always coming back, then going on again. The morning sun was warm on their shoulders, and the two men slouched comfortably in their saddles, relishing the freshness of the morning air. The horses sensed their riders' relaxed mood and moseyed along with their heads swinging in time with their steps. Overhead the vivid colors of a rainbow arched across the crystal-blue sky, its multicolored arc seeming to touch ground miles to either side of the trail. For all the crash and splatter of a few short hours before, the day had turned into one of those days that make both man and dog glad to be alive.

Up ahead, the long ears of a jackrabbit suddenly came into view through the tall grass as Dog flushed the speeding rodent from his sheltered hide under a low-growing sage bush. In a flash, the chase was on as the shepherd put on a burst of speed, trying to overtake the fleeing hare, but it wasn't to be. With a flirt of white tail-hair the jack bounded away, easily outdistancing its pursuer. Dog trotted up to Jesse with her tongue lolling in a grin, wagged her tail then was off again, looking for some other critter to chase.

Howdy Baxter looked up from where he sat contemplating the future. A vague plan for taking his revenge on Harvey Palmer and Jesse Thompson had been stirring in his mind for several days, and now it began to gel in his devious brain. The sound of hooves brought his attention back to the camp; Montez was riding into camp leading a string of horses. The Mexican seemed to have a sixth sense when it came to finding stray horses, and this time had been no exception. He'd found them, still mostly tied together, about three miles west of the camp, grazing on a rich patch of grass in a clearing in the brush. It had been a simple matter to capture his own horse and use that one to lead the rest back to the camp. Baxter rose to his feet and tipped his hat back off his head. "Good man, Montez. Now I've got a job for you: I want you to ride into that town and see what you can find out. I'm of a mind to think Harvey Palmer may have a girl there, seeing as how he's been around there so long. I really don't think there's much else in that part of the country to keep him there. Keep your mouth shut and your ears open."

"*Sí*, Howdy, I can do that," Montez answered, "but those people, they seen me before, when that Thompson *hombre* whip Marty."

"I kind of doubt anybody but Harvey Palmer and maybe the bartender would remember you," Baxter assured him. "Marty's the one they'll remember. Just be quiet and see what you can find out."

"Eef you say so, *jefe*," Montez answered, turning turned toward his gear. He quickly saddled his horse and rode out. Baxter watched him go, an evil smile quirking his lips. If everything went according to plan, he'd be having his revenge in a matter of days.

Cholo Montez drifted down the main street of Watsonville. The sun was out, and the mud was nearly dry. His horse's hooves kicked up puffs of dust here and there. His wide-brimmed *sombrero* was pulled low as he slouched in the saddle. He was riding a different horse and wearing a different shirt than the last time he was here so he felt at least somewhat at ease. His black eyes were constantly moving under the stiff brim of his steeple-crowned hat. He half expected someone to point him out as one of the outlaws who had been with Marty Bannon, but no one so much as glanced his way.

Watsonville had seen its share of traveling cowhands, including Mexican ones, so one more wasn't anything to write home about. It seemed that Howdy was right about that.

Tying his horse to the rail in front of the Bluebonnet Café, Montez stepped up onto the boardwalk, spurs jingling on the pine boards. He crossed to the café and opened the door. A few of the seats were occupied, but most were empty, as folks had to be out and about making a living. He moved to a chair at a table near the wall and sat down. He removed his hat, placing it on a nearby chair. The morning waitress picked up a coffeepot and cup, raising them in his direction. He nodded, so she brought the pot to his table and poured the cup full. "*Gracias*," he murmured.

Montez sipped his coffee and contemplated the menu chalked on the slate hanging on the far wall near the kitchen door. Several of the items were crossed off, indicating that the supply had run out, but ham, spuds, and cornbread were still on the list. The waitress came back to his table and he ordered some of each. It wasn't long before she set a platter with a big slab of ham and some fried potatoes in front of him, accompanied by a plate of cornbread and a pot of honey. She poured his coffee cup full as he again murmured, "*Gracias*". Montez was a man of few words.

Even though he was seemingly engrossed in his breakfast, Montez missed very little that went on around him. When the bell over the door rang and a pretty brunette came in, he noted her presence then ignored her, until the waitress commented, "Haven't seen you in here for breakfast since Harvey lit out, Lila. Got any idea when he'll be back?" Montez figured there couldn't be more than one Harvey spending time in

Watsonville, so he listened carefully while appearing to ignore the conversation as he continued to eat.

"He should be back in a day or two, Missus Parkman," Lila answered. "He went over to Mason to send a telegram. I've been cooking for myself the last couple of days, but I've kind of gotten spoiled, coming to breakfast with Harvey every day. This morning I decided to splurge and come over, instead of staying at the hotel."

"Well, sit right down and I'll have a pot of tea for you in a jiffy." Carol Parkman, the widow who owned the café, was also the waitress this morning. She bustled into the kitchen and returned shortly with a pot of tea and a cup and saucer. "There you are, Lila."

"Thank you, Missus Parkman. I believe I'll just have a small piece of ham and some of your good cornbread, if I may."

"Coming right up." The older woman had known Lila Foster since she and her now-deceased husband Bertram had come to Watsonville. She liked the younger woman, who had not let circumstances bring her down but had instead rebuilt her life, and prospered. She herself had been widowed twice, and it did her heart good to see Lila with Harvey. No one should have to be alone.

Montez finished his meal and rose, donning his hat. He reached into the pocket of his short jacket and brought out four bits, dropping the coins on the table and turning toward the door. When the women looked his way, he nodded and touched a finger to the wide brim of his *sombrero* then made his way to the door and out.

"What a polite fellow," Lila commented as the two watched him leave. She was surprised at the gracious manner of the stranger--many drifters had the manners of hogs--and so she wondered why she suddenly felt a shiver of foreboding trace an icy finger up her spine.

She shrugged off her unease as Missus Parkman declared approvingly, "It's about time one of these cowhands showed a lady a little proper respect!"

Forty

Mort was doing some hard thinking. He knew Baxter had a plan in mind, and that somehow that plan involved women, but Mort didn't know what it might be. All he knew was that he didn't want any part of it. In this part of the world a man could get hung, or otherwise seriously killed, for even saying the wrong thing to the wrong woman. And Kitty Moynahan was definitely the wrong woman for any of these gents to mess with. These boys were looking to get dead, and every man around who could raise a hand would be there to pull the rope. Mort wasn't all that tall, but he really didn't have much of a hankering to have his height increased by having his neck stretched.

Mort yawned as he got up from his seat against his saddle, saying, "I'm about ta fall asleep, Grant." He looked over to where Grant leaned against his own saddle, sipping from a bottle of whiskey. "I'm gonna make a circle, see if anybody's out and about. I'd hate ta have some lawman or some such come on us an' find half of us nappin'." He reached down for his saddle and blankets and sauntered toward the picket line. His saddlebags and bedroll were already tied behind the cantle of the saddle along with his slicker, which had finally dried after the downpour he'd been out in. His Winchester was in the boot under the offside stirrup.

"Where do you think you're going, Bales?" Howdy barked from his position across the clearing. He rose to one knee with his hand on his pistol.

"I'm goin' for a ride, see if anybody's out yonder sneakin' up on us, Baxter," Mort answered coolly. 'Seein' as how nobody's been on sentry watch all damn day, I thought it might be a good idea to have a look around. Is that alright with you?" Mort stopped with his saddle on his hip and waited for Baxter to call his bluff.

"I suppose that would be a good idea," Baxter relented. "But be back before dark."

"Yeah, yeah," Mort said more confidently, now that he was fairly certain that he wouldn't get a bullet in the back. From what he'd seen of Baxter, a man could never be a hundred percent sure. He strolled to his horse and set the saddle on the ground. He pulled a currycomb from his saddlebag and worked over the horse for several minutes. He picked some burrs from the paint's tail, and brushed the mud from the gelding's back and belly. As he slung the blankets into place and smoothed them down, making sure there were no wrinkles, Mort looked for all the world like a man just going for a leisurely Sunday jaunt. But inside he was stretched tight, sure that he would still have to fight his way out of the camp.

Mort cinched the saddle in place, kneeing the

paint in the barrel to make him let out the belly full of air he'd sucked in when he felt the cinch. Mort pulled the cinch tighter, dropped the stirrup he'd hung over the horn while he worked, and reached up to gather his reins. He stepped into the saddle and turned away from the camp with an airy wave of his hand. He was soon out of sight behind the wall of brush at the side of the clearing; only then did he let out a breath he hadn't realized he was holding.

Mort held the paint to a walk, resisting the almost overwhelming urge to run the horse out of there as fast as the animal could move. But he knew that the horse's hoof beats would tip Baxter and Grant that something was wrong, and he didn't want them any the wiser until he had a good head start. He figured that once he got to Watsonville, the two men would have a lot more trouble killing him and getting away with it than they would out here in the wide-open lonesome.

Montez rode loose in the saddle, his horse pacing lightly over the rolling terrain in a ground-eating jog that felt like sitting in a rocking chair. Montez prided himself on the quality of his horses, and went to a lot more trouble than most to make sure that they were well-trained and well-cared for. The grulla he was riding today was no exception. As he rode, the Mexican outlaw sang softly to himself, a sad song of unrequited love and the young *señorita* who was the cause of it all. His dark eyes were never still, always seeing what was around him. He'd been on the outlaw trail too many years to ever completely relax. But even his keen eyes didn't see Mort hidden back in the brush, watching the tall, pointed crown of Montez' *sombrero* pass by. Mort had stayed off the trails, preferring the brushy hollows and sandy washes that would hide his horse's tracks to the easier traveling of the open meadows and trails. It might take him longer to get to his destination, but it would also take anyone who might decide to trail him that much longer to work out where he'd gone.

From the sound of Montez' singing, and the fact that he was on his way back to camp already, Mort figured the Mexican must have gotten whatever information it was that Baxter had sent him after. As the sound of singing faded away, Mort heeled the paint into motion, continuing on his way to town. *By this time, that Thompson gent should be at least somewhere in the vicinity of Watsonville, if what Jode heard was true,* he thought as he rode. Mort intended to find Harvey and Jesse and tell them about the outlaws, then keep on traveling until he was clear out of the country. He had a hunch that if Palmer and Thompson went on the warpath, things would get pretty hot around here in one hell of a hurry. Anyone who didn't want to get scorched had better be a long ways away, and Mort liked his hide in its current, un-scorched condition.

Forty-one

Harvey and Jesse jogged along the road from Mason to Watsonville with their hats tipped back, enjoying the day that was slowly drawing to a close. Ahead of them, the sun was disappearing behind the mountains and its red glow spread from horizon to horizon. "We aren't but about ten or fifteen miles from home, Harve," Jesse said. "What say we ride on in instead of stoppin'?"

"That sounds good to me," Harvey answered. "I'd kind of like to sleep in my own bed again." He smiled. "And have breakfast with my "hotel lady", as you so quaintly put it."

Jesse smiled back. "When are you gonna make an honest woman out of her?" he asked suddenly. "I think she'd say "I do" in a heartbeat if you asked her."

Harvey's head turned with a jerk. "I don't think that's any of your business," he began stiffly. He stopped, suddenly realizing how he sounded. He grinned sheepishly and said, "I think you're right. Soon's I get a chance, I'm gonna ask her. There's more than Orville Hanneman's money comin' on the stage tomorrow night. I ordered a diamond ring all the way from Frisco, an' it's supposed to be on that stage. When I've got it in *my* hand, it's gonna go on *her* hand. Or at least I hope so. I've been trailin' through the country by myself for way too long. It's time I settled down, an' that horse ranch is where I'm plannin' on doin' my settlin'."

Montez walked his horse into the outlaw camp. Carson was hunkered down near the fire turning sputtering strips of bacon in the big fire-blackened skillet. The enamelware coffeepot steamed gently nearby. Montez stepped down and led the grulla to the spring to drink, then to the picket line. He uncinched the saddle, lifted it off of his mount's sweaty back and turned the horse loose for a moment to roll. When the horse got up and shook the big chunks of grass and dirt from it's hide, Montez led it to the picket line and tied the gelding with enough rope that it could reach the knee-high grass growing there.

Turning toward the fire, Montez noticed Baxter and Grant watching him intently. "Well, what did you find out?" Baxter demanded. "You weren't gone very long. I didn't expect you back until tomorrow at the earliest."

"I foun' out thee hotel lady an' Harvey Palmer, they been sharing the uh, how you say, the *amor*."

"Love... So, the woman from the hotel is Harvey Palmer's lover? How do you know that's who she is?" Baxter questioned.

"I see her there when we were een de town

before," the Mexican answered simply. He bent down to fill his cup with coffee. "An' she say she from dee hotel een dee café dis morning."

"All right, that's the last piece of the puzzle. I've got a plan!" Baxter declared. He looked around and noticed how dark it was getting to be. "Did you see any sign of Mort Bales on your way here?" he asked suspiciously. Montez' shook his head, with a decidedly puzzled look on his face, and Baxter cursed viciously. "I knew I should have shot that little weasel!" he snarled. "He's taken off on us!" As quickly as it came his anger subsided. There was nothing he could do about Bales now. Raising his voice he called, "Every body get over here! It's time for us to get even!"

As the outlaws moved toward Baxter, they looked at each other questioningly. Baxter kept silent until the men were gathered in an uneasy semicircle in front of him. "Anybody else know much about this country?" he demanded suddenly. Jode raised his hand gingerly, not at all sure he wanted to be the focus of the crazed outlaw's attention.

"What are ya wantin' ta know, Howdy?" he asked diffidently.

"Are there any abandoned ranches, or ghost towns, or anything of the sort anywhere close?" Baxter queried.

Jode thought about the question for several moments; the answer came to him, and his face brightened. "Yeah, now that ya mention it, there's an old minin' camp about twenny miles or so north of here. I think there's still a few buildin's standin' about. Or there was the last time I was by there. Why?"

"Never mind why!" Baxter snapped. "How far is it from Watsonville? How easy is it to get to? What kind of terrain is it in?"

"Near as I can figure the place is about thirty or so miles out of Watsonville," Jode replied, carefully considering his words. "It's in a box canyon that's kinda hard to find. Ya gotta know where it is an' be lookin' for it, or you'll miss the trail."

"Good, good," Baxter chuckled. He was actually rubbing his hands together with glee. "That sounds like it will do very nicely. Tomorrow morning we'll ride up there and take a look at it. It sounds like just what I'm looking for."

"What're you gonna do in a ghost town, Baxter?" Grant wanted to know.

"I'm going to use it to set a trap for Harvey Palmer and Jesse Thompson. And Kitty Moynahan and the hotel lady are going to be the bait."

Forty-two

The first rosy flush of dawn was painting the eastern horizon when a shadowy figure raised its hand and halted the procession of shadows following behind. Jode's voice drifted back to Howdy Baxter, where he waited impatiently with his fingers drumming on his saddle horn. "The turnoff's here somewheres, but I gotta have more light to find it. We're gonna hafta wait."

"What is this place we're lookin' for, anyway?" Grant growled.

"It useta be a minin' camp called Horton," Jode answered. "Called that after a gent name of Zacharia Horton. Somehow or other he stumbled over a vein of silver in a box canyon up yonder. Folks found out about it an' came flockin' in here, only it turned out the vein weren't near as big as Horton thought it was. The town purty well sprung up an' died out all in less than a year. There never was more than half a dozen buildin's an' a mine tunnel, an' I don't expect too many of the buildin's are still standin'."

By the time Jode's slow drawl stopped there was enough light for him to start recognizing terrain features. Jode heeled his horse forward, looking not at the ground but at the surrounding rock formations. The others silently sat and watched until he turned in his saddle and waved them forward. He faced forward again, kicked his horse ahead and disappeared behind a protruding shoulder of rock where no opening seemed to be.

As the outlaws approached the stone wall, it soon became apparent that what appeared to be one big boulder actually consisted of two outthrust shoulders of rock with a gap between them big enough to admit a small wagon. One of the outcroppings sat at right angles to the face of the second formation. The brush growing in front of the rocks obscured the passage further, making it easy for a traveler to pass by unless he knew where to look.

Behind the rocks the sandy trail swung gently back to the right, then meandered through a slot in the bluff before opening out into a flat area of a few acres. Here and there, a few stunted mahoganies stood silent sentry duty, while alongside a small, trickling stream cottonwood leaves rustled in the fitful breeze.

Along what had once been Horton's main street, a false-fronted building advertised *"Cards, Liquor, Women"* in faded weatherworn gilt. A set of deer antlers framed the words *"Buckhorn Saloon"* painted on a sign hanging by one creaking hinge out over the sagging roof of the building's front porch. To either side, other buildings in various states of disrepair leaned drunkenly on their neighbors, or stood in solitary disarray. The men spoke in low tones as they surveyed what had once been, for a short while, a bustling mining camp. They had been in enough similar camps to read the story of Horton's demise for themselves, even without Jode's earlier tale.

Baxter's grating voice broke the stillness. "Where's the mineshaft you were telling us about, Benson?"

Jode pointed up the canyon past the buildings. "It's up yonder. Most likely caved in by now. It's been a coon's age since it's been worked."

"Well, let's go find out, shall we?" Baxter spurred his horse up the street as the others straggled along behind. When they rounded the last heap of fallen lumber, the outlaws found the mouth of the shaft yawning at the foot of the sheer cliff that blocked the end of the canyon. A pair of rusty narrow-gauge rails protruded like a tongue from the opening, ending at a chute that had been used to dump the rock from the mine into the wagons that transported the ore elsewhere for processing. A rusting ore-cart lay on its side near the chute, its last load of rock spilled alongside.

Baxter rode up to the shaft and stepped down, trailing his reins on the ground. He took a stub of candle from his shirt pocket, struck a match and touched it to the wick. When the wick caught flame, he blew out the match, ground it into the dirt underfoot and walked forward between the rails. Shortly after disappearing into the dark hole, his voice echoed eerily out of the side of the cliff. "This is perfect."

Baxter emerged from the darkness and blew out the candle. He waited a moment for his eyes to adjust to the bright sunlight then stepped forward. "Benson, is there any way up that cliff?" He pointed at the sheer face behind him. "Game trails or whatever, that will let a man with a rifle up there?"

Jode thought for a minute. "I ain't sure, Howdy. It seems to me there might be one off over yonder." He pointed to Baxter's left, toward where a boulder jutted from the face of the cliff and appeared to have an opening behind it. Baxter walked that direction and looked behind the rock; a narrow hint of a trail, pocked with the tracks of deer and coyotes, started at the foot of the boulder and wound its way up through an eroded crack toward the top of the cliff. As the outlaws watched, Baxter strode a few yards up the trail, then turned and looked down at them.

"Who's the best rifle shot here?" he called.

"I reckon I'm alright," Carson volunteered.

""Good. Get up top and find a vantage point that lets you see the whole town and the trail into this canyon," Baxter ordered. "You'll want to build a parapet to get behind. Surely there's something up there you can use."

"What's a parapet?" Carson asked in a puzzled voice.

"I... am... surrounded... by... illiterate... " Baxter began angrily, then subsided. "Just build a wall you can get behind, unless you don't mind getting shot." He turned back to the others and saw a quizzical look on Grant's face.

"Just what exactly do you have in mind, Baxter?" Grant questioned.

"We, or rather some of us, are going to pay Miss Kitty Moynahan and the hotel lady a little visit. While we're there, we're going to invite them to visit our humble abode here. The rest of us will be preparing a welcoming reception for Harvey Palmer and Jesse Thompson, who are sure to follow."

Forty-three

In the loft of Johansen's smithy Jesse sat up and stretched. From the look of what few shadows there were outside the barn, it had to be close to noon. He had a horrible taste in his mouth and his eyes were grainy. He and Harvey had gotten into town long after the moon was down; he'd unsaddled his horse, climbed into the loft and dropped on his blankets fully clothed. He'd fallen asleep instantly.

A rustling in the hay near him made him look around. The thump of a furry tail on boards and the sudden appearance of two furry ears and a head with one blue eye and one brown eye told him who the culprit was. "How in the world did you get up here, Dog?" he asked as he reached out to ruffle the shepherd's ears. Dog just looked at him with her tongue out and didn't answer. Jesse stood and picked up his hat, brushed the bits of hay from the crown, and settled it on his head.

"Well, I reckon if you got up here, you can get back down, he told the dog. "Let me know if you need help." Jesse climbed down to the floor and waited. A moment later Dog appeared at the head of the sloping ladder and carefully scrambled down a few rungs before jumping to the ground, tail waving happily. "I think it's time we went and found some breakfast, eh?" Jesse remarked.

"Breakfast?" rumbled Lars as he came through the doorway from the wagon yard. "It's almost noon!"

"I know, I know, but I got in late."

"I t'ought you young folks vas tough," Lars chuckled.

"We are; some of us are just tougher than others!" Jesse replied with a laugh. "But not before breakfast. Right at the moment, I'm feeling a bit puny from hunger. I'll see ya later, Lars. Come on, Dog."

Mort was hanging on the horns of a dilemma, so to speak. On the one hand, what little bit of conscience he had was prodding him to do something to warn Harvey and Jesse that Howdy Baxter had something bad in mind, and that it involved at the very least Kitty Moynahan. On the other hand, the last time he'd seen Harvey, the man had told Mort, Jode, and Grant that if he ever saw them on his back trail he'd shoot 'em and leave 'em for the buzzards. That was not exactly the most promising future a fellow could have, so Mort was camped in the brush out east of Watsonville, thinking. A camp by himself was a good place to think. He figured that if Baxter and company came into town, it would be from the west and they wouldn't find him. That gave him an unknown amount of time to try coming up with a plan that would let him keep his hide intact. He sat leaning back on his saddle and contemplating what future he might have. If he walked up to Harvey, Harvey would shoot him. He'd said so, and Harvey had always been a man of his word. But if Mort rode away without doing anything at all, he might as well shoot himself because he'd never be able to live with the thought that Kitty had gotten hurt--or worse--and he hadn't done anything to stop it. His sainted mother would turn over in her grave. So he sat some more, and he thought some more.

After a while, like the slow dawning of the sun, an idea came to him. He'd leave a note at the hotel for Harvey, and ride away in good conscience. And, better yet, he'd ride away alive, knowing he'd done what he could. Immediately acting on the thought, he reached into his saddlebag for an old tally book he kept there in case he needed something to start a fire with; a fella never knew when he might need a piece of paper. He took out the book and a stub of pencil he found alongside of it, licked the tip of the pencil, and began to write laboriously:

Deer Harv: Howdy baxtre an grant Morgan ar plannin sumthin bad to git bak at you an that tomson fella. I dont hav no idee whut, but its got sumthin ta do with wimmen. I aint that kind so I left an im ridin out of the terittory an aint comin back. You aint gunna see me agin.

Mort Bales

When he read back through what he'd written, Mort sighed. He knew he couldn't write very well, but the note was the best he could do and he hoped it would get his point across. Now he just had to figure out where to put it. While he was figuring, he saddled his horse. He pulled the cinch tight, stepped into the leather and eased the horse toward the town. A short time later he pulled the paint to a halt, still under cover, at the upper end of Watsonville's main street. He took a spyglass from a saddlebag and sat and watched the comings and goings of the townsfolk while he looked for Harvey or Jesse. He really didn't want to run into either of them.

A pair of figures coming out of the hotel caught Mort's attention. Harvey and Lila were strolling along the boardwalk toward the café. There was his chance: he'd come up on the hotel from the back, go in and leave his note on the counter and be gone. A matter of just a couple of minutes and he'd be a free man. Or at least he'd be free of Baxter and the rest. Better yet, he'd be free of a kidnapping charge. After collapsing the spyglass and returning it to his saddlebag, Mort heeled the paint into motion and began to skirt the town, headed for the hotel.

A few minutes later Mort reined in behind the hotel and cautiously peered all around, but the town was still in the midday heat. A cicada buzzed nearby and a few small birds flitted about or picked at things in the dirt, but no human was in sight. Mort stepped down and moved stealthily to the back door of the building. He tried the knob; to his relief it turned easily, and the door swung inward on silent hinges. A short hallway led to the lobby and the counter. He tore the note from the tattered tally book, hurriedly laid it on the counter near the bell where he figured it couldn't be missed, and left. Five minutes later, the only signs that he'd ever been there were a few horse tracks in the dirt and a fading plume of dust in the distance.

Forty-four

The bell over the cafe door jingled when Harvey opened the door for Lila. Jesse looked up from the steak he was finishing and grinned. "Looks like I'm not the only one gettin' a late start to the day," he said cheerfully. Dog lay on the floor at his feet catching the occasional bite that Jesse dropped for her. The shepherd's tail thumped the boards as Harvey and Lila came up to Jesse's table.

"Well, we did get in kind of late," Harvey replied with a smile on his face.

"You know, that's pretty much the same thing I told Lars down at the livery when he commented on me going to breakfast at noon. All he did was make some smart crack about young people supposedly bein' tough." Harvey laughed as he seated Lila at a nearby table. A short time later, they were eating as well.

Mandy Hooper was a perky redhead whose husband taught school when there were children to teach, and did carpentry and that sort of thing when there weren't. She was a good friend of Lila's. They had met soon after Lila and Bertram arrived in Watsonville, and the two young women had hit it off right away. Today she had a few spare minutes, since her husband had returned to the schoolhouse for the afternoon session, so she decided to drop in at the hotel for a visit. It never dawned on her that Lila would be gone at this time of day. She had no way of knowing that Lila had gone to eat with Harvey.

Holding her skirts up out of the dust of the street as she crossed, Mandy stepped up onto the hotel's boardwalk. The hotel door was closed. She figured that in this nice weather that was a good sign that Lila probably wasn't there, but just on the off chance that the breeze had blown the door shut, she opened it and stuck her head in. "Hello, Lila. Are you here?" she called. Silence greeted her. Not finding any sign of her friend, Mandy closed the door. Inside the small lobby, the sudden draft from the opening and closing of the door lifted a small piece of paper from the counter and drifted it off the back of the plank top. The small grubby slip fluttered towards the floor and settled gently down, coming to rest between a pile of old newspapers and the wall. Unbeknownst to Mort, his good deed was about to go for naught.

Kitty strode purposefully from the Bar M ranch house, pulling on her riding gloves as she went. Before she closed the door she called back to Dennis, who was just finishing his coffee after the noon meal, "I'll see you tomorrow, Dad. I'm going to spend the night in town with Melody. She's supposed to have some new fabrics coming in on the afternoon stage."

"Don't be spendin' all me money, daughter,"

came the gruff reply, with a hint of laughter underlying the tone. "Those cows don't raise themselves, y'know." Kitty's reply was a lilting laugh as the door banged closed. No matter how hard he tried, he couldn't get his daughter to close the door in a ladylike manner; she always slammed it.

Kitty walked lightly toward the barn with her spirits high. The big blue horse with the spotted rump stood in the first stall watching her come, nickering a welcome. "Are you ready to go, Socorro?" she asked gaily. She held out an apple for the big Appaloosa to take from her palm. While he crunched the treat, she headed to the tack room for a brush and currycomb. For the next several minutes, she hummed to herself as she fussed over the flashy gelding, brushing and combing until his coat shone and his sparse mane and tail were tangle-free. A short time later, her saddle was cinched tight and she was trotting out of the barn. Socorro was sidestepping and prancing as the pair took the road toward Watsonville.

Forty-five

Harvey and Lila made their way unhurriedly up the street toward the Desert Inn, her hand resting easily on his arm. It was a beautiful day; the sun slanted gently down on the couple as they ambled along enjoying the warmth after the cold rain and wind of the morning before. In the distance, a cloud of dust rolled across the land, belying the fact that just thirty hours before, the road into Watsonville had been practically a swamp.

The afternoon stage from Ellsworth rolled over a rise, the horses trotting tiredly as they swung into the final stretch toward home and feed. Up on the box, the shotgun guard sat up a little straighter, and dropped his hand to the grab rail at the side of the seat, when he saw Barley Masters, the driver, swing his whip into the air above the horses' backs. The lash cracked like a pistol shot, and the six-horse hitch lunged into the harness. "Heeyah, you brutes!" Masters yelled. "Let's come inta town in style!" The whip cracked again, and the horses lunged into a gallop, the coach swaying around the last turn onto the main street of Watsonville.

Hearing the rumble of wheels and the jingle of trace chains as the coach swung into the end of the street Harvey and Lila stopped, and watched the horses move smartly past the first buildings. "My down payment on Hanneman's ranch should be on that coach, Lila," Harvey said softly, looking off into the distance. "I'm finally settlin' down."

Beside him Lila's heart raced, though her hand on his arm remained relaxed. *Harvey was settling down! Near Watsonville!* She had met that nice Mister Hanneman, and she'd heard a number of the locals comment that his horse ranch was one of the best around. Now Harvey was buying that ranch. Suddenly the day was even brighter than it had been, as Lila pondered her dreams of a future she once thought could never be hers.

The coach came to a stop in front of the Emporium in a cloud of dust with the trace chains jingling. Barley Masters shoved the brake down with his foot and wrapped the reins around the lever. He climbed down from the box and turned to where Jack Logan waited to drop the strongbox down to him. "Get 'er down here, Jack," he said. "I'm ready to put these critters to bed, and have a drink. It's been a long day."

"Hell, Barley," Jack replied with a chuckle. "It ain't even four o'clock yet. We're early for a change."

"Yeah, but I been hoorawin' these cayuses for the last ten hours, an' I'm ready for a long break. Come on." Logan handed down the strongbox and began unlashing the rest of the bags and boxes from the roof of the coach. Masters turned to enter the store building. The closest thing Watsonville had to a bank was the big iron safe at the back of the Emporium, and that's where he was bound. Five minutes later he was back at the boot, unbuckling the dust curtain and pulling out a sack of mail and the last of the baggage for the three men and one lady who had ridden the coach from Ellsworth.

The passengers stood on the boardwalk stretching the kinks out of their backs and trying to knock the worst of the dust from their clothes. One of the men used his hand to slap the dust from his wool trousers, straightened his vest and cravat, checked to make sure the sweep of his watch chain was just right and shrugged into his frock coat. "Pardon me, sir," he said to an unshaven fellow leaning against a porch post.

The man looked the newcomer up and down, then said in a surly tone, "Whatcha want, stranger?"

"My name is Noonan, my good sir, Shanghai Noonan," the stranger replied. "I was wondering if you could tell me where I might find one of the better saloons in town?"

"I ain't your good nothin', tinhorn," the man replied, "An' there ain't but one saloon in town. It's down yonder." He jerked his chin in the general direction of the Nugget.

Seemingly taking no offense at the label "tinhorn", Noonan answered crisply, "Thank you," and turned toward his carpetbag on the boardwalk. As he bent to pick up his bag, the sound of a boot grating on sand caused him to swing his backside away from the flight path of the mate to that boot. The booted foot missed its intended target and instead swung high into the air. Noonan reached out, hooked his wrist under the offending member and lifted briskly upward. A thoroughly satisfying crash, accompanied by the grunt of expelled air and the thud of a skull hitting pine boards, signified the ungraceful landing of the unshaven fellow from the porch post. Noonan picked up his bag with his left hand, turned and looked down at his erstwhile assailant.

"Having trouble standing, my good man?" he asked, while a smile flickered under his neatly trimmed mustache. He got no answer from the supine fellow on the boardwalk, so he stepped over the reclining form and strode confidently down the street.

The other stage passengers, and Harvey and Lila as well, watched in amazement as the gambler, if indeed that was how the man made his living, sauntered down the street, whistling. As they resumed their walk to the hotel, Harvey and Lila chuckled at the picture of the unshaven man's comeuppance. "I don't believe I've ever seen anything quite like that," Lila remarked.

"Me neither," Harvey said. "But I'd be willing to bet that Hobie Parks will think twice before he tries to hooraw a stranger again." He laughed out loud. "He sure made a thump when he came down, didn't he?" When they arrived at the hotel Harvey opened the door for Lila. "I need to go to the Emporium and get my bank draft. I'll see you later." Looking around to make sure no one was watching he leaned down and kissed her on the cheek. "I'll have a surprise for you when I get back," he whispered. He turned and headed up the street, humming to himself.

Forty-six

Lila stepped through the door of the hotel, leaving it ajar behind her. She was lost in thought, wondering what Harvey's surprise could be, when a callused hand suddenly clamped over her mouth from behind and a rough voice whispered in her ear, "Not a sound, hotel lady."

Lila froze. Her eyes were wide above the hand covering her mouth. Across the room a man in a tall-crowned *sombrero* was rifling through the shelves under the counter. For a moment she couldn't decide why the man looked so familiar then it dawned on her: he was the Mexican who had been so polite in the café yesterday.

A whip-thin man dressed in black, with a mad gleam in his eyes, stood at the end of the counter with her quill pen in his hand. The intruder looked at Lila thoughtfully for a moment, then smiled to himself and dipped the pen in the pot of ink in front of him. He began to write on a blank page from her register. The scratching of the nib on the coarse paper seemed to echo in the room, even more so than Lila's frightened breathing. When he finished, he laid down the pen and took a small folding knife from his pocket. He flipped the knife open, drove it through the paper and deep into the counter top. "There, that should get some attention," he announced as he looked around at Lila and her captor.

"Alright, get her on a horse and let's get moving," the black-clad stranger ordered. "Ma'am, my man there is going to remove his hand. If you try to run or shout, or if you do anything other than what we tell you to do, he will knock you unconscious and we will take you out of here belly-down over the back of a horse. Is that clear?"

Lila nodded as best she could and the hand relaxed its grip on her jaw. "Who are you people and what do you want?" she demanded angrily when she could talk. Her only answer was a rough hand on her arm that began dragging her toward the back door of the hotel. Once outside, Marty Bannon yanked Lila over to a saddled horse and all but tossed her into the saddle. He reached into a pocket and brought out a handful of rawhide pigging strings. He quickly lashed her hands to the saddle horn while Montez shoved her feet into the stirrups and tied them tightly to the rawhide-covered wood. The hem of her dress had ridden up above her shoe tops due to her position in the saddle, and Montez couldn't resist running his hand along her ankle and up her calf. She kicked the offending hand away, narrowly missing Montez' jaw with the heavy stirrup.

Baxter snapped, "Montez, that's enough!" Then to Lila he said, "Do we need to gag you, or will you be quiet? It will be much easier to breathe without the gag."

"I'll be quiet," she answered. She was regaining her composure as the initial shock of her capture wore off. "I have no wish to be knocked unconscious," she said calmly. She was thinking that it would be much easier to know where she ended up if she were conscious when she arrived there. "But keep that man away from me." She looked away as Montez grinned insolently at her sauntered toward his horse.

"Good, good. You are as intelligent as you look," Baxter said. He pointedly ignored her comment about Montez. The men mounted and the four of them rode slowly away from Watsonville, taking care not to stir up dust. Baxter led, followed by Bannon leading Lila's mount. The Mexican, turning half around in his saddle, brought up the rear. He wanted to be sure that there was no pursuit.

The afternoon was warm; a slight westerly breeze moderated the temperature and cleared the dust raised by Socorro's prancing hooves. After a mile or so of dancing and sashaying, Kitty swaying lightly in the saddle, the blue horse settled into a ground-eating jog that was easy on the seat. Kitty hummed softly to herself as she rode, letting Socorro set the pace. Her thoughts were on nothing in particular, but were definitely on one tall, good-looking deputy in general.

Rounding a bend in the trail she came face to face with two men she didn't know, although she quickly recognized Jode Benson as the nondescript drifter who was in the Emporium the last time she was there. The men sat their horses in the middle of the trail, blocking the way. Reining Socorro to a stop she said calmly, "I would appreciate it if you men would let me pass. I have places to go."

Neither of the men spoke; nor did they make a move to clear the trail. She looked around for another way past them, but they had picked the site for their ambush carefully. The trail was hemmed in by a rock outcropping on one side and a wall of tall brush on the other, leaving no exit but back the way she had come. Lifting the reins, she clucked to Socorro and the big horse began backing up with his ears laid back against his skull. He had only taken a few steps when an insolent voice behind Kitty asked, "Just where do ya thing you're goin', missy?" Kitty eased the pressure on the reins and the big horse stopped. She turned to look over her shoulder and saw a buckskin horse standing cross-wise in the trail. Its rider was leaning casually on his elbows on the saddle horn.

"What do you want?" She tried to keep her voice from shaking.

"Why, we came to invite ya for a visit," Carson answered. "A friend of our'n wants ta meet a friend of your'n, an' he wants ya to introduce 'em ta each other." Baxter had decided to send Grant and Jode with Carson, and leave Hank back in Horton to tend the camp.

"And if I don't want to visit this friend of yours, then what?"

"Ma'am, you ain't got no choice in the matter other'n to come along peaceable. Benson, tie her hands an' feet an' let's get goin'."

Jode and Grant crowded their horses forward, and Jode stepped to the ground with several short pieces of rope in his hand. He reached for Kitty's left wrist but she jerked that hand away and drew her pistol with the other. Before she could bring the pistol to bear, Carson's rawhide quirt popped her on the wrist. The pistol flew from her hand to drop into the dust of the trail as she cried out in pain. "None of that now, missy!" Carson snapped. "You'll only git yourself hurt." She cradled her wrist in her other hand while tears of anger and pain gathered in her eyes. Jode roughly pulled her wrists to the horn of her saddle and lashed them tightly. A few moments later her feet were tethered together under Socorro's belly and the three outlaws led Kitty away from the trail.

Forty-seven

After Harvey left Lila at the hotel, he went back down the street toward the Emporium. He was pretty sure that his money and Lila's surprise were on that day's stage, and if they were, they'd be in the safe at the store. When he stepped up onto the boardwalk in front of the door, he could still see the imprint in the dust that Hobie Parks had made when the stranger had tipped him over. He chuckled to himself and stepped through the door into the cool, shady interior of the building. Delbert Hoskins, the proprietor and Melody's father, was putting away the last of the goods that had arrived on the stage. The shipment was mainly a selection of pretty bolts of cloth and a few fancy fixings he'd bought with the idea that some of the local ladies might like them. "I suppose you've come for the items that came in on the stage, eh, Harvey?" Del said. He straightened from where he'd been squatted down to put an ebony comb in the glass fronted display case.

"Yep. That is if everything I was expectin' got here."

"Tell me what it is, and I'll tell you whether or not it came," Del countered with a knowing smile on his face.

"You know good an' well what at least one of those things was, Del," Harvey challenged, a mock scowl on his face. "You helped me pick it out of the catalog."

"Oh, that. Yep, it's here. Along with an envelope made out to you from the bank in Ellsworth. Hang on a minute, and I'll get 'em." The storekeeper walked to the iron safe that was bolted to the wall in the back of the room and spun the dial. He returned a couple of minutes later and handed Harvey the envelope, along with a small parcel wrapped in brown paper and tied with stout twine. "I guess this must be it," he said casually.

Harvey took the small package from Del and untied the twine. When he unfolded the paper, he found a small velvet box inside. He carefully tipped back the hinged lid to reveal what lay nestled in silky cloth inside. The small diamond on its delicate gold band caught the light from the windows at the front of the store and flashed brightly as Harvey tilted the box from side to side. "That look like what you thought it would, Harvey?" Del wanted to know. Harvey just nodded, spellbound. In his hand lay his future, if all went the way it should. A future he would build with his own two hands and the help of a good woman: a woman he'd left once before, but would never leave again.

Just then, Melody came from the back of the store. "Dad, have you seen any sign of Kitty? She was coming into town to spend the night, and she should have been here long before now. I'm getting worried."

"I haven't, my dear," Del replied. "But maybe since it's such a beautiful day, she's just taking her time getting here."

"Perhaps you're right," Melody sighed. "I guess before I call out the cavalry, I should give her a little more time. But not much more--it's getting late." She turned on her heel and went back to her task, but the thought that Kitty might be in trouble wouldn't let her be. Her mind would not be at ease until she saw Kitty's big blue horse pull up at the rail out front.

Harvey stuck the bank envelope into an inside pocket of his vest. "I reckon I'd best get moving," he said. "I think I'll take this down payment out to Hanneman's today; then I won't have to worry about it. He's got the papers all drawn up, and he's just waiting to have the money in hand so he can head back East. See you later." Harvey stepped onto the boardwalk and saw Jesse turning into the saloon. He wanted to show Jesse the ring; at the same time, he wanted to get his down payment to Orville Hanneman, so he turned toward the livery instead. The horse ranch was just as much a part of his future as the ring in his pocket. He had no way of knowing that his immediate future was going to be nothing like what he had planned. Things were about to get complicated. *Real complicated.*

Forty-eight

Jesse and Dog strolled into the Nugget. On a hot afternoon like this a cold beer, if one was to be found, sounded like a good idea. Jesse stopped just inside the door for a moment to let his eyes adjust to the sudden dimness then went on up to the bar. "What can I get ya?" asked the bartender, a chunky sort with slicked-back hair whose upper lip was generously adorned with a wide handlebar mustache.

"Cold beer, if you've got such a thing," Jesse said.

"As a matter of fact, we do," the fellow replied. "We found an ice cave back yonder," he pointed back over his shoulder, "so we keep the kegs cold all the time. I'll be right back." He picked up a mug and disappeared through a door behind the bar. A few short moments later Jesse was taking his first sip of the first truly cold beer he'd had in quite a while.

"Now that's good," Jesse sighed to no one in

particular. The riffling of cards drew his attention to a table in the back corner of the room. A frock-coated figure who appeared to be only slightly older than Jesse's twenty years sat shuffling and dealing a less-than-pristine deck of cards, laying out a game of solitaire. When the bartender returned from the man's table Jesse asked, "New gambler?"

"Yep. Come in on the afternoon stage. Says his name's Noonan."

"Ever seen him before?"

"Can't say as I have."

"Well, maybe I'll wander over and say hello." Jesse picked up his mug and walked to the table. Indicating a chair at the side of the table he asked, "Is this seat taken?"

"If you sit down there, it is. What can I do for you?" The man gazed mildly at Jesse, but Jesse had the feeling there was more to this gent than met the eye.

"I noticed you were new in town, and thought I'd come over and say hello." Jesse pulled the chair around so that he could see all of the doors, and sat down. The glint of amusement in the stranger's eyes told Jesse he'd noticed. "Jesse Thompson," he offered, extending his hand across the table.

"Shanghai Noonan." They shook hands. Jesse looked the other man in the eye.

"What pedigree would a handle like that one come from, if you don't mind my asking? No offense intended, of course." Jesse gave Noonan his most innocent smile.

"You may have noticed that my tan is natural," Noonan said with a smile of his own. "I'm part Chinese, part Apache, and the rest Irish. That's where the Noonan comes from. My mother named me something only someone who speaks Cantonese can pronounce, so I ended up with the nickname Shanghai early on, and it's pretty much stuck."

"I reckon the Irish part explains the freckles," Jesse quipped.

"I reckon," Noonan drawled, "that I'm what you might call one of a kind."

"I'd say," Jesse answered.

Harvey strolled down the street toward the smithy, intending to saddle the dun and head for what was soon to be his ranch. Things were definitely looking up, as far as he could tell. He rounded the corner of the building and noticed a buggy sitting idle near the building. When Harvey stepped in the door Lars was bent over the forge. "When did you get the wagon?" he called to the smith.

"It ain't a vagon, it's a buggy!" Lars declared. "I've had it for a while, just been doin' some vork on it. T'ought I might be able to rent it out."

"Have you got anything you can hitch to it?" Harvey asked with surprise and speculation in his voice.

"Of course I do. How else you t'ink I'd be able to rent it out?" Lars replied. "Got a real pretty bay mare out yonder dat'll make dat t'ing stand up and race if you let her."

"How much to rent it for the rest of the day, if I bring it back tonight?" Harvey had just gotten an idea that really appealed to him. He'd rent the buggy and take Lila with him to Hanneman's; then he could propose along the way. It'd be perfect.

"For you, two dollars. Anybody else, dey have to pay more dan dat. And de price includes me hitchin' de horse to it."

"Sold," Harvey said. "Get 'er hitched up an' I'll be on my way." The smith put down his hammer and went out into the complex of corrals behind the building. He returned in a few minutes with a sleek bay mare whose coat gleamed from brushing. Lars moved to the back wall of the building and took down a set of harness; Harvey was soon sitting in the buggy with the reins in his hand, ready to go. "See ya tonight, Lars. It'll probably be after dark when I get back." Lars lifted a hand as Harvey clucked to the mare. With a flip of the reins, Harvey was off to the hotel. The mare trotted smartly along with her head high.

Bringing the buggy to a stop in front of the hotel, Harvey climbed down and tied the mare to the hitch rail. He noticed that the door was nearly closed. Lila normally kept it open this time of day if the weather was decent. Harvey stepped up on the porch and moved to the door. Just inside the entrance, where the braided rag rug should have been was a patch of dust on bare floorboards. Things were getting stranger all the time.

Cautiously Harvey reached out with his left hand and gave the door a gentle shove. His right hand hovered over his holstered pistol. The door swung open silently and Harvey slipped quickly inside, flattening his back against the wall. The rug lay in a crumpled heap in the middle of the floor, and the back door leading outside--behind and to the left of the counter--was standing wide open, swinging slightly in the light breeze. Harvey drew his gun and called, "Lila? Are you here?" When there was no answer Harvey stepped away from the wall. His head swiveled as he tried to look everywhere at once, foreboding rising in his mind.

"Lila!" There was still no sound so Harvey advanced further into the room.

The fluttering of paper turned his attention to the counter top and the knife stuck there. He hurried to the counter and the paper pinned to the pine boards. He holstered his gun, reached out to yank the knife from the wood and dropped it onto the counter. Unable to believe what he was seeing, he picked up the paper. The note was written in a fine copperplate script.

My dear Misters Palmer and Thompson,
I cordially invite you to the fair city of Horton for a discussion of past, present, and future evils that have been perpetrated against me and mine by the two of you. Come alone. The lives of Kitty Moynahan and the hotel lady depend on it. Be there three days from today at noon.
Most Uncordially Yours,
Howdy Baxter

Harvey could hardly accept what he had just read. He glared at the paper in his hand, anger pulsing through him as he realized what Baxter's foul plan meant; a curse escaped his lips when he reread the part about Kitty and Lila. Baxter had taken the two women and was using them as bait to get his hands on Harvey and Jesse. He knew Baxter wanted revenge on him for his brother's death. From the tone of the note in his hand, it was also obvious that Baxter intended to kill Jesse. And if the stories were true, Baxter wouldn't stop there. Kitty and Lila were sure to be killed as well.

Exhaling slowly, Harvey gathered his thoughts. There was no sense in rushing off half-cocked. He had been to Horton before, so he already had a fair idea of how the land lay. With three days to plan, surely he and Jesse could figure out something. But first, he had to find Jesse.

Harvey folded the paper, stuck it in his vest pocket, and started for the door. When he felt the ring box in the same pocket he turned back. Taking the box from his pocket, he opened the door to what Lila loosely referred to as her "office", and placed the ring and the bank draft in one of the pigeonholes of the rolltop desk which sat against the near wall, then rolled the desktop closed. He closed the door behind him and pulled his Colt from the holster to check the loads. It hadn't changed from this morning, but it was something he always did before he went to war.

Forty-nine

There was no sign of Jesse in either the Bluebonnet Café or the Emporium as Harvey hurriedly searched the town for his partner. He strode rapidly toward the Nugget. As he stepped inside he heard Jesse call out, "Hey, Harvey. There's somebody here I want you to meet." Jesse waved from his seat at a table with the dandy Harvey had seen dump Hobie Parks on his head. When Harvey got to the table Jesse said, "Harvey Palmer, meet Shanghai Noonan."

Impatiently shaking the proffered hand without even a glance at its owner, Harvey said, "I need to talk to you outside right now, Jesse. It's important." Jesse's smile vanished at Harvey's tone.

"What's wrong?"

"Outside!" Harvey snapped as he turned toward the door.

"Harvey!" Jesse's voice rang out.

Harvey turned back and saw that Jesse was still

seated. "What is the matter with you?" Jesse demanded.

Harvey yanked the folded sheet of paper from his pocket and slammed it down in front of Jesse. "That's what's the matter with me! Read that!" Jesse quickly scanned the note that Howdy Baxter had written, then looked up at Harvey who stood with his arms crossed on his chest and storm clouds rising on his features.

"What do you propose we do next?" Jesse said in a steely tone.

"I 'propose' that we ride to Horton and kill Howdy Baxter!" Harvey retorted. "Does that work for you, or do I have to go alone?"

"If I may stick my nose in someone else's business, did you just mention Howdy Baxter?" Shanghai suddenly interjected. Harvey nodded suspiciously, and Noonan went on. "I don't suppose there's a Mexican gentleman named Montez riding with him, is there?"

"I don't know what his name is, but there's a Mexican with Baxter. Or at least there was," Harvey replied roughly. "But if he's ridin' with Baxter, it's pretty likely he ain't a gentleman."

"Either way, I'd like to draw cards in this game, if I may," Noonan said calmly. "I have a score to settle with *Señor* Montez."

"Suit yourself. But if you can't keep up you'll get left behind. Come on, Jesse."

Jesse had been watching this exchange with some concern. He was pretty sure they were going to need help of some sort, but the note had said that they were to come alone. They'd have to figure out a way to use this Noonan fellow, if they could do it without letting Baxter and whoever was with him know they had an ace in the hole. And here life had been looking so simple and uncomplicated just a few minutes ago.

He let out a sigh as he addressed his partner.

"Wait a minute, Harve," Jesse said quietly. Harvey stopped with an impatient look clouding his face.

"Are you comin', or aren't ya?" Harvey demanded.

"I think we'd best sit and contemplate for a minute," Jesse replied. "We need a plan."

"My plan is to ride in there and kill Baxter and anybody else I have to kill to get Lila back!" Harvey declared as he turned angrily toward the door.

"Harvey." He kept on walking. "Harvey!" Still his pace didn't slow. "Dammit Palmer, I said sit down!" There was no denying the steel in Jesse's voice. Harvey stopped as if he'd been slugged in the back, and swung around slowly.

"What did you say?" he asked mildly, but the thunderheads behind his eyes told a different story.

"I said sit down!" Jesse was equally as adamant. "If we go off half-cocked, we'll just get Lila and Kitty both killed. We need a plan other than just riding into Horton, wherever that is, and killing Baxter, no matter how soothing that would be. Now are you comin' back here to help me get something figured out, or am I coming over there and kickin' your butt hard enough to make you listen?" Harvey stood with his fists clenched, glaring at Jesse. After a moment, he finally relaxed.

"You'd try it too, wouldn't you?" he asked as the storm clouds in his gaze began to clear.

"I'd not only try it, I'd get it done," Jesse said with conviction. "But it'd hurt us both and we don't need that right now. So come on. Let's figure out a way to get Lila and Kitty out of there, and get Baxter and whoever else's with him in a jail cell at the same time, without getting ourselves or the women killed."

"A jail cell or an unmarked grave." Both Harvey and Jesse turned toward the source of the measured, icy words. In the heat of the moment, they'd both forgotten about Noonan. His remark stopped them both in mid-stride.

"I assume your talkin' about your beef with Montez, correct?" Harvey asked as he approached the table and pulled a chair around to face Jesse and his companion. Noonan nodded. "Just what is it you've got against him?" Harvey went on.

"He was one of a band of renegades who killed my sister," Noonan said, cold hatred in his voice. "She was living in a convent near a small village down on the border while she tried to decide whether or not she had a true calling as a nun. Montez wasn't riding with Baxter then, but he and the crew he was with raided the village, killed a lot of people, and burned the convent after having their way with several of the postulates." He stopped for a moment and studied his hands where they lay on the table.

He took a deep, shaking breath, then continued in a heavy tone. "The bastards shot the priest and three nuns, and the girls, then rode off. One of the girls lived long enough to identify Montez and one other man. That other man is feeding the ants in the desert down near Nogales. He was still screaming when I rode off on the trail of the others. He was more than happy to give me their names." Noonan paused; his earlier smile had been replaced by a snarl of feral rage, which quickly disappeared under a gaze of pure ice. "I made a vow to my mother and grandmother that I would find those men and avenge my sister. Montez is the only one left. I heard in Las Vegas that he's riding with Baxter."

Jesse and Harvey both stared at Noonan, stunned by his story. At last Jesse took a deep breath and said, "I understand why you're out to get Montez. But I want him in jail, not staked down in the middle of an anthill. If you can't live with that you'd best not come with us."

Noonan returned Jesse's gaze and said, "If that's what it takes to keep Montez from hurting any other young girls then I'm in. But if I shoot, I shoot to kill. Agreed?"

"Agreed," Jesse answered. "Now, we need a plan and we need to know where we're going. The note says we've got three days. Has either one of you ever been to this Horton place?"

Harvey began to describe Horton and the surrounding area to the two men but as he talked he was watching Noonan closely. It never hurt to know as much about a man's riding companions as possible. Noonan had already told them a good bit about himself but what they didn't know could get them killed.

"I've been there. It's a ghost town," Harvey volunteered. He went on to describe Horton and the surrounding terrain, watching Noonan intently as he talked. What they didn't know about the man could get them all killed. "It sits in a box canyon about thirty miles or so from here. It was a boomtown for a little while, then the riches ran out an' everybody left. Last time I was through there a few of the buildings were still standing but they were pretty well fallin' down. I don't know what's left there now."

"How do we get into the canyon?" Jesse asked as a plan began to form in his mind.

" There's a winding trail just wide enough for a wagon leading into that canyon. The trail's hard to find, and it's a prime site for an ambush. There's an old mine shaft that goes back into the bluff at the head of the canyon an' he'll probly have the girls there, 'cause it's easy to guard."

"Hold on a minute," Jesse interrupted. "I've got an idea. Is there a way up to the top of that bluff?"

"If I recall correctly there's an old trail that comes in from over back of Granite Peak," Harvey told him. "It comes up through a steep-sided draw, and ends up on top of that bluff. There's also a trail up from the Horton side. I don't know if Baxter knows about it but we have to figure that he does."

"We need to get somebody on top of that bluff, 'cause Baxter'll damn sure have somebody up there. Maybe more than one somebody," Jesse put in. He looked over at Noonan. "How quiet can you be?"

"Ask Running Deer," Noonan replied enigmatically.

"Who in the world is Running Deer?" Jesse asked, taking the bait.

"Running Deer *used to be* an Apache warrior who thought he was better than me because I'm not full-blooded Apache. He challenged me to a duel in the desert. The war chief of his band put us out at night, a mile apart, with nothing but a pair of moccasins and a knife each. Only one of us could come back." He sat back and lapsed into silence. Since he was the one telling the story, he was obviously the only one who had returned from the desert, in which case it sounded like they'd seriously underestimated the man.

"Here's what we're gonna do," Jesse said suddenly. His two companions sat forward in their chairs, listening intently. "I don't think Baxter will ambush us on the trail; he'll want to look us in the eye when he kills us. Noonan, I want you on top of that bluff well before we go into the canyon. I think you can be pretty damned sure there'll be somebody up there; it'll be your job to take him out before we ride in. The note says we're to be in Horton at twelve o'clock, so you'll need to be in place by eleven or so. With you on the high ground, we'll have a better chance of getting ourselves and the girls out of there alive. Just make sure you don't get killed before we have them out."

"If it's all the same to you, I'd really rather not get killed afterward, either," Noonan commented dryly.

"That's not up to me," Jesse told him. "So, are we set?" Both men indicated their agreement with Jesse's plan.

Harvey stood and stretched. "Are we gonna send word to the Bar M?"

Jesse looked at him for a few ticks of the old Regulator clock over the mirror back of the bar. "I owe that much to Dennis," Jesse said thoughtfully, "but I'm afraid if we just send someone out there, he'll come riding in here with all his hands and that's the last thing we need. I'll ride out there and tell him myself. I'll try to convince him to let us do it our way." With a crooked grin, Jesse stood and put on his hat. "I need to pay him for the horse anyway. I'll be back tonight some time. Dog, you stay here." Jesse left the saloon and headed for the livery stable.

Fifty

The shadows were long around the ramshackle buildings of Horton. Although it wasn't especially late, the lay of the surrounding ridges caused dusk to come early. The two groups of outlaws came together just outside the mouth of the passageway into the box canyon; Carson and Montez smiled evilly at each other secretly as the men examined each other's prizes. Lila sat erect in her saddle, her chin held high, refusing to acknowledge the leers the two vicious gunmen aimed toward Kitty and herself. Kitty's eyes were downcast, and she seemed to be looking at nothing in particular; when her horse shifted sideways, however, Lila caught a flashing glance from those intelligent blue eyes. The young woman was anything but downhearted; it was obvious to Lila that she was already planning some vengeance of her own. She'd never been handled in her life as she'd been handled today, and somehow these men were going to pay. And they were going to pay in blood, if necessary.

Jesse took the trail to the Bar M at a trot. As he rode his eyes scanned the surrounding terrain but his thoughts were on Kitty. He was examining his feelings. He knew how much she meant to him, and he was mad at himself for being the cause of her kidnapping. As he rounded a bend in the trail, the glint of sunlight on steel caught his eye. He reined the gray to a stop and bent down from the saddle. It didn't take much of a tracker to read the story in the dust. Here was where Kitty had been kidnapped. Her pistol was still lying half-concealed by the dust that her captor's horses had kicked up. Jesse stepped down and picked up the gun. He blew the dust out of the action and slipped it into a saddlebag then continued on toward the Bar M.

When Jesse drew the gray to a halt in front of the Bar M porch, Dennis was leaning against a post waiting for him. "There'd best be a good reason that horse is lathered up the way he is," Dennis said lightly, but the tension in his big frame revealed that he sensed that things were not right.

"There is, sir," Jesse answered. "I don't believe in beating around the bush so I'll say this straight out: Kitty's been kidnapped and I'm the ransom."

Dennis sprang bolt upright and a vehement curse split the air. "Who did it and where is she?" he growled. "We'll be on the trail in an hour with a hangin' rope!"

"If you do, you'll kill her as sure as if you had pulled the trigger yourself!" Jesse exclaimed. His tone caught the attention of the distraught rancher.

"What do ye mean, lad? And this better be good!"

"Howdy Baxter and his men ambushed her on her way to town. They also rode off with Lila Foster from the hotel. They're demanding that Harvey Palmer and I be in a ghost town called Horton at noon three days from today. We have to go there alone, but we've got an ace in the hole. I can't let you ride in there with your crew..."

"What do ye mean, ye can't let me ride in there?" Dennis demanded. "Ye're talkin' about me daughter here, y'know!" he thundered.

Without pausing, Jesse reached into his pocket for his badge. He held the star up for Dennis to see as he said, "Baxter said he'd kill both of the women if he sees anyone but me and Harvey. You'll have to trust us. Not only is this my job, but I think you know how I feel about Kitty."

Dennis stood with his fists clenched. His Irish temper blazed as he contemplated his daughter's perilous situation, and the despicable animal who had instigated it. Moments later, an icy calm washed over him as he reined in his rage. "Alright, deputy, we'll do it your way. But if anythin' happens to me daughter, and I do mean anythin', I'll be huntin' down every one of those mongrels and stringin' their guts from a bobwire fence! I care not how long it takes, nor how much money I'll be spendin' to do it."

"Nothing will happen to her, I promise," Jesse assured the angry rancher, while mentally kicking himself for making a promise he wasn't sure he could keep.

By this time, the gray was cooled out enough to let him drink his fill from the trough near the horse corral. Dennis followed the pair across the ranch yard and now he stood near the corral fence. "I'd like to buy this horse if he's for sale, sir," Jesse said.

"He's not for sale, lad, unless you decide to sell

him," the big rancher replied. "Take him, with my blessin'. But remember ye this: if Palmer and yourself aren't out of there with me daughter by sundown three days from now, we're comin' in. I've known that scum Howdy Baxter for twenty years, and I know he'll do just what he says. He's just as crazy as he acts. By sundown either you and Kitty will be dead, or he will."

Recovering from his surprise at hearing that Dennis knew Baxter, Jesse asked, "How'll you know where to go?"

"I've been livin' here a long time. There's only one ghost town that I know of around here, and that's Horton. I was there a number of times back when it was boomin'."

The gray lifted his head and gave himself a shake. "You'd better either take a different horse or take it easy on that one," Dennis observed.

"I'll just take it easy on this one," Jesse assured him. "He's tougher than mule hide, I'm thinkin', and he and I have an understanding." He tightened the cinch and stepped aboard. Lifting a hand to Dennis, he reined the horse around and heeled him into a jog out of the ranch yard.

Fifty-one

Flickering orange light made eerie shadows dance across the walls of the ramshackle buildings of Horton. The greedy flames of the campfire hungrily devoured the old boards they were fed, snapping and popping in satisfaction. A sudden flare of heat and light signaled the demise of a handful of greasewood stems as the orange of the flames turned brilliant blue for a moment. A scorpion, driven by the heat from its refuge in a pile of sticks, stood for a moment with its whiptail curled over its back and pincers raised in challenge. Immediately the flames enveloped it, shriveling then bursting its hard carapace. The scorpion's demise went unnoticed by the men who lounged around the fire.

"What do they want with us?" Lila whispered apprehensively to Kitty as they lay, trussed and immobile, at the edge of the pool of yellow light.

"It's pretty obvious they're going to use us to get at Harvey and Jesse," Kitty murmured back. "I heard one of the men say that they'd get even in three days." The two women sat with their hands bound in their laps. Their feet were bound with rope, and a set of leg shackles looped from Lila's right ankle to Kitty's left.

It had delighted Rule Carson no end to get the job of shackling the two together, but it had cost him. When his hand had strayed above the top of Kitty's riding boot she had lashed out and her bound feet had slammed into Carson's chest. He had been squatting, and the powerful blow had rolled him onto his back. As he fell, the rowels of her spurs had raked across his arm and hand, tearing skin and flesh. With her bound hands, she had partially blocked the open-handed slap he gave her in return, but she had still gotten a split lip out of the encounter. Before he could hit her again, Howdy Baxter had intervened. "Keep your hands to yourself, Rule, and that sort of thing won't happen."

Carson now sat across the fire from the women with his crudely bandaged hand in his lap. He was staring sullenly at them as they sat against the relatively solid wall of what had once been the rather grandiosely named *Palace Saloon*. He was muttering threats under his breath. "Whatsa matter, Rule?" Marty Bannon spoke up. "'Fraid we'll tell the boys back at the ranch you got whupped by a girl?" At the best of times, Carson was pushy, always questioning Bannon's orders. And since Marty himself had gotten his clock cleaned by Jesse Thompson in the Nugget, Carson had steadily become more rebellious and insolent, at least when Baxter wasn't around. So, from Bannon's point of view, it was nice to see him get his comeuppance. And it was even nicer to see Kitty give it to him.

"Don't mess with me, Marty!" Carson snarled. "I'll shoot your ass and leave ya ta rot, Howdy or no Howdy. What's he gonna do with them women, anyway?"

"In case you don't remember, I'm using them for bait, you idiot!" Baxter snapped from where he sat in the shadows with a blanket around his shoulders. "You two can kill each other on your own time. Your time is mine until after we kill Palmer and Thompson. Until then both of you pull in your horns. If anybody shoots anybody other than those two around here, it will be me. So both of you just shut up."

Fifty-two

Besides the carpetbag he'd taken off the stage with him, Shanghai Noonan had a small ironbound trunk he'd asked the stage driver to deliver to the hotel for him. The trunk now sat at his feet with its lid hinged back against the front of the bureau that stood in his hotel room. He was perusing the trunk's contents absently while thoughts swirled through his head. He sensed that he was finally going to come to a reckoning with Cholo Montez. He'd been on the bandit's trail for two years, and he'd killed several men along the way. A couple of them had just been in the wrong place at the wrong time and had backed the wrong play. The rest had been in on the raid on San Sabalo that had killed his sister Bella...

Sighing, he reached into the trunk and pulled out a pair of Apache moccasins and a pair of deerskin breeches. A beaded, long-sleeved hunting shirt came next. Under the shirt, each nestled into its own velvet-lined box, lay a matched pair of Smith & Wesson Model 3 Russian revolvers. He looked down at the gleaming metal, then drew out a holster rig and laid it on the bed beside him. He lifted the heavy guns from their nests and opened each of them one at a time and spun the cylinder. After listening to the well-oiled sounds they made he laid them on the striped brocade bedspread.

He stood and removed what he thought of as his "gambler disguise", carefully folding the garments into the trunk. He kept out only a derringer in a small holster which he strapped to his wrist with the butt of the gun pointing down. He stepped into the breeches and pulled the shirt over his head. He slung the gun belt around his waist and loaded the guns from a box of cartridges in the trunk then holstered them. The loops on the belt were full.

Noonan reached up and twisted his long black hair into a braid that hung down to his shoulder blades. He tied the end of the braid with leather string, then bent and stepped into the moccasins. Settling the gun belt on his hips, he reached for the doorknob. If he was going to be hunting, he'd need a horse. A hidden pocket in the lining of his gun belt held more than enough cash to finance one last hunt, and then he could get on with his life. He just hoped he could return to some semblance of a normal life after all he'd done in the last few years to avenge his sister. The Good Book said that vengeance belonged to the Lord, but Noonan hadn't wanted to wait on the Lord's timetable. He may have damned himself to Hell for all eternity; but all that had really mattered to him for the last two years was finding the men who'd killed Bella. And now there was only one left.

Lars was putting his shop to bed for the night when a man in buckskins, his dark hair hanging in a braid down his back, appeared in the doorway. "Help you?" Lars asked cautiously.

"I'll be needing a horse for a few days," the man's deep voice replied. "I'll want something that's trail-broke and won't spook at every little thing. And I want something with some bottom. I might need to cover some country."

"I've got vhat you're after, but it ain't gonna come cheap," Lars replied. "Dere's a sorrel out yonder dat I t'ink'll vork for ya, but ye'd best go look him over. Let me know vhat you t'ink."

"I'll do that." Noonan headed to the horse corrals and found the only sorrel horse there. He slid through the rails and walked slowly up to the short-coupled, easy-moving animal. He spoke to the horse, then grabbed a handful of mane and vaulted lightly to its broad back and heeled the horse into a trot around the corral, using his legs for control. He nudged the horse into a lope, then let him drop back to a walk. After a few circuits of the corral, he swung his leg over the horse's neck and slid to the ground. "You'll do," he told the sorrel. Noonan returned to the barn and asked, "How much for a week, with a saddle and bridle?"

"Vith a McClellan an' a hackamore he'll cost you ten dollars. Don't need anyt'ing else on dat fella."

"You have a deal, friend. That's pretty much of a horse." Noonan reached into his pocket for the money. He handed the coins to Lars and extended his hand to close the deal. "I probably won't need him for a couple of days, but one never knows. When I do, it will be on short notice."

"Not a problem, Mister, uh..."

"Noonan. Shanghai Noonan. Call me Shanghai."

"Alright, Shanghai it is. De saddle is on de rack over yonder," Lars pointed to the back of the shop. "An' de hackamore's on a peg alongside of it."

"Thanks." Noonan strode from the shop. Lars watched him go, scratching his chin. From the looks of things somebody was going to be in deep trouble, and soon. It was easy to see that the young man in the buckskin clothing was on the hunt.

Harvey sat at the table in the saloon long after Jesse and Noonan left. He sat staring at his hands on the table in front of him for at least an hour before he came back to himself with a shake. He felt like he should be doing something, but there wasn't really anything to do until Jesse got back, which wouldn't be for several hours yet. Finally he stood and said, "Come on, Dog," and went out into the early evening twilight, heading toward his rental house, followed by the shepherd. He was passing the Emporium when he remembered what Melody had said about Kitty being late. As much as it pained him to have to upset Melody, he knew it would be better for her to know than to wonder.

"May I help you, Mister Palmer?" Melody asked brightly as he stepped inside. Her father was waiting on another man whose back was to Harvey. The man was dressed in buckskins and had a black braid hanging down his back, and a pair of pistols belted on his hips. At the mention of Harvey's name Noonan swung around. Harvey was startled when he realized who it was.

"What are you doin' dressed like that?" he asked, not sure quite what to think.

"We are going hunting, are we not?" Noonan asked.

"Well, yeah, some of us are." Harvey still wasn't sure just what he was seeing.

"I'm getting ready to hunt. I needed some

more cartridges, and Mister Hoskins just happens to have them, along with some other things I need." He indicated the two boxes on the counter. "What about yourself?"

"I came to talk to Miss Melody." Harvey turned toward the young lady in question, who stood with a puzzled look on her face. "Miss Hoskins, I'm afraid I have some bad news," he said stiffly. "Kitty Moynahan has been kidnapped, and is in serious trouble. Jesse Thompson and I, with some help from this gent here, are going to get her back."

"What?" she exclaimed, although Harvey was sure she'd understood every word. "Why? Who would do such a thing?"

Del Hoskins cursed and started for the door. "I'll get some men together and we'll get her back. You two wait right here."

Noonan stopped him with a firm hand on his arm. "I'm afraid I can't let you do that, sir," he said gently as Del tried to yank his arm loose. "Howdy Baxter has her and has said he'll kill her if anyone other than Harvey and Jesse are seen; I have no doubt he'll do exactly what he says."

"Howdy Baxter!" Hoskins spat. "Somebody should have shot that son of a..."

"Father!" Melody exclaimed. "I don't think that's necessary!"

"We may end up doing exactly that, sir, but for the moment, you'll have to let us handle it our way. We..."

"You just said that Harvey and Jesse are the only ones Baxter will let close without killing Kitty," Hoskins interrupted. "What about you?"

"I don't plan on being seen, sir." Noonan's flat

statement stifled Hoskins's protests, cutting them off abruptly. "I lived in an Apache *rancheria* as a boy. Discerning my presence will take more than those men have to give. What do I owe you for the cartridges?"

Hoskins looked over at Harvey. "You goin' along with what this fella is sayin', Harvey?"

"I reckon," Harvey drawled. "We can't do it alone, but we can't take a whole herd of men with us either. If we don't do this Baxter's way, he'll kill the women."

Melody picked up on the word 'women' immediately. "What do you mean, 'women'?" she demanded. "Who else have they taken?"

"They also have Lila Foster," Harvey said bitterly. "They say they'll kill them both if…" He stopped, unable to continue. He didn't see the look father and daughter traded. Del of course knew about the ring, since he had ordered it for Harvey. But Melody hadn't known a thing until her father had told her.

"So you see, that's why we can't have you alerting the town," Noonan said firmly. "Jesse has ridden out to talk to Miss Moynahan's father and will be back later tonight. Until then, and probably longer, we have to keep this quiet."

"I understand, young man," Hoskins said. "In consideration of the fact that you're going to be helping to bring back both Lila and Kitty, and to bring Howdy Baxter and his men to their just rewards, I will give you those cartridges free of charge. Just get those women back safely."

"We will sir, we will." And like Jesse, Shanghai was uneasy about promising something he wasn't one hundred percent sure he could deliver.

Fifty-three

The moon was down when Jesse turned the tired gray into the main street of Watsonville. "Almost there, horse," he said quietly, patting the horse on the neck. A shadowy figure tilted back in a chair against the wall of the hotel chuckled, though there was little humor in the sound. "Does that critter answer back when you talk to it?" Harvey asked as he brought the chair's front legs back to earth. Before Jesse could answer, Harvey went on. "What'd Dennis say?"

"We've got until sundown on the third day to get the women out. After that, all bets're off. It was all I could do to keep him from stormin' in there right now with his whole crew and hangin' everybody. If Baxter hadn't threatened to kill Kitty and Lila, I think Dennis would have gone stormin' in there anyway, whether I wanted him to or not." Harvey stared at him in disbelief. "It was the best I could do." Jesse stepped down from the saddle and stood with his hands on his hips trying to stretch the kinks out of his back. "Where's Noonan?"

"You ain't gonna believe what I saw this afternoon after you left for the Bar M," Harvey answered obliquely. He stopped and was obviously waiting for Jesse to say something. When nothing was forthcoming but a blank stare, he went on. "I went over yonder to Hoskins's store, an' when I went in there was this gent all dolled up in buckskins--moccasins and all--with a braid hangin' down his back an' a pair of .44 Russians on his hips. When he turned around, it was your so-called 'ace in the hole'. I didn't know whether to laugh or cry."

"I think it might behoove a fella not to laugh at that gent," Jesse said thoughtfully. "I kind of suspect he might not take it kindly."

"Thank you for the vote of confidence, Jesse," Noonan's deep voice called softly. Both men flinched and reached reflexively for their guns. They relaxed minimally when they recognized the voice, and relaxed further when Noonan stepped out into the open. "I'll try not to disappoint you, Harvey."

"See what I mean?" Jesse laughed.

Lila had at last fallen into a fitful sleep when a hand sliding down her cheek and onto her shoulder awakened her abruptly. Her eyes flew open wide and she drew a deep breath, opening her mouth to scream. As she did, a bandanna was shoved roughly into her mouth, stifling the sound before it could begin. "Ah, ah, ah, *señorita*," an accented voice whispered thickly in her ear. Foul breath brushed her cheek. "You don' wan' to wake up thee whole camp, eh?" She stiffened when she felt Montez' hand began to slide further down her body. She drew her legs up to kick, as Kitty had done to Carson earlier, only to have them pinioned by Montez' own legs. While she struggled, his other hand moved down her leg and grasped the hem of her skirt. He began lifting it toward her waist as she tried to shrink away from the hand that was roughly exploring her upper body. Montez had begun to fumble with the buttons of her bodice when a sudden thud stopped his pawing and the outlaw's weight was lifted from her. She watched him tumble across the sandy clearing and it took her a moment to understand what had happened. Then she saw Howdy Baxter, pistol in his hand, draw back his foot to deliver another kick to the ribs of his hapless henchman.

"I thought I told you and Carson to keep your hands to yourselves, Montez!" Baxter hissed. His eyes glittered madly in the last remaining firelight. "I can kill Palmer and Thompson without you if need be. If you so much as look crossways at either of these women again I'll gutshoot you and feed you to the ants, which I will go get myself. Is that clear?" Montez was silent except for the harsh rasping of his breath as he tried to draw some much-needed air into his lungs. Baxter raised his pistol and thumbed back the hammer. "I said, is that clear?" The chorus of clicks yanked Montez' attention from his aching ribs to the gun.

"*Sí*, Howdy," he mumbled, vowing silently that his day would come. He rose shakily to his feet and stumbled toward his bed.

Baxter watched him go, then bent and pulled the bandanna from Lila's mouth and tossed it distastefully into the night. "I am truly sorry about that, Miss Foster," he said formally. "I don't believe it will happen again." He pulled her skirt down over her legs, turned and disappeared into the shadows. She spat, trying to get the taste of the cloth out of her mouth. Right then Lila knew beyond a shadow of a doubt how it felt to want to take the life of another human being. And she hated these men for making her feel that way.

A movement nearby caught Lila's attention. Beside her, Kitty whispered, "Are you alright?"

"Yes. Where were you? Why didn't you say something?"

"I couldn't. That animal gagged me before he grabbed you," Kitty explained. "By the time I got rid of the gag it was all over." She stopped. Her eyes were searching Lila's face, hoping for some trace of understanding. Lila nodded and Kitty let out the breath she was holding. "Let's try and get some sleep. I don't think he'll try anything more tonight." The two lay side by side and closed their eyes. Each was praying that sleep would come and let them forget, if only for a short time, where they were and why they were there. "Hurry, Jesse," Kitty whispered to herself. "Please hurry."

Fifty-four

Daylight crept into the outlaw camp a little at a time. A low ceiling of clouds muted the sun's light and warmth, casting a pall over the ghost town of Horton. The men slowly stirred, glancing at the women from under down-tilted hat brims. It was in each man's mind that Howdy Baxter seemed to be changing, day-by-day. Each minute that passed seemed to be carrying him closer to the brink. It was entirely possible that something could snap in Baxter's unstable psyche, and they would all end up dead long before Harvey Palmer and Jesse Thompson got anywhere close to Horton.

"Hey, Howdy," Marty Bannon called, pointing at the women. "How 'bout we untie these two an' let 'em do the cookin'?" Baxter raised his gaze from the sandy soil between his boots.

"Very well, but tether them short. I don't want them running off. And do it yourself. I don't want to have to shoot one of these other idiots." Baxter continued to mutter under his breath, shaking his head as the men traded looks.

Bannon rose to his feet with a nod. Yawning and scratching, he walked over to where the two women lay feigning sleep. "Up an' at 'em, ladies. You ain't in some fancy hotel," he said, lightly kicking the sole of Kitty's boot. When she opened her eyes and shot a disdainful look his way, he grinned and said, "You two gotta earn your keep somehow, so you're gonna be doin' the cookin'. It's time for breakfast. Your hands'll be loose, but don't get any ideas. We don't necessarily need ya alive, we just need them boys back yonder in Watsonville to think you are. So behave yourselves."

He squatted at their feet. "Don't move. You try to do to me like you did ta Rule last night an' that clout he gave ya'll feel like your momma's kiss." The two women soon found themselves able to move their feet, but the rope that still linked their ankles allowed them to take only short steps. Grabbing an arm of each woman, Bannon effortlessly lifted them to their feet. He untied their hands and allowed them a minute to rub the circulation back into their numb fingers, then pointed to where the packsaddle and sacks of supplies were stacked. "There's the grub. Get at it." Until the scheduled arrival of Harvey and Jesse, cooking would be the two women's reason for living.

Kitty moved gingerly to the canvas-covered cache. Under the canvas she found bacon, potatoes, flour, and coffee. As she was rummaging around in the various bags and pouches, her questing hand found something that seemed out of place. Using her body to shield the object from the men's view, she quickly drew out a small sheath knife. Undoing a button on her blouse, she slipped the knife inside and under the waistband of her skirt. Now she could do some real planning. As she and Lila prepared the food, Kitty's thoughts were churning round and round, looking for a way out of this predicament. She was confident that something would occur to her; she still had a couple of days.

The moon was down and the land was cloaked in deep darkness when three shadowy riders slipped cautiously away from Johansen's shop. They were silent, each lost in his own thoughts, each wondering what the day would bring. It was the third day of Lila and Kitty's captivity, and the grim determination on each man's face told Lars Johansen that today, men would die. Heeling their horses into a trot Harvey, Jesse, and Shanghai moved into the night, set on a mission they all hoped would be successful, although each man would measure success in a different way.

To Jesse, success would be seeing Howdy Baxter, Grant Morgan, and the others in the territorial prison. Harvey's idea of success was bringing Lila back safely and settling down to raise horses and possibly a young Harvey to carry on the Palmer name. And to Noonan, success would be the death of Cholo Montez and the chance to at last lay the spirit of his sister to rest.

The sun had barely begun to lighten the eastern sky when the three drew rein at the mouth of a shallow canyon. "This is where the back door into Horton opens," Harvey said quietly. "You follow the trail up this canyon for about a mile, then it climbs up steep an' levels on out. It'll top out on a butte. That butte's the head end of the box canyon Horton sets in. There'll be a man on top of that butte where he can see the two of us the whole time. You have to make sure he don't get a chance to shoot us."

"What makes you so sure they'll have somebody up there?" Noonan questioned.

"Because that's what I'd do." Harvey turned the dun and rode off without another word. Shanghai and Jesse exchanged looks, then Jesse shrugged and turned the gray to follow Harvey as Noonan heeled Lars's sorrel into the canyon and up the trail.

"Are you ever gonna cut him a break, Harvey?" Jesse asked as he brought the gray alongside the dun.

"If he helps us keep Lila alive, I'll shake his hand and thank him. But if anything happens to her, and I have the first, foggiest idea it was even a little bit his fault, I'll kill him myself." It was obvious from the tight look on Harvey's face that he was deadly serious.

"Suit yourself," Jesse replied. "But that gent's gonna take a sight of killin'." The two rode on in the growing light. At their present pace, they would be early for their rendezvous with Baxter.

Noonan rested his horse. They had been climbing steadily for the better part of an hour, and from the slope of the land he couldn't help but feel that he was getting close to his destination. He searched for a place to leave his horse and found a shaded patch of grass, in a small cove situated out of sight behind a stand of tall sagebrush. He reined the sorrel into the cove, stepped down and picketed the horse where it could reach a trickle of water that seeped out of a crack in the rocks into a small pool. Noonan squatted and cupped some water to his lips, letting the cool liquid slide down his throat. He looked at the position of the sun, nodded to himself and rose, wiping his hand on his pants. He drew his pistols from the holsters and blew some imaginary flecks of dust from the actions, then started forward afoot.

The slope ahead seemed to reach into the blue vault of the sky. As he neared the crest, Noonan sank lower and lower until he was covering the last several yards on his hands and knees. He finally sank completely to his belly and edged forward to where he could look over the top of the bank with only his eyes and the top of his head showing. The ground in front of him was flat and broke off sharply on his left, toward what appeared to be a trail up out of the canyon where Horton had to be. At the far edge of the butte, he could see a small pile of stone amidst an area of brush and tall grass. He scanned the rocks and brush for a long time but nothing moved; he rose, crouching, and slipped into a hiding place near the rocks. It was time to wait for whoever and whatever might come along. He settled down in the grass, out of sight of anyone coming up the trail from below.

About an hour short of midday, Noonan heard a pebble rattle on gravel, followed by a muffled curse. Rule Carson appeared at the head of the cut where the trail rose from Horton, carrying a Sharps rifle slung on his back. The outlaw gave a cursory look around but completely missed seeing the few small signs that Noonan had left of his passage. Satisfied the he was alone at the top of the bluff, Carson unslung the rifle, settled down behind the largest rock and spread a pad of canvas across the top. Cushioning the forearm of the Sharps on the pad, Carson sighted on various objects on the ground below, both near and far, so he would be ready to fire without hesitation. He settled down to wait, invisible to anyone in the canyon below.

The man's back was to Noonan. Shanghai slipped soundlessly from his nest in the grass and rose to a crouching position, a long-bladed knife held securely in his hand. The haft was heavy and made for striking. Noonan held the knife with the blade pointed up. He moved silently up behind Carson with his hand drawn back. Some sixth sense, or possibly some small unconsciously sensed sound, caused Carson to turn his head so that the blow that should have struck him at the base of the skull instead slammed into the side of his neck, stunning him. Shaking his head and trying to push away the effects of the impact, Carson tried to come to his feet, but his body wouldn't obey what his head was commanding. He swung one arm up in an attempt to ward off the second blow. The long blade of Noonan's knife plunged in up to the hilt under Carson's upraised arm as Noonan brought it around in a backhand stab. Carson tried to yell, but only gurgled as the blood flooded his lungs. He spasmed once, then lay still.

Noonan cursed, shaking his head. He hadn't wanted to kill this man, but reflex had taken over after the first blow hadn't connected where he had intended. One man was now out of the fight; he dragged Carson's body off to the side, then went back and kicked loose dirt over the pool of blood. The women were one step closer to safety, and he was one step closer to Montez.

Fifty-five

Harvey took a deep breath and squinted up at the sun. "It's time. I'd rather be early than late." A quick glance of understanding passed between the two men as they mounted their horses and turned toward the passageway. They had already checked their guns; they had each loaded a sixth cartridge in the normally empty chambers of their pistols, then let the hammers down carefully. That extra round might be the difference between life and death for one of them, or for one of the women they were here to save.

The trail was easy to follow. Baxter's men had made several trips through the cut in the rocks, enough to churn up the loose soil. As they rode, Harvey quietly described the terrain and buildings to Jesse as best he could remember. He ended with, "The mineshaft's clear at the far end. I think you were right--that's where Baxter'll be with the women. Noonan should be above and behind them by now if he did his part. Either he's there or he isn't. I reckon we'll find out soon enough."

They rounded the last shoulder of rock and Horton lay in front of them. Alongside the remarkably intact saloon a fire burned, sending up a thin column of smoke. Bedrolls and saddles were scattered about. The outlaws' horses, and Kitty's big blue Appaloosa, were grazing inside a rope corral strung between some of the tumbledown buildings. The horses' heads came up and Carson's buckskin nickered a greeting to the newcomers.

Hank Jenkins stood near the fire. "Howdy's up yonder." He pointed up the canyon.

"You go up ahead of us," Harvey ordered. "I don't want anybody behind me." Hank started to protest and Harvey said, "Walk or die."

"Mister Palmer," Hank began again, "You can believe me when I say I din't have nothin' to do with kidnappin' them two ladies, an' if you give me a chance I'll be outta here so fast it'll make yer head spin." He waited for Harvey's response; Harvey stared at him silently. "I admit I was trailin' you. But huntin' a man is one thing: kidnappin' women is a whole other bucket of fish. I don't wanna git hung."

"Why didn't you just leave?" Harvey asked harshly.

"'Cause Howdy woulda kilt me, that's why." Hank answered simply.

"Go on, git!" Harvey snapped. "But don't let me see you anywhere near me or mine again!" Gratefully Hank bobbed his head and picked up his saddle.

Harvey and Jesse started up the canyon. Harvey looked over at Jesse. "You alright with that?"

"I don't have a warrant for him, just Baxter."

"Good enough."

As the two men went on toward the mine, a

furtive movement in a second story window caught Jesse's eye. He gave a short quiet whistle.

"I saw him." Harvey said quietly as they rode on. They passed the last of the buildings and came into sight of the yawning mouth of the mineshaft. Howdy Baxter, Grant Morgan, and Marty Bannon stood in a line in front of the opening; Baxter was standing in the middle of the ore cart track.

The dun and the gray stopped of their own accord twenty yards from the three men. Jesse gave each man in turn a quick, appraising look that easily took stock of guns, position, and available cover. Then he smiled and said, "Hello Grant. Ready for me to arrest you again?" His voice rang from the rocks of the bluff.

To Jesse's surprise, Baxter jumped like he'd been bee-stung. He shot a poisonous look at Jesse then turned to glare at Morgan. "What does he mean, 'arrest you again', Morgan? Did you forget to tell me something I should possibly know?"

Sullenly Grant mumbled, "He's one of Judge Martin's deputies..."

"What? I don't think I heard you correctly."

Grant raised his voice and repeated his words.

"This man is one of Judge Martin's deputies?" Baxter snarled. "And you didn't think I needed to know this?" A storm of mixed emotions broke across Baxter's face, then he was calm again. "No matter. He'll just have to disappear and the Judge will have to find another deputy. Montez!" Baxter raised his voice. "Montez! Bring out our guests!" There was a squeaking of un-lubricated bearings and an ore-cart appeared in the mouth of the tunnel. Seated in the cart back-to-back with their hands tied behind them were the two women. Lila sat facing forward, blinking in the sudden glare of the noon sun. Montez pushed the cart out into the open then stepped up alongside the cart with an insolent grin on his face and his hand on his holstered pistol. His hip was nearly touching the side of the cart next to Lila's left shoulder.

While the women had been waiting in the tunnel, Kitty had told Lila about the knife she'd stolen. She had managed to cut Lila's hands loose and give her the knife before Montez had come back. When the outlaw had appeared, they had settled into stillness and waited under the watchful eye of the outlaw for what would happen next.

The cart came to a stop behind Baxter; almost of its own volition Lila's hand swung the knife up and around, and drove the short blade into the outlaw's back just above the kidney. Montez' hand flew to his back, reaching for the source of the unexpected pain, and Lila reached over and yanked the Colt from the holster on his hip. She jammed the muzzle of the gun against his side and shot Montez twice with his own pistol. Harvey yelled, "Lila! NO!" as guns began to blast all around her.

Fifty-six

Noonan rose up from behind the rocks on top of the bluff when he heard Harvey's shout. He saw Montez fall to the ground with blood covering his back and side and his hand still grasping the hilt of the knife. Noonan had time only to think that Lila had saved him some trouble, when a bullet caromed off the rocks in front of him and whistled past his head. He spun to look toward the saloon and saw the cloud of powder smoke drifting from the upstairs window where Jode Benson knelt with his rifle lifted for another shot.

Noonan reached down and picked up the Sharps that Carson had left when he passed on to his reward, and snugged the butt against his shoulder. With a quick prayer that the sights would be close enough, he cocked the hammer and squeezed the set trigger. He quickly shifted to the other trigger, let out the rest of the breath he had been holding, and touched just the tip of his finger to the trigger. The blast sent a five hundred grain, soft-lead bullet through the wall just below the windowsill, ripping away most of Jode's left hand. His rifle fell from the window to clatter on the hard ground below as he screamed and clasped his mangled hand between his thighs.

As Montez fell, Harvey and Jesse dove from their horses, drawing their pistols as they scrambled for cover. Each scanned the area for Howdy Baxter, but he was nowhere in sight. Grant Morgan, shooting as he ran, was lumbering toward a pile of ancient timbers that lay stacked near the mine entrance. He took cover behind the pile and quickly reloaded. A bullet notched the crown of his hat and he flinched. How things could have fallen apart so fast was beyond his understanding. At the moment all he could think of was how fast Jesse had killed Cutter Davis, and just how easy he himself could get dead in the next few minutes. Those were not comforting thoughts.

Lila sat in the ore cart holding the smoking pistol in her hand, stunned by what she had just done. She stared at the gun with her eyes wide; the thought ran frantically through her head, over and over, that she had just killed a man. She had taken a human life. Never mind that the man was an outlaw who had killed who knew how many innocent people; never mind that he had fondled her body and that she had only been saved from something worse by Howdy Baxter's intervention. She had killed Montez, and she was unsure of what to do next. Dimly she heard the gunfire around her, but she was lost in confusion until Kitty shouted her name. When that still didn't get Lila's attention, Kitty reached out and kicked her foot.

Startled, Lila came to her senses. The pistol fell

from her hand into the bottom of the ore cart. "Untie me, Lila!" Kitty was shouting. "We have to get out of here!" Lila reached for the ropes that bound Kitty's wrists, and soon the young woman was rubbing the circulation back into her hands and reaching down for the dropped pistol at their feet. "Come on!" Kitty yelled, grabbing Lila's arm with her free hand. The two women helped each other out of the cart, and Lila let out a shriek when she stepped on the still, limp body of Montez. "Back to the tunnel!" Kitty told her. "We should be safe in there!" They disappeared into the tunnel, bullets kicking up dirt at their heels.

Placing her back against the tunnel wall, Kitty peeked back outside with the pistol raised. Baxter appeared beside the ore-cart, turning his guns toward Harvey and Jesse. She leveled the Colt in his direction, but before she could pull the trigger, he disappeared behind a pile of mine tailings. "Damn," she cursed to herself. It wouldn't have hurt her feelings one bit to shoot Howdy Baxter dead on the spot.

Bannon heard the boom of Carson's Sharps and expected to see either Harvey or Jesse slammed to the dirt. He was astonished to see splinters fly from the saloon wall instead. There had to be someone besides Carson up on top of the bluff, but Bannon was too close to the wall of rock to see who it was. With a curse he ran for the trail to the top of the bluff. If he could get up there without getting shot, he'd have Palmer and Thompson right where he wanted them.

Jesse saw Bannon lunge toward the boulders marking the start of the trail and snapped off a shot, but the bullet ricocheted from one of the rocks. Chips of granite and bits of lead sprayed Bannon as he scrambled up the trail. Jesse decided to leave Shanghai to take care of Bannon; he had his hands full down here. He rolled over next to Harvey, behind a small rise in the ground, and yelled over the gunfire, "Cover me! I'm goin' after Baxter!" Jesse lunged from the ground and ran for the abandoned ore cart. If he could get to the cart, he should have an angle on Baxter and Morgan. As he ran his Remingtons were blasting. He was hoping to keep the outlaws' heads down long enough for him to reach his goal. Behind him, Harvey picked up the Winchester he had yanked from its scabbard on his way to the ground and was blasting rounds into the piles of timbers tailings sheltering the two outlaws as fast as he could work the lever.

Jesse dropped to the ground behind the ore-cart. He reached up and took off his hat, sticking a finger into a hole in the crown; He thought, *Man, that was close!* He shucked the empty cartridges from his pistols and reloaded them from his belt, then dropped one of the Remingtons into the left hand holster. He eased himself closer to the ground and peered around the back end of the cart toward where Baxter and Morgan should be. He could see Grant sitting with his back to the pile of timbers, reloading his own pistol.

In a brief lull in the gunfire, Grant heard the telltale clicks of the hammer of the Remington in Jesse's right hand coming to full cock. He looked to his right and saw his own death looking back at him. The bore of the pistol looked bigger than the mineshaft, and the blood drained from Grant's face. There was no way he was going to be able to get a shot off before he was killed. He would have to spin the cylinder, close the loading gate, draw back the hammer, and swing the pistol around, all before Jesse could fire. And that just wasn't going to happen.

Carefully, so as not to be misunderstood, Morgan laid the Colt on the ground between his feet with the loading gate still open. Jesse motioned with the barrel of the Remington; Grant rolled to his knees and began to crawl toward the cart. Just before he left the shelter of the timbers he stopped. "If I go out there your partner is gonna kill me," he whined.

"You shoulda thought of that before you drew cards in this game!" Jesse declared. "But I'll see if I can cover your butt for you. Harvey!" Jesse yelled.

"Yeah!"

"Morgan's comin' out, an' he's unarmed. Don't shoot him! I wanna take at least one prisoner back to Judge Martin."

"If you insist!" Harvey yelled back. "At the moment I'd just as soon kill him as look at him!"

Morgan didn't appear to be especially reassured by Harvey's words, but Jesse told him, "On your feet, Grant. Don't do anything stupid, and you just might live to go back to prison." Morgan rose to his feet and started walking toward Harvey. He held his hands at shoulder level and as he walked he stared at Harvey. He was ready to dive for whatever cover he could find if the barrel of the rifle swung toward him. But when the gunfire came, it came from behind him.

"Morgan, you coward!" Howdy Baxter screamed. Baxter rose from his hiding place in the rocks and triggered three shots into Grant's back, slamming him to the ground. Before Harvey or Jesse could get a shot off Baxter dropped back behind the pile; bullets whined off the rocks. The last thing they'd expected was for Baxter to shoot one of his own men, and they'd been too shocked to fire until it was too late.

Marty Bannon ran hard up the trail to the top of the bluff. The cuts on his face from the rock chips thrown up by Jesse's bullet stung as sweat ran into them. He rounded a curve in the winding trail and slowed to look back. He was out of sight of the fight below, so he stopped and stood, panting. He ejected the empties from his Colt and reloaded it, then started up the trail with the pistol in his hand. There'd been no shooting from the top of the bluff since that one blast from the Sharps, so he wasn't sure if whoever was up there had stayed or gone, and he didn't care. He was headed to the top. If anyone was there, he'd kill him first then kill Palmer and Thompson. If nobody was there he'd just go on and kill Harvey and Jesse and be done with them.

Noonan knelt behind the rocks. From his vantage point he could see Montez' body but little else. He'd heard Baxter's yell, and three shots, but now things were quiet. He stifled the urge to climb down and make sure Montez was dead; that could pretty easily get him shot by Harvey or Jesse, who were expecting him to be on top of the bluff.

He came to his feet and started moving closer to the edge of the bluff. As he took the first step, he heard the faint sound of boot leather scraping on rock. Someone was coming up the trail from below. Noonan holstered the pistol he was holding and drew his knife from the sheath. He ghosted back into the brush to wait.

Bannon eased up the last few yards of the trail as silently as he was able. He stopped just below the top and removed his hat, then moved up just far enough to see the top of the bluff. The first thing he saw was Carson's body. He swore silently and moved up a little further. Now he could see into the nest of rocks where Carson had been, but it was deserted. Moving just his eyes, he continued to survey the area. Whoever had killed Carson was still here somewhere, Bannon was sure of it. And whoever it was, he had to be good to kill Carson without anyone being the wiser. Rule Carson might have been hard to work with, but he'd been tough and canny.

The tiniest movement caught Bannon's eye. Something had disturbed a clump of brush yonder which from Bannon's viewpoint didn't appear to be big enough to hide a rabbit, but he knew looks could be deceiving. He ducked slowly back out of sight and holstered the Colt. He dug his toes in, ready to lunge. He wanted this one alive so he could kill him slowly.

Noonan could see Bannon surveying the clearing. He watched the outlaw's eyes hesitate on Carson's body, then move on. When Bannon's tousled hair slowly slid from view Shanghai listened, waiting to see what the hulking outlaw's next move would be. The answer wasn't long in coming. With a rush, Bannon charged up over the bank with his arms spread to grapple. He covered the distance to the brush in a moment, his teeth bared in a snarl. He was going to get even with somebody and he didn't care who it was.

Shanghai rolled to his feet to meet Bannon's rush but he had no time to get set before they came together with a thud. Bannon's shoulder drove into Noonan's lean belly and slammed him backward and down. The knife flew from his hand, and it skittered away out of reach as the two men rolled across the clearing. They were punching and hammering, each trying to gain an advantage over the other. Bannon was the bigger of the two, but Noonan was faster and in better condition.

The two men rolled apart and sprang to their feet, circling warily. Bannon's shirt was torn and Noonan's braid had untwisted, leaving his hair hanging down around his shoulders. "Why, you ain't nothin' but a worthless 'breed," Bannon snarled. "I've killed better men than you with one hand. You ain't nothin'."

Noonan's temper flared. "My mother didn't think so," he grated and went on the attack. He slipped past Bannon's roundhouse right to smash Bannon's lips with a snapping left. He followed the left with a right to the belly.

Bannon grunted and stepped back, wiping the back of his hand across his mouth. Seeing the blood, Bannon said grudgingly, "But you can hit a little." He swung a ponderous left that caught Noonan in the ribs as he was coming in, stealing his breath. Noonan spun away, but not before a following right caught him on the shoulder blade and knocked him staggering. He caught his balance and charged in, and the two men stood toe-to-toe, punching with both hands. They shuffled back and forth as they continued to land blow after blow. Bannon's right eye was swollen nearly closed from an overhand left; Noonan had a cut on his cheekbone that washed blood across the lower part of his face, and he was sure in a lucid moment that several teeth were loose. His ribs ached with every punch he threw, but he ignored them in the heat of battle.

Noonan threw a right to Bannon's heart, then another. Bannon's hands sagged for a moment, but he brought them back up, only to have Shanghai slam a left to the same place. Bannon's hands dropped, and a slashing right slammed into his already-broken nose, smashing bone and tearing skin. Blood fountained from Bannon's mangled face, but before Shanghai could step away, Bannon rushed with his arms spread. The snarl on his face was fearsome to behold.

Noonan threw a quick glance over his shoulder. He could see the edge of the bluff and knew instinctively what Bannon would try to do. He backpedaled swiftly, trying to give himself some room to maneuver, but a lucky grab by Bannon caught the shoulder of his buckskin shirt. Knowing how little space he had, and with a mental shrug and apology to Jesse for what he was about to do, Shanghai reached up and got a double handful of Bannon's shirtfront. He dropped to the ground on his back and brought the outlaw down with him. He shoved his heels up into the big outlaw's belly and pushed upward and over his head. With a yell of pure terror, the big gunman soared out and over the edge of the bluff. Noonan lay panting, trying to draw a deep breath but his ribs wouldn't allow it. He ached all over, but forced himself into a sitting position, feeling of his teeth with the tip of his tongue. He struggled to his feet and moved gingerly to the edge of the bluff to see what had become of Marty Bannon, although he had a pretty good idea already.

Fifty-seven

Bannon's scream echoed through the box canyon. There was a thud and a clang and the crackle of broken bones as the big outlaw struck the ore-cart rails crosswise. The impact instantly broke his neck and back, and shattered his skull. Harvey, Jesse, and the two women all stared at this sudden apparition that had appeared in front of them; Howdy Baxter did not. He had been belly-crawling through the thick grass near the mine entrance, trying to reach the women, and Bannon's sudden arrival gave him the chance he needed.

With a lunge, Baxter came off the ground and leapt into the tunnel where Kitty stood transfixed by the sight of Bannon's broken corpse. The pistol in her hand was forgotten. Baxter slammed her against the rough rock wall, banging her head and knocking her nearly unconscious. The pistol was jolted from her hand and skittered into the daylight outside the tunnel. Baxter spun her around and shoved his left hand under her arm and around her chest. His hand reached up and gripped her chin. He pressed himself against her back, pulling her tight against him, tucking the muzzle of his Colt into the soft flesh at the corner of her jaw. "You're coming with me, young lady!" he hissed.

Lila saw Kitty sag as her body slammed into the wall. She watched in horror as Baxter prepared to use Kitty as a human shield. Without a thought for her own safety, Lila jumped to her feet and attacked Baxter, screaming and clawing at the arm that held Kitty upright. When Baxter turned to look at her the madness gleaming in his eyes nearly drove her back, but she took a deep breath and kept clawing. His turn swung Kitty, head lolling, between them. Baxter carelessly backhanded Lila into a heap against the far wall of the tunnel with the hand holding the pistol. His knuckles crashed against her jaw and she dropped limply, blackness welling up and blocking her vision. She desperately wanted to lift herself up and continue her attack on Baxter until he released Kitty, but her muscles wouldn't obey. She sagged against the wall and could only watch through tear-blurred eyes as Baxter forced Kitty into the bright sunlight outside the mineshaft.

Jesse saw Baxter's dive into the tunnel and heard Lila's agonized voice as she fought to save Kitty. He rose and started for the tunnel, but before he could move away from the ore cart Baxter appeared with his body pressed tightly against Kitty and his arm and hand holding her in front of himself as a shield. The Colt was pressed tightly against her jaw. Jesse took a step forward; the Remington in his right hand swung up as he turned sideways and stepped into a perfect target stance.

"Stop right there, Deputy Thompson!" Baxter snapped. "Or I will spread this young lady's brains all over this canyon. And I don't think you want that now, do you?"

Harvey appeared in the corner of Jesse's narrowed vision, Winchester at the ready. "You stop right there too, Palmer!" Baxter snarled. "If I have to kill both of these lovely ladies to get your attention, I will. You have my word on that."

"What have you done with Lila?" Harvey grated. "If you've touched one hair of her head..."

"Those are big words for someone who will be dead soon!" Baxter suddenly laughed, a high-pitched caw that brought the hair on the back of Jesse's neck to attention. "Throw down your guns and I'll only kill the two of you. The ladies can go free. And the same goes for whomever you have on top of the bluff."

Jesse thumbed back the hammer of the Remington. The front sight was steady on the small sliver of Howdy Baxter's head that he could see. At the same time, he saw that the hammer of Baxter's Colt was back and the knuckles of his trigger finger were white. Baxter was on the edge of pulling the trigger and killing Kitty.

"Drop the gun, Baxter," Jesse said evenly. "If you kill her, the whole territory will be hunting you and you know it. Even your own men will track you down and kill you."

"But that won't matter to you, will it?" Baxter crowed. "You'll be dead."

"So it looks like a standoff," Jesse said. His gray eyes narrowed as he tried to figure the odds of shooting

Baxter without Baxter killing Kitty.

"I think not. Drop the gun!" Baxter commanded. His voice was rising and he was getting further and further from sanity. Jesse's finger tensed on the trigger. Then something caught Jesse's eye that kept him from firing.

Lila struggled to her knees. Her head was reeling as she pushed herself heavily to her feet. She stood leaning against the wall of the tunnel, heart pounding and cheek throbbing. She reached a hand up to where Baxter had hit her and winced at the bolt of pain that went through her head when her fingertips gently touched the bruised skin. Her face was swollen and felt lopsided, and it was all she could do to keep from screaming.

Lila heard Baxter's ultimatum to Jesse and Harvey. She forced herself to walk toward the bright sunlight outside the tunnel. She tried to move quietly; she didn't want Baxter to know she was coming. She saw an old pick handle lying near the wall of the tunnel and she carefully bent and picked it up, nearly falling in the process. Wrapping her fingers around the weathered piece of hickory, she used it to push herself back to an upright position. When she was sure she wasn't going to fall, she took the handle in both hands and stepped unsteadily forward. When she stepped out into the afternoon sunlight, she looked into Jesse's eyes past Baxter's shoulder. She knew he'd seen her and was waiting for whatever she was going to do.

Once again Baxter snarled, "Drop the gun or I'll kill this fine looking young woman. It would be such a shame to have her lying on the ground here at my feet, bleeding and broken, due to unnecessary valor on your part, Deputy. Trust me, I will do what I say."

Jesse stood silently and didn't lower the gun. He was watching Lila move carefully toward Baxter. Slowly she brought the stick of hardened wood up, around and back over her right shoulder. She swayed for a moment with her eyes closed and Jesse prayed silently, "Please Lord, give her the strength to do what she's trying to do."

Lila's eyes opened and she stepped forward. She watched Baxter's gun hand sag ever so slightly, and swung the pick handle as hard as she could. Though not a ranch girl, she washed all the hotel sheets herself on a washboard and had built up a fair amount of arm strength; it was impossible not to. The thunk of wood on skull-bone echoed across the face of the bluff and the stinging impact rolled through her arms and into her throbbing head, causing her trembling hands to lose their grip on the still-vibrating pick handle.

Howdy Baxter was aware only of a crushing impact before his world went dark and he dropped in a heap. His gun hand swung wide, and his finger involuntarily squeezed the trigger, blasting a shot into the blue sky above the canyon wall as he fell. His fall dragged Kitty off her feet. His entrapping arm fell clear as she tumbled across the hard ground, forcing herself to roll away from him. She scrambled to her feet and ran to Lila, catching the other woman as her eyes rolled up into her head and she fainted dead away.

Harvey and Jesse ran forward with their pistols pointed at Baxter but the outlaw was out cold on his face in the dirt. Blood oozed from a cut and a sizeable lump on the back of his head. The two men holstered their pistols and anxiously moved to where Kitty had of relief shook her.

Kitty stood and moved to where Jesse was tying Baxter's hands behind his back. She waited quietly, looking down at the two men. Jesse finished trussing the outlaw and rose, dusting his hands. "Kitty, I, uh..." he stammered, at a loss for words now that she was safe. She looked at him steadily. Her eyes were wide and she was trembling slightly. He looked over to where Harvey knelt holding Lila in his arms. He had the sudden urge to reach out to Kitty, but her sober look kept him still. He began to speak again. "Did those men hurt you?"

She shook her head silently and continued to look at him. He finally reached out his hand and touched hers where she held them clasped in front of her. Her skin was cold when he slipped his fingers under hers and gently pulled her toward him. She moved up against his chest and his arm went around her. Her back was stiff under his hand and she kept her head turned to one side, looking past his shoulder. After a moment, she leaned back and looked into his eyes. Quietly, she asked, "Does this sort of thing happen to you often, Jesse?"

"It doesn't happen often, but it has happened once before," he answered softly. Another one of Judge Martin's deputies was the bait that time."

"I was afraid of that," she murmured. Something deep inside of Jesse turned cold. He was sure he knew what was coming next. "I think you know how I feel about you by this time," she went on. "But I'm not sure I'm strong enough to live with knowing that there are men out there who would go this far to kill you." She stopped again and heaved a deep sigh. "I think you should kiss me; then I will go home, and you can take *that*," she indicated the unconscious body of Howdy

Baxter, "back to Laramie. I need time to think." She raised her arms and her gentle hands moved to the dark hair at the back of his neck. She pulled his lips down to hers in a lingering kiss then stepped back. Jesse watched her, his heart dying inside of his chest.

"Kitty..."

She reached up a finger and touched it to his lips, silencing him. "Don't say anything, Jesse. Just take me home."

Fifty-eight

The rattle of displaced rock signaled Shanghai Noonan's arrival at the bottom of the bluff. As one man, Harvey and Jesse spun around, their pistols pointing in the direction of the sound. Shanghai jolted to a stop next to the boulder at the mouth of the trail with his hands raised. "Hold on there, gents," he said. "It's just me." With a sigh of exasperation, Harvey holstered the Colt and turned back to Lila.

Shanghai walked forward and stopped next to Montez' body. He knelt down and applied two fingers to the man's neck, seeking signs of life. Finding none, he rose and dusted off his hands. "One of them was holed up in the saloon," he said. "I'll go see if he's still around." He moved off down the canyon, favoring his battered ribs.

He silently stepped onto the back stoop of the ramshackle saloon building and slipped through the door with one of his pistols in his hand. He scanned the interior until he located the stairway leading to the top floor. Slipping silently across the room, he eased his way up the stairs, keeping his back pressed against the wall and stopped, with just his eyes clear of the landing. Listening intently, he heard a rustling sound, followed by a pained whimper, coming from a doorway at the end of the short hallway. His moccasin-clad feet made no sound as Noonan continued up, stopping once he arrived on the landing.

Hearing another whimper from the room ahead, Noonan ghosted forward with his pistol raised alongside his shoulder until he reached the doorway. He leaned forward just far enough to peer into the room; Jode Benson was seated against the wall, his ruined hand wrapped in a grubby, blood-soaked bandanna. His face was pale, and a slowly spreading pool of blood oozed across the floorboards beneath him. The wall nearby was covered with spatters of red. His eyes were wide and he was staring, unseeing; his harsh breathing echoed in the empty room, catching on every inhalation.

Noonan brought his pistol to bear, ready to order the wounded man to stand and come forward, but he stopped when Jode took a deep breath and toppled onto his side. He exhaled slowly, and silence filled the room. Jode's sightless eyes stared blankly into space, his pale face slack, and he seemed to somehow shrink into himself as he died.

Shanghai holstered his pistol and turned back into the hall to make his way down the stairs and outside. He squinted his eyes against the bright sunlight after the comparative darkness inside the building as he turned toward Harvey and Jesse, who waited expectantly. "Was anybody there?" Jesse asked.

Noonan nodded curtly. "He's dead. Bled to

death. I'm going for my horse." He walked past the two couples and started up the trail behind the boulder. Harvey and Jesse just watched him disappear from sight.

Shanghai walked slowly up the trail. His only thought was that now, with Montez dead, he could get on with his life. His problem was that he wasn't exactly sure what "his life" entailed; he'd been on the vengeance trail for what felt like forever. He didn't want to go back to the *rancheria*; there was no future for him there. All he knew was horses, guns, and hunting, but he wanted more than the hand-to-mouth existence the Apaches led now that they'd mostly been defeated by the cavalry. With his life's goal achieved, he felt as though his spirit had been set adrift to wander the world without a purpose.

"I'll go saddle some horses," Jesse said in the stillness. "We'd best be started out of here before too long, or Dennis Moynahan is gonna come hellin' in here with a lynch rope." He caught up the gray's reins and started toward the rope corral where the other horses were pastured. For some reason the animals had not broken out despite the recent explosion of gunfire. He glanced once at Kitty, but she was staring off into space with her hands clasped. Shaking his head in resignation, he headed for the horses.

At the rope corral, he dropped the gray's reins and took his lariat down from his saddle. He shook out a loop and eased forward, waiting for his chance to catch Kitty's horse. "That won't be necessary, Jesse," Kitty said quietly from behind him. "Come here, Socorro." Kitty stepped forward with her bridle in hand and the big horse walked up to her, nickering a greeting.

When the Appaloosa stopped beside her, she slipped the bit into his mouth and the headstall over his ears, then turned to lead him toward her saddle. "That black is the one Lila rode in here." Kitty pointed out a fine-boned, easy-moving mare in the back of the pack. "And the chestnut is Baxter's."

Jesse nodded and stepped forward. His hand shot out as the horses began to move. The loop settled over the black's head and came up tight under her chin. Jesse led her out and over to where the saddles lay, threw a saddle on and cinched it up. He picked up another rope and caught Baxter's horse and saddled it.

Harvey and Lila came around the corner of the building, Harvey's arm supporting arm around his fiance's waist. "What do you think we should do with the rest of the horses?" Harvey asked.

"Let's just take down the ropes and let 'em go," Jesse said absently. "There's plenty of grass and water here to keep 'em. Maybe Dennis'll come in an' get 'em; right at the moment I really don't care a whole lot one way or the other. We'll get Baxter on his horse and head out of here; it's getting along toward sundown." Jesse led the chestnut gelding over to where Baxter lay blinking his eyes groggily. "On your feet, Baxter," Jesse ordered. "Unless you wanna ride out of here belly-down over your saddle."

Fifty-nine

Shadows were stretching across the ghost town as the sun dropped lower. Jesse knew that the Bar M's crew would be coming, but for some reason he couldn't seem to work up a sense of urgency. It might have been simpler to just let Harvey shoot Baxter, but he knew that in the long run it would have just complicated things more than they already were.

Heaving a quiet sigh, he turned to where Baxter sat with his hands lashed to his saddle horn and his feet tethered together under the horse's belly. The sight of the captured outlaw suddenly reminded him of something Kitty had said earlier about taking Baxter to *Laramie*. He looked over to where Kitty stood with her reins in her hand, ready to mount up and go. "How did you know about..."

"About Laramie?" she broke in. "I found your badge and the warrant for that, that, *animal*,"--she pointed at Baxter--"in your pockets when you came to our ranch that night. I decided that you must have a reason for not saying anything about it, and I honored that. Dad doesn't know."

As if the mention of her father had been a signal for him to arrive, the clatter of hooves echoed against the canyon walls as Dennis Moynahan and a dozen of his crew burst out of the passageway into Horton. Rifles in hand, the men of the Bar M spread out into a skirmish line and came on at a trot. "Your father knows," Jesse said grimly. "I told him when I went to tell him about this." He waved his hand to indicate the ghost town. He reached into his vest and brought out the silver star and pinned it to his lapel. He stepped forward and the last rays of the lowering sun flashed on the points of the star, bringing the riders to a halt in a cloud of dust.

Dennis gazed at Jesse without expression for a moment that seemed to stretch to forever. He nodded curtly, once, then his eyes went to Kitty. Dennis stepped down and strode to her, placing his hands on her shoulders. "Are you all right, daughter?"

"I'm fine, Dad. I just want to go home."

Dennis turned to Jesse with his arm around Kitty's shoulders. "Is Baxter the only one left?" At Jesse's nod, he raised his voice. "You boys find the bodies and put 'em in yonder," he said, pointing at the saloon. "And burn it down. Burn the whole town. I don't want a single stick still standing when we leave."

Jesse started to protest, but Dennis silenced him with a glare. "My men have better things to do than bury scum like that, and I'll be damned if I'll cart 'em twenty-five miles to town for somebody else to worry about. And I want to send a message: *don't mess with the Bar M*. I'd've hung them all if I could. The only reason Baxter's still alive is out of respect for the law.

You men," he called to the silent group of riders, "take a good, long look at this coyote." He pointed at Baxter. "If you ever see him again, shoot him down like the mad dog he is." He looked back at Jesse. "And you'd better make damned sure he gets to jail and stays there!"

The Bar M riders scattered, and soon returned with the bodies of the dead outlaws draped over saddles. They unceremoniously dumped the bodies on the porch of the saloon, then dragged them inside. A short time later, a few fine wisps of smoke and the crackle of flames announced the lighting of the funeral pyre. As the flames began to devour the sun-dried lumber, men picked up flaming brands and torched the surrounding buildings. The outlaws' horses scattered away from the heat and smoke, and the other horses had to be held under tight rein. Dennis watched silently as the second story of the saloon collapsed into the conflagration below, sending sparks and smoke billowing into the air. Flames danced joyously over the new tinder. Soon nothing was left but a heap of burning timbers.

Dennis mounted his horse and led his men from the canyon. Jesse and his prisoner, then Harvey and Lila, followed behind. Kitty rode silently beside Jesse. Her expression was blank and she sat staring straight ahead, lost deep in thought.

When the cavalcade emerged from the rocks into the open air again, Kitty looked over at Jesse. "I meant what I said, Jesse. I love you, but I need some time. Take Baxter to Laramie, and then, if you can, come back and we'll talk." She reached up and touched his cheek, then spurred Socorro ahead to catch up with her father. Jesse reached his hand up to where her fingers had rested for a moment. He stared after her then turned the gray's head toward Watsonville. He would pick up his gear, and Dog, then he would ride for Laramie. But he would be back.

Shanghai Noonan materialized from the brush astride Lars Johansen's sorrel horse. "What are you gonna do now, Shanghai?" Jesse asked as Noonan eased up alongside the gray.

"As soon as I take this horse back to the livery, I'll be leaving. I have to get word to my family that it's over."

"What about after that?" Jesse queried.

"I don't know for sure," Noonan answered. "But I need to find something."

Jesse looked over at him. "Have I got a deal for you..." he began.

"Why does that make me think he'd better start looking to his hole card?" Harvey cut in. He and Lila rode close together; Lila wasn't willing to let him too far away. Harvey stuck out his hand to Noonan.

"I want to thank you for helpin' us," he said. "I had my doubts at first, but you done good."

"Thanks, Harvey. I'm glad I didn't let you down."

Ignoring Harvey's comment, Jesse went on. "Judge Martin's always looking for deputies, and we make a good team. Will you at least think about it?"

"I'll need a horse."

"There's a pretty good paint gelding back in Watsonville that needs a rider."

Noonan rode for a few yards in thoughtful silence, then looked up at Jesse. "I guess Laramie's as good a place as any to send a telegram from. You've got a deal." He reached across his saddle and clasped hands with the deputy.

Harvey just shook his head and snorted, "Lord,

help us. The complications never end." He heeled the dun ahead, with Lila's black mare trotting alongside.

Jesse nudged the gray into a trot as Shanghai Noonan fell in alongside. His usual mischievous smile was beginning to show as his normal good humor returned. "Come on, horse, let's get this weasel to jail. I've got a girl to come back and visit." He yanked Baxter's horse ahead and moved out on the trail to Watsonville.

THE END